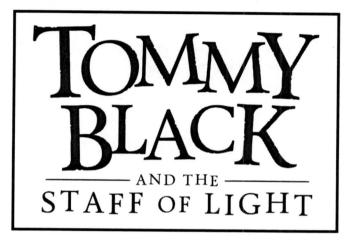

TOMMY BLACK
— AND THE —
STAFF OF LIGHT

JAKE KERR

Currents & Tangents
Press

Praise for

Tommy Black and the Staff of Light

The action almost never stopped, which made this book very hard to put down. A simple trip to a restaurant turned into a battle for survival when Tommy gained a great power, and his grandfather lost it. Through the course of the story, some secrets were discovered, while others were hidden. Overall, this book could not be better.

A Litpick Top Pick book
Litpick Kids Reviews
litpick.com

An Indie book that Wows! you.

Middle Shelf magazine, January/February 2015

I read a lot and I read a lot of magic stories. It is very cool when I come across something very different. This is an amazing book. I was really blown away by the story. Mr. Kerr has created a unique world of magic.

This Kid Reviews Books
thiskidreviewsbooks.com

I highly recommend Tommy Black and the Staff of Light to Fantasy lovers of all ages.

The Reading Wench
thereadingwench.com

Also by Jake Kerr

The Tommy Black Series

Tommy Black and the Staff of Light
Tommy Black and the Coat of Invincibility

The Guildmaster Thief Series

The Guildmaster Thief
Crossing the Bridge
Blade of the Guildmaster
Blood on the Bridge

Cover design and illustration by M. S. Corley

ISBN 978-0-692-31666-5
[1. Fiction: Fantasy-General. 2. Juvenile Fiction:
Action & Adventure-General, 3. Juvenile Fiction:
Historical-United States-20th Century]

10 9 8 7 6 5 4 3 2 1

Published by Currents & Tangents Press

Dallas, Texas

For Lea, Zoë, Willow, & Mia

Chapter One

SHADOWS IN MANHATTAN

L et's be honest, my Grandfather drove me crazy. He was a kind man and all, who truly cared and looked out for me, but I was pretty much a prisoner in his townhouse. Sure, I could walk outside, but what was there to do? It took all my willpower not to sneak away on a regular basis. The only relief was the day when Grandfather and I would see the latest motion picture at the Ziegfeld Theater and then walk to the Persian Garden restaurant for dinner.

I lived for those days, and it was during one of them

when I forever left the prison of my Grandfather's apartment behind. It was a Saturday, and it started out ordinary enough. We had just watched Errol Flynn in The Adventures of Robin Hood, and were on our way to the Persian Garden. I grabbed a broken broom handle off the curb and pretended I was Robin Hood, practicing sword thrusts and swings against mailboxes and trees along Sixth Avenue. Sometimes I'd have to pause as the passing horses and automobiles stirred the dust and made me cough, but I didn't mind. It was better than the dry stale air of my grandfather's townhouse.

We were walking along, and Grandfather didn't seem to mind my antics until we turned into the alley leading to the restaurant and I smacked one of the metal drums stacked at the entrance. Dark brown fluid splashed over the edge. My nose was assaulted with the noxious smell of rotting straw and horse manure.

Grandfather stopped, turned, pointed his cane at me, and growled, "Watch it now, Tommy! You're wearing your nice clothes." I looked at my khaki pants and white cotton shirt and then at the brown liquid on the cobblestones. While the length of the alley was mostly empty, the entrance was stacked with large metal containers filled with dirt and horse waste scraped from the streets and only emptied once a week. "Mind your step," he added and started walking again. I stepped over a pool of liquid manure, glad none had splashed on my leather shoes.

He took particular joy in our trips down the quiet alley. He once told me that before my parents passed away they had forbidden him from taking the shortcut to the restaurant, as if that would stop him. He talked of taking the dangerous lonely road, and I humored his belief that an alley could be dangerous by stabbing at imaginary thieves as I rushed to catch up.

Grandfather was a tall man, with the same grey eyes we all seem to have in my family, and he had wild white hair that he kept slicked back in the style of his youth. His hair would resist his efforts however and often stuck out in odd directions, causing him to constantly slide his fingers across the top of his head in an attempt to tame the unruly mess. He didn't smile much, or laugh, and there was an intensity about him that was often scary. But he was a kind man, and for as much as he drove me crazy I did love him dearly.

The alley was long, running the length of the theater and the department store that backed onto it from Seventh Avenue, and was always empty, the drums of manure and dark brown clotted liquid pooling beneath them acting as an effective deterrent to everyone but my grandfather. As always, he set a pace that was a brisk walk for his long legs and a gangly jog for me, my fourteen year old legs always a half step behind and trying to catch up. The sharp "tap, tap, tap" of his cane whenever he walked had become another part of his character, like his firm handshakes and the constant fixing of his hair. The taps were so loud and distinct that everyone in the neighborhood knew when Grandfather was approaching long before they saw him.

I matched Grandfather's stride a few steps behind him and returned my attention to stabbing and parrying imaginary foes. We were more than halfway down the alley when the rhythmic swinging and tapping of his cane ceased. My grandfather stopped so suddenly that I almost ran into him. As I regained my balance, he tossed his cane to his right hand, and with his left arm, pushed against my shoulder and maneuvered me behind him as he slowly turned to his left.

"Stay directly behind me," he whispered. "Don't run. Don't

hide. Just stay behind me." I had no idea what was happening but I did as my grandfather said, his voice calm but commanding. He glanced at me, and I saw a look in his eyes that I had never seen before. He turned away and looked at the wall across the alley. I peeked around, but saw nothing but a dark elongated shadow from a small balcony on the second floor. It was a sunny day, so it was easy to see everything along the wall. There was nothing out of the ordinary. I gripped the broomstick in my hand, prepared for anything.

Grandfather stared at the shadow, unmoving. He crouched down slightly, holding his cane in both hands like a staff. His knuckles were white.

"Grandfather, what is it?"

"Shhh. Stay behind me."

I thought I saw a flicker in the shadow, and my grandfather suddenly stood upright.

"Vingrosh, I know you are there. You may as well come down. I don't know why you are skulking about, but your efforts were obviously for naught." The normal-looking shadow started to move. It was not the slow, natural movement of shadow reacting to light. It moved as if it had a life of its own.

The darkness was so alien and unnatural that my hands started to shake. I grabbed Grandfather's arm and steadied myself.

"Please let go, Tommy. I may need to move with some suddenness, and—as I said—it is safer for you behind me, not holding onto me." He nudged me with the end of his cane. I felt an immense power as the cane touched me. If you've ever been near a lightning strike or inside an electricity station you'll know what I mean. It wasn't being touched by power; it was being touched by the presence of power.

I peered again at the wall in the direction my grandfather was staring. The shadow spread like a black stain. "What is it, Grandfather?"

"Shhh, Tommy.

"Vingrosh, I am late for a dinner appointment with my friends from Persepolis. Or perhaps we should join them together?" My grandfather slammed the brass tip of his cane to the ground, where it let out a loud crack.

Immediately the shadow on the wall started to drip, like fresh paint. It oozed down, crossed the alley toward us, and then coalesced in front of my grandfather, who was still tense but glanced back at me and winked. The shadow on the ground was roughly circular and looked like a hole in the alley. A deep baritone voice came from the hole. It had a barely perceptible echo, almost like it was spoken from the end of a long pipe, its voice echoing off the sides until it got to us. I couldn't understand what it was saying, but the accent was oddly English sounding.

"None taken," my grandfather responded. "Although I expected more from you, Vingrosh."

The shadow spoke some more, sounding almost apologetic as its words echoed from the ground.

My grandfather laughed. "You presume to ask me for my staff? Do you forget all I have done for you?" He tapped his cane to the ground again, and the shadow appeared to get smaller, but only for a moment.

The shadow responded with a short phrase, and my Grandfather let out a short laugh. "Be reasonable? What is reasonable about giving up the staff?"

The shadow then growled and spoke again. My grandfather no longer sounded amused as he stated in a clear, firm voice, "Baseless threats do not become you, Vingrosh."

The creature growled again and with purposeful slowness

rose from the alley into a vague human-like form. An arm reached out and pointed over my grandfather's shoulder behind us. I looked around and saw another shadow seeping down the wall.

My grandfather saw it, too, and in a blur, twirled the cane in his left hand and then plunged it down against the cobblestone. It let out a crack like thunder. The shadow creature in front of us fell back a few feet, while my grandfather yelled, "Run, Tommy!"

I held my ground.

Errol Flynn would not flee and neither would I. My Grandfather was old. It was time for me to take care of him. I moved forward a step and swung the broomstick at the shadow. There was no resistance. The end of the stick swung through the black air, followed by my hand. As my fingers touched the shadow they immediately went numb. My momentum carried the rest of my hand into the creature. I cried out and yanked my hand back. The broomstick fell from my fingers into the depths of the blackness. Thankfully, my hand emerged, but it was cold and without feeling.

"Tommy, no!" Grandfather grabbed my other arm and

hauled me away. The force of his grip was painful. He dragged me behind him as he sprinted toward the theater alley entrance.

I looked over my shoulder but could only see blurs of black.

As suddenly as he had stopped earlier, Grandfather stopped again. This time I did collide with him, but before I could fall to the ground, he grabbed me and held me close.

"Tommy, that was a very foolish thing you did. Now you must listen to me. Whatever you do, do not move. I need you to stay as close to me as possible." I couldn't tell why we had stopped. We were just outside one of the emergency exits from the theater, standing close to the door. I looked back, and squeezed my hand into a fist even though I couldn't feel it. The entire alley was an oozing mass of black, moving toward us.

The horrific thought of being engulfed by unfeeling nothingness took away any thought of fighting the shadows off. "Grandfather, shouldn't we try to run? Or maybe break in through that door to get away?"

My grandfather looked at me. He didn't seem scared, but he had a grim look on his face. "No, Tommy. These are Shadows. The only thing that can stop them is light."

I looked around. The entire alley was bathed in light. The sun wasn't directly over head, but it was still well before nightfall. "But we're surrounded by light!"

"Artificial light, Tommy. Artificial light." He pointed with his cane, and above the exit door was a floodlight, which glowed dully. It was meant to illuminate the door and surroundings at night, but had little effect during the day. I looked down and couldn't see the outline of the floodlight on the ground even though I knew it was shining down on us.

"You may not see it, Tommy, but the light from that bulb above is protecting us from the Shadows. " He paused, as if considering his options. He ran his hand over his head, putting his disheveled hair back in place. In a quieter tone, seemingly more to himself than to me, he added, "Now, how to escape? Shadows are powerful." He nodded grimly. "Powerful."

"What are Shadows? Should we call for help?" We weren't far from the theater end of the alley, and I was certain we could get someone's attention.

"They are magical creatures, Tommy. And, no, we cannot call for help. We would just put others at risk."

Magical creatures! Of course they were. I had always been

told that they had disappeared from Earth decades before I was born, and yet here they were. I looked up at my Grandfather. He stared intently down the alley. How could my grandfather, who walked with a cane and rarely left our apartment, know anything about magical creatures?

My curiosity left me as I followed my grandfather's gaze down the alley. From a distance, what looked like a wall of black was actually an approaching collection of individual moving shapes. Several came directly up to us, but wouldn't get any closer than a couple of feet. Two of them grew into the vaguely human shape I had seen earlier, while the rest surrounded us in a sea of black.

One of the Shadows spoke, but my grandfather didn't reply. "What did he say, grandfather?"

"He said I'm clever." He paused. Clearly the Shadow said something else that Grandfather didn't want to relay to me. I looked around. A Shadow oozed toward us from further down the alley. I watched as it stretched and twisted itself into a human form. It pulled its arm back, and then whipped it forward. A rock clattered off the wall above the door.

They were trying to break the lightbulb.

They could do it, too. It was a bare bulb, unprotected from vandals by a cover or metal cage. Another rock flew over our heads.

Grandfather stood tall and grasped his cane in both hands. He pulled his arms in opposite directions. Over his right shoulder I could see the top of his cane, which now ended in a bright sword, while in his left hand was the bottom of his wooden cane. The engravings glowed.

As soon as the sword was free, I noticed that my grandfather was twisting it oddly in his hand. There were murmurs coming from the Shadows, and as I looked out I saw several of the standing ones dart one way or another.

Another rock flew, but as it clattered off the mark I realized what my grandfather was doing. He was using the bright steel of his blade as a mirror, reflecting the light from the floodlight out toward the Shadows that were throwing rocks. The light didn't appear strong enough to do more than cause pain, but it was working.

More Shadows joined in throwing rocks, but my grandfather's hand waved like a symphony conductor wielding a baton, sending invisible light across the alley in all directions.

Even more Shadows arose. I felt like I was on some alien landscape, surrounded by black stalagmites.

To my horror, a rock struck my grandfather in the shoulder, twisting his body back. The blow clearly hurt, but did not knock him off his feet. Grandfather smiled. "I wondered how long it would take them to think of that."

He made a gesture with the fingers holding the wooden part of the cane in his left hand. Immediately, a warmth surrounded us. Another rock flew toward grandfather, but it thudded, as if it hit a mattress or heavy draperies. It slid harmlessly to the ground.

"What was that?"

I whispered the words to myself, but Grandfather answered. "It is my sad excuse for a shield spell. Never was much good at magic. About the only thing I can stop are slowly thrown rocks. Never thought it would actually come in handy."

Seeing that their rocks couldn't harm us, the Shadows redoubled their efforts at smashing the light bulb. They made very little progress with my grandfather reflecting rays of artificial light at them.

"Can you stop them from hitting the light?" I asked.

In a grim voice, Grandfather replied, "We're lucky I am stopping them from hitting us." I asked him what he meant, but he ignored me.

After what seemed like an hour, my legs were burning. The feeling was returning to the hand that had touched the Shadow while it was leaving my legs. I don't know how long a human can stand in one spot, but I felt that I was near my limit. All the while, my grandfather held his ground, waving his sword around in a series of graceful and never ending arcs. I couldn't imagine how his arms, let alone his legs, felt.

He must have been tiring, however, as a rock hit the floodlight with a horrifying clink. It flickered but did not break. This seemed to spur the Shadows on, and more of them braved the reflected light from my grandfather's sword to hurl rocks.

Several of the Shadows were within arm's reach, waiting for our protective light to shatter into darkness. I couldn't stop myself from staring at them, their black so complete that I felt myself on the edge of a bottomless dark pit. They made no sound, but I felt warm air, like a breath against my cheek. The urge to run was nearly overwhelming.

The Shadows became too much for my grandfather to

control with his sword. Another rock hit the light, but again it didn't break. I looked up at him; his face was frozen in intense concentration.

I heard the sound of glass shattering and prepared myself for whatever death a Shadow would deliver, but I didn't feel glass shards falling on us, and when I looked up I saw that the light was still glowing. It wasn't the sound of glass shattering I heard, but a shriek. All around us the Shadows flowed with great speed up the walls and down the alley. Toward the restaurant end, a large smiling man approached. It was Mister Oz, the maître d from the Persian Garden restaurant. His name was actually Baraz, but I had called him Mister Oz for as long as I could remember. He was carrying a box flashlight, and as he pointed it at a Shadow he would laugh and say, "Boo!"

My grandfather sheathed the sword back in his cane and walked up to Mister Oz, who seemed to find the whole situation quite amusing. I followed, with my hand gripping my grandfather's shirtsleeve. Every shadow we passed looked ominous.

"My goodness, what is the world coming to? There isn't a worse race I can think of for assassinating someone in the city that never sleeps than Shadows." Mister Oz laughed again. "They should have just waited for you to take a camping trip!"

He turned to me. "What do you think, Tommy?" He flipped on the flashlight and shone it in my face. "Boo!"

Grandfather wasn't amused. He stopped in front of Mister Oz and replied, "Well, apparently they didn't want to wait." Sighing, he added, "I'm getting old and careless, Baraz. Why would I leave the house without a flashlight?"

Mister Oz slapped Grandfather on the back and held up the box connected to the electric lamp. "You would walk around the city carrying this?" He smiled. "Besides, why would you leave the house with a flashlight? We've had twenty years of peace, and much of that is due to your kindness to the Shadows."

My grandfather grunted. "Peace, kindness… the fact that we are using these words tells me how old and careless we have gotten, Baraz."

Mister Oz nodded solemnly, but immediately smiled again. "You are too hard on yourself. Who would expect the Shadows to do such a thing? They have been quiet for all this time."

"No, Baraz. I was foolish to expect—to hope—for peace

and quiet." He looked at me and his frown lessened a bit. I could feel the tension leaving his body under the iron grip I had on his sleeve. "This is no one's fault but my own."

He reached down and put his hand on my shoulder. "It's about time Tommy learned about his legacy. Come, let's talk about this over dinner. It is dangerous business when the Shadows not only break their treaty but attack the one who saved them."

Mister Oz fell in step with Grandfather. "Indeed, my friend. The Shadows are lucky Vingrosh was not there. He would have torn them to shreds for attacking their savior."

"Vingrosh was there." The news must have stunned him, as Mister Oz stopped suddenly, grabbed my grandfather's shoulder, and spun him around to face him.

"Are you sure, *Pehlivan*? I find this almost impossible to believe."

"I am sure. He said that my time was done in this world and that he wanted the staff." My grandfather shrugged and started walking toward the restaurant. "He was surprised I didn't just give it to him, and I can't blame him. My time *is* done, Baraz."

Mister Oz was quiet, but I noticed him shaking his head. As he entered the door in front of us, he turned over the sign in the window so that it showed "closed."

Chapter Two

THE CHEF'S TABLE

My parents died in a subway crash when I was three years old, which led my grandfather to never use the subway again. Even trains made him nervous. As a result my life centered around locations within walking distance of his apartment in Manhattan Valley or, on special occasions, a horse-drawn carriage down Central Park to Midtown.

The closest theater to us was the Ziegfeld, and our weekend carriage trips to the theater were a welcome escape from my Grandfather's claustrophobic apartment.

But even the glamorous Ziegfeld couldn't compare to the excitement of the Persian Garden.

Entering the Persian Garden was like entering a foreign country, a place marked not just by strange furnishings and people but also new and exotic smells—rich spices and incense that caused my head to spin. Everything made all the more intense by the subtle lighting of candles and gas lamps.

In the past, the carved wood of the chairs and the booths and the rich and colorful tapestries led to flights of fancy over every meal, but after my experience with the Shadows, the subdued lighting gave everything the potential of being something sinister. Every flickering light cast a moving shadow, and I wondered which would be the one that would flow across the floor and envelop me in darkness. To make matters worse, as I looked around I noticed for the first time that there wasn't a single artificial light. Grandfather seemed unconcerned, however, and he strode purposefully through the main dining room toward the back, followed by Mister Oz.

Normally we ate at a large booth near the front of the restaurant, but we passed right by it. In fact, we passed all of the booths and tables and entered the kitchen through a doorway filled by hanging beads. As the beads slapped against the back of my head, I took in a room that could have come right out of the previous century.

The kitchen was a mixture of wood preparation counters and large iron ovens and stoves, the kind which have long since been abandoned for smaller and more modern equipment. The walls were stone and the floor a colorful tile. Four men were busy preparing meals, all of whom were wearing robes and sandals and intent on their work.

There was a small wooden booth in the back which looked like it could fit about four people. My grandfather slipped into a seat, followed by Mister Oz, who sat across from him. My grandfather snapped his fingers and then patted the seat next to him when I looked his way. "How's your hand?" he asked.

"Almost back to normal."

"That will teach you," he replied as I slid beside him. He reached above my head and flipped a switch on the wall which I hadn't noticed. The table was immediately bathed in white neon light. In the environment of the warm restaurant and its archaic kitchen, the effect was cold and ugly.

Mister Oz smiled and said, "Your paranoia is returning."

Grandfather shrugged as a young man came up to the table and slid glasses of water in front of us. He said something in Farsi which I couldn't understand. Mister Oz nodded and answered him. The waiter strolled off, and Mister Oz turned to my grandfather. "Should we call for my father?"

"No." Grandfather shook his head. "He didn't understand before, and I doubt he understands now. He'll just bring up pointless distractions." Mister Oz nodded.

Grandfather took a long drink from his glass and then set it on the table in front of him. He ran his fingers through his unruly hair, and then folded his hands, resting them on the table, slow and deliberate. He peered at Mister Oz. They were silent as I looked from one to the other.

"What is happening, Grandfather?" I asked. I thought of the magical creatures, which I had considered long extinct. The fear of the attack was starting to fade, and I had to admit that I was rather excited about the possibility of magic—real magic—in Manhattan.

He reached over and tousled my hair without looking at me. "That's the question now, isn't it?" I considered a more specific question, but he was no longer paying any attention to me.

— 22 —

"For twenty years all I have wanted was to be left alone. I left England, rejoined my family, dealt with tragedy." Grandfather paused, tapped his glass with his finger, and then continued, "You and your father have been great friends, honoring my request and defending my privacy." He leaned forward. "But I hear things, Baraz. I know there is trouble on the Continent. I hear of an illusionist with great power in Germany. I know that young fool Cain is consolidating his power in England. And now this," Grandfather waved a hand toward the front of the restaurant, "with the Shadows."

He leaned back and sighed, while Mister Oz remained quiet and attentive. "I have been foolish, Baraz, to expect that the burden of the staff could just be forgotten, to think that magic would just fade away along with my family's legacy." My grandfather took another drink from his glass.

"Magic *is* fading, Declan." I looked over my shoulder, startled. The voice came from an older man dressed in colorful robes standing to the side and behind me. He was short and stout, with a wrinkled face. Despite his age, his hair was thick and black, without a hint of grey. It was wavy, but cut short. His eyes shone, and more than anything he looked like a kindly old man lecturing a child. I had seen him before in the restaurant but had never met him.

"And to think they say that wisdom comes with age," Grandfather stated.

The old man smiled, and I immediately knew who he was. His smile was broad and identical to one that I had seen many times, that of his son. "You're Mister Oz's father!"

The old man looked at me. "Indeed I am, and you are Thomas, the grandson of the *Pehlivan*."

"What's a *Pehlivan*?" I asked, as Mister Oz mirrored his father's smile. I remembered that Mister Oz had called my grandfather that in the alley.

Grandfather raised his hands and in an exasperated voice said, "Oh, now you've done it, Ali. You may as well join us and spin a tale or two."

Mister Ali laughed and sat down across from me. He turned to my grandfather. "So Master Thomas knows nothing?" Grandfather nodded, and Mister Ali laughed again, but it wasn't the deep joyous laugh that marked his son. This was one of resignation. "It is why the staff usually skips a generation, Declan. I should have expected this. You all hold on too long."

"Does it matter? You are the one that says magic is dying." Grandfather shrugged and took another drink of water, finishing it off.

Mister Ali nodded. "This is true." He paused and then added quietly, "Perhaps it *is* time to give up the staff."

My grandfather replied with a cold stare. No one said anything, and I could feel the tension in the air. Grandfather eventually spoke. "That is what Vingrosh told me."

It was Mister Ali's turn to stare. I couldn't tell if he was surprised or worried or shocked. My grandfather remained quiet and stern, and Mister Ali eventually shook his head and then looked across the table at me. "We can discuss that later. I owe an explanation to young Master Thomas."

The waiter stopped by with some bread, which delayed whatever Mister Ali was going to say. I found the waiting intolerable. I had known of magic, of course. Everyone knew of the exploits of Merlin and how he changed the history of England, but that was centuries ago, and, like most people in 1938, I found magic so watered down that it was more of a sideshow curiosity than anything worth my attention. There hadn't been a truly great magician since Merlin himself, and like every boy my age I was more interested in movies, auto-mobiles, airplanes, and guns. But all of this talk of magical creatures, illusionists, Shadows, and a legacy involving me pushed every other thought and interest aside.

I picked at my bread, my appetite drowned by curiosity and adrenaline. Mister Ali smiled warmly. He had the kindest eyes and smile I had ever seen. "*Pehlivan* is Persian for hero, Master Thomas. To many in the world, your grandfather is considered a great hero."

"A hero?" I immediately thought of Errol Flynn. The thought of my grandfather as a swashbuckling adventurer captivated me. I had only known him as the old man who didn't like to leave his apartment and moved slowly with his cane when he did. "What did you do?" I turned to Grandfather, but he nodded toward Mister Ali.

"It is a long story, but the essence is that your grandfather helped the allies win the Great War."

"Ha, 'helped' is an odd way of putting it," Mister Oz interjected, spitting out bits of food in his hurry to make his point.

"Yes, Baraz," his father said patiently, "But 'helped' is how we want them to put it."

"Helped? How? I thought that it was America joining the war with our troops that helped end the war." I was getting an idea that the truth was being hidden on purpose, and I wanted to know more, especially as it appeared my grandfather had a large part in the Great War that no one knew about. That didn't seem right.

Mister Ali looked like he was going to say something but his son spoke up first. "The truth is that your grandfather is the greatest Archmage to ever wield the staff. He destroyed the Kaiser's troops. He broke the Kaiser's will. He laid waste to—"

"Enough!" Mister Ali exclaimed. "Master Thomas doesn't need to know more than his legacy." I looked at my grandfather, but he seemed detached from the conversation and just continued to eat.

Mister Ali gave his son a stern look and turned to me, "You know of magic, of course?" I nodded, although in truth I knew precious little. "Well, there are few, very few, great magicians still in the world, but they avoid attention for reasons that we can discuss later. The important thing to know is that all of the magicians in the world pale in power to the one wielding the staff that your grandfather wields.

"My son was correct. Those that wield the staff are called Archmages, and your grandfather is one of the greatest. But your grandfather, to his credit, also realized that such great power is dangerous, and he left England and rejoined your parents twenty years ago to let the magic of the world fade away as it was meant to."

My bread lay uneaten in front of me as I was focused wholly on the story. "So my grandfather's a great magician?"

"No, Master Thomas. He wields the staff, and the staff is a source of powerful magic. That makes him greater than the greatest magician. Very few can wield the staff. In fact, only members of your family can wield it, for reasons lost to history."

I looked over at my grandfather, who was wiping his mouth with a colorful napkin. "But where is the staff?"

At this Grandfather laughed. "Why it's right next to you, Tommy." He looked at me and patted the cane, which lay on the seat between us. "It can change form, but I've never been able to figure out how to do it. My own father made it a cane before he gave it to me. I believe it was his idea of a joke, but I've grown quite fond of it."

"Does that mean I'll have it someday?"

I was speaking to my grandfather, but Mister Ali interjected, "I'm afraid not. As we mentioned, magic is fading, and the staff is now more of a danger than a benefit to humanity. Best to let it fade away, as well."

"In that you are wrong, Ali." My grandfather looked across the table, his eyes focused and intense. "Vingrosh and the Shadows appeared just outside your doors. They threatened me and my grandson. Things are changing, and I'm afraid now is not the time to give up the staff."

Mister Ali shook his head. "Shadows? What did they want?"

"The staff."

Mister Ali banged his hand on the table. "Then why didn't you give it to them, Declan? Can't you see? Shadows can't use the staff, and they can make it disappear forever. It's exactly what we talked about twenty years ago!"

My grandfather looked at Mister Ali. "You've always been too soft to understand magic, Ali. When a Shadow demands the staff is exactly the time when we can't give it up. Why can't you understand that?"

Mister Oz broke in, "He's right, father. We can't give up the staff until magic has left the world. It's our only defense."

Mister Ali looked angry, his face turning red, the smile nowhere to be seen. Pulling himself out of the booth, he stood and turned toward us. "Declan, you and I have seen too much together for you to believe such nonsense." He then turned to his son. "Baraz, you've listened to too many of the *Pehlivan*'s stories. You are both wrong." And with that, Mister Ali left the kitchen, pushing aside the beads in the doorway with such violence that one of the strings fell, clattering to the floor.

There was an awkward silence, broken by Mister Oz. "He doesn't understand, *Pehlivan*." He sighed. "He never did."

My grandfather nodded and turned to me. "Tommy, now is not the time, but you will someday wield the staff." He nodded toward the cane lying beside him. "I've been too complacent, too trusting. It is time that I prepare you for the challenge that awaits. I don't know what is going on in the world, but it appears we are once again facing troubled times."

Just then I heard a deep resounding boom, and the entire restaurant shook.

Dust fell from the ceiling onto the table. There was a silent pause as Mister Oz and my grandfather looked at each other uneasily.

One of the waiters ran in, the beads clattering against the door frame as he shoved his way through. "We are under attack!" He pointed to the front of the restaurant.

A second boom shook the building.

I looked at my grandfather, thinking back to his concentration and concern over the attack from the Shadows. This time he was smiling.

Chapter Three

THE OLD FORTRESS
UNDER ATTACK

S liding out from his seat and moving briskly toward the beaded door leading to the dining room at the front, Mister Oz moved with a grace and speed I had never seen him use before. The restaurant workers, so recently chopping greens and stirring soup, arranged themselves behind him. There were no words spoken, no commands given. They didn't appear any different than when they were working in the restaurant, other than they now wielded wicked-looking knives pulled from under their robes. One grabbed a staff from a corner that I hadn't noticed.

I felt a shove and half-fell out of the booth as my grandfather pushed himself to his feet. I looked up at him. He cut a fierce figure, his knuckles white as they gripped the cane in his right hand, his eyes glinting in the neon light.

The restaurant shook again, but I didn't hear a sound, which only made it more frightening. I scrambled to my feet and looked around. My perceptions changed. I noticed the solidity and mass of the place. Without the decorative trappings out front, the Persian Garden had the look of a fortress. The walls were hewn from huge pieces of rock. There were two windows recessed in the wall along the side of the kitchen, which appeared more like windows you would find in a castle wall than a restaurant.

More men arrived in the kitchen. Dressed in the colorful costumes of the Persian Garden wait staff, the men rushed to the front of the restaurant bearing scimitars and knives rather than plates and glasses.

The restaurant was quiet, and I wondered if Mister Oz's workers had beaten off whatever had made the percussive noise when a screeching filled the air. In the midst of the din and a harsh light outlining his frame, my grandfather stood still. And then it came: Another boom, louder than the others, shaking the restaurant so much that I feared the heavy stones above our heads would fall.

Grandfather leaned down and looked me in the eyes. He was smiling and looked excited. I don't think I had ever seen him happier. "Tommy, just like in the alley, there is danger outside, but I don't want you to be afraid—you are in the safest spot in all of New York, and while I am powerless against Shadows, this—" He waved his hand toward the front of the restaurant. "This I can handle. So just sit here and wait for me to come back. I need to go help Mister Baraz." He put a hand on my shoulder and gently tapped my chest with his cane. "Be brave."

I watched as he turned and sprinted through the beads to the front of the restaurant. Part of me was terrified from the memory of the Shadows, but part of me wanted to follow him. How dangerous could it be? He said it himself: This was something he could handle.

Besides, I felt cheated. My grandfather had kept me cooped up in his apartment even though he was some kind of mighty magician warrior. What else did he lie to me about? And now that I was finally experiencing excitement, he left me behind in a kitchen.

In the end, the urge to run out and show him that I was not a child wasn't enough. I kicked at the floor as I walked back to the booth. The terrifying nature of the Shadows and other unknown creatures weighed too heavily on my mind, as did the prospect of my grandfather's anger if I disobeyed. I sat down. I was useless. A coward.

As I turned my attention back to the kitchen, Mister Ali entered from the front. He ignored me and went to one of the large iron ranges where he started to work on some food that had been abandoned in the chaos before.

I was so stunned by the contrast of him calmly cooking amidst the desperate preparations for some kind of battle that I momentarily forgot we were under attack. A clash of metal served as a jarring reminder, however, and the shrieking from earlier increased in volume. A human scream pierced the air and then the otherworldly shrieks quieted down again. It sounded nothing like the battles I had seen in the movies. Feeling lost, I said to Mister Ali, "Can you tell me what is going on?"

"Shhh," was his reply, spoken over his shoulder.

A horrible caterwaul sounded from above my head. It was muffled by the stone, but even the stone couldn't stop me from feeling the pure wrath in that sound. I still wanted to think of the attack as part of an exciting adventure with my grandfather, but fear kept me in the booth.

The loud booming explosions stopped and were replaced by smaller ones of greater frequency. I looked up and noticed shapes flitting across the windows. Intermittent wails came from above, each one making me cringe. I didn't know if I could ever get used to that sound. Three men arrived and began to twist and contort their hands over a crack in one of the walls. They soon stopped and, unlike all the others, moved back toward the rear of the restaurant.

Mister Ali started spooning dark rice into a bowl. A particularly loud boom resounded through the walls, but he looked completely unconcerned. He grabbed a fork and a napkin and approached me. Without saying anything, he slid the bowl in front of me, placed the fork next to it, and dropped the napkin onto my lap.

"Thank you," I mumbled.

Mister Ali shrugged, and replied, "You'll need the energy." He smiled and waved his hand toward the rice.

There was a sudden series of explosions that weren't as loud but felt much more powerful, like the air was pressing against my chest. More dust fell from the ceiling, but Mister Ali continued to stand and watch me, a smile never leaving his face. I looked around, and the massive stone walls didn't seem quite so formidable anymore. As every second passed my excitement lessened and my fear increased.

Every so often people would rush through the kitchen, and in the midst of the shrieks, the explosions, and the activity I felt like I was in a sanctuary in the middle of a storm.

Mister Ali motioned toward the bowl again. "Eat."

I took a tentative bite of the rice. Mister Ali continued to stand quietly, and realizing I was being rude, I asked him to take a seat.

He slid into the seat across from me. "Master Thomas, we appear to have time, so why don't I tell you a story."

I stammered out an "okay,"

"Wonderful. I take it your grandfather tells you stories at night?"

"Sometimes."

"Fantastic!" Mister Ali leaned his elbows on the table and folded his hands together. He kept his eyes on me. A heart-rending scream sounded from outside the windows. I dropped my fork and looked up. The windows were clear, and there was a silence that lasted a few seconds. It was broken by the loudest boom yet, a sound that didn't appear to be an explosion but rather as if something huge had slammed into the building. The walls, ceiling, and floor shook, dust billowing from the gaps in the stones. To my horror, a crack formed in the stone above our heads. I looked at Mister Ali in alarm.

He scratched his head and then peered at me, as if nothing at all had happened. "Has he told you the story of Aladdin?"

I pointed at the ceiling. "There's a crack," I whispered.

Mister Ali shrugged. "It's old," he said.

A whistling came from the front of the restaurant. "Aladdin?" Mister Ali asked again.

"Uh, yes. He has told me the story of Aladdin."

"Excellent. Ali Baba and the thieves?" I nodded and put my fork down, more full of fear than hunger. "Very good. A trifle of a story, but there are lessons to be learned even in those."

He scratched his chin and then peered at me closely. "How about Ahmed and the mighty stone?"

"Yes," I replied as the shrieking resumed with the ferocity of a hungry lion, unleashed in a field of gazelles.

"Very good, Master Thomas. It seems that your grandfather hasn't completely ignored your education."

Two men burst into the room from the front. They were covered with dust and were dragging a third man, who appeared to be unconscious. They went to Mister Ali and gently laid the man at his feet. They spoke to him in Farsi. Mister Ali nodded and the two men departed just as quickly as they entered.

"Excuse me, Master Thomas," Mister Ali knelt down and examined the man. I couldn't see anything wrong with him. Mister Ali stood up and walked deeper into the kitchen. He opened a cabinet that appeared to be rarely used, and I glimpsed a multitude of bottles inside. Some were dusty, some were shiny. There were a few that contained fluids a myriad of colors—deep dark red, pale milky blue, pure green, and others. Mister Ali pushed them aside and selected a bottle from the back. It was dusty and dull looking, the green glass of the bottle hiding whatever was inside.

Mister Ali pulled the cork and poured a clear fluid into the closest glass he could find. He came back to the table and knelt beside the wounded man. Lifting his head with one hand, Mister Ali poured half the contents of the glass into the man's slightly open mouth. He immediately woke up, coughing.

The man looked around to get his bearings, and then, realizing what had happened, thanked Mister Ali in Farsi. Rubbing his head, he once again entered the front of the restaurant. Mister Ali placed the cup on the table and sat across from me. I looked at the fluid left in the glass in awe.

Mister Ali leaned back in his seat. "I have the perfect tale for the occasion," he stated casually, continuing as if nothing had happened. "It is the story of Harun Al-Rashid, who once ate in this very kitchen, although it was in a different city at the time. This was many years ago, but the times were similar—"

At this point, there was a whistling sound that quickly got louder and ended in a deep thud from the front of the restaurant, followed by a rush of air that rustled the beads in the doorway. Mister Ali paused. It wasn't the loudest impact I had heard, but it was different than the others, a jarring that seemed to penetrate the deepest parts of the thick stone walls of the fortress. It didn't even shake the building. The rush of hot air was new, however, and it had a distinct smell, sharp like gunpowder.

Mister Ali looked as if he was concentrating intently, his eyes squinting. Everything had gone quiet. He stood up and looked at me, his carefree look gone. "I'm sorry, Master Thomas, but I may be needed up front." More than the explosions, more than the shrieks, more than the wounded man, Mister Ali's change from indifference to concern frightened me the most. He walked out of the room, his step steady and sure.

I waited a few minutes, the sounds from the front of the restaurant a chaotic mix of violent impact and unearthly screams. I couldn't stand not knowing how the battle was going, so I slid out of the booth with the idea of just peeking through the door to see if everything was okay. The thought was frightening, but the thought of being alone was even more so. I pretended I was Errol Flynn as Robin Hood, bravely facing the Sheriff of Nottingham, to help steel my nerves.

The doorway was more like a short hallway of stone, so I slid along to the front. It didn't take more than a few steps for me to see that the entire front of the restaurant was blown away, and large parts of the roof were missing.

The restaurant was charred from explosions and flames, tables and chairs were in pieces throughout the room. The decorations I loved were shattered. In the distance the street itself was full of wreckage. The front of the department store facing the restaurant was badly damaged. The skies were full of flying creatures that stayed at a distance, while the streets appeared to be empty. Dominating it all was the towering form of my grandfather. He stood tall on the sidewalk, wielding his cane. Whole swaths of figures in the sky would disappear as he aimed it at them. The air would shimmer as if I was looking through heat rising off the desert floor, and then the creatures would just disappear. Grandfather laughed and looked around.

Approaching along the street was a reddish creature of massive size. Flames burned along its skin. It appeared to be attempting to sneak up on my grandfather. I looked around and grabbed a knife off of one of the tables that was still standing. I inched forward, confident in the knowledge that I would be able to save my grandfather by surprising the fiery creature.

I had taken two steps when it turned and looked at me. The malice in its eyes, the deep red depths of its power and hatred froze me.

The next thing I knew I was on the floor, dust falling on my head. My white shirt was singed at the shoulder. When I was younger I had fallen off of a tree and landed flat on my back. I felt the impact across my whole body, and it knocked all the air from my lungs. This felt the same way. I struggled for breath as I crawled to my knees.

"Tommy, you fool, get back in the kitchen!" My grandfather was peering back at me. Mister Oz stood next to him, making motions with his hands.

"*Pehlivan*, my shields will hold, but the light is faltering." It was then I noticed that the Persian Garden restaurant sign was shining on them both. It flickered.

"Now, Tommy!" I don't know if it was anger or concern in his voice, but Grandfather's tone was not one I could ignore.

I stumbled back to the kitchen and pulled myself back into the booth. After a few deep breaths, I drank some water. Grandfather burst through the bead-covered door into the kitchen. He was covered in dust, his suit was torn, and he was wet with perspiration, but what struck me the most was his white hair, which was no longer slicked back but disheveled and wild.

Mister Ali came in right behind. Before my grandfather could say anything, Mister Ali stated, "We have sustained too much damage to handle Shadows."

Grandfather nodded, and tapped his cane on the floor. Small sparks flashed with each tap. "Of course." He sounded terse and dismissive.

"What of the Ifrit in the streets?"

Grandfather shook his head. "If I'm not there to hold them off, the walls won't hold." This began a rapid exchange between Mister Ali and my grandfather.

"The alley?"

"Shadows." Mister Ali nodded.

"The sky?"

"Djinn. I could destroy them but in these close quarters I would put too many innocent people in danger."

"Shadows? Ifrit? Djinn? I warned you of this Declan!" Mister Ali started pacing. "What are our options now? The Ifrit or Djinn will destroy the rest of our lights, and then the Shadows will destroy us!"

Mister Oz ran in. He was bleeding profusely from a cut above his brow, and I could see metallic armor shining through rents in his robes. He had a curved knife in his right hand. As he approached, the casual joy he showed in the alley was gone. He bowed to my grandfather.

"A Marid approaches, *Pehlivan*."

My grandfather closed his eyes, tapping his cane on the tile. After a moment, he opened his eyes and whispered, "We have no choice; we must take the river."

There was a pained expression on Mister Ali's face. "I cannot argue, but I don't know if that is due to wisdom or despair." He approached me and gently took my arm. "Come, Master Thomas. I'm afraid we have misled you. You are not safe here, and we need to take a journey underground."

I stood up and looked around. Everyone but my grandfather looked in shock. My grandfather put his arm on my shoulder and said, "I cannot join you, Tommy. I have battled the river before and..." His voice trailed off before he continued. "Let me just say that it will be better for you if I don't come."

"Archmage, you can't be serious!" It was Mister Oz, who held a piece of his robe against the gash on his brow.

There was another explosion, and my grandfather stood up. He looked magnificent and terrible. His eyes were cold and steady, a stark contrast to his wild hair and torn suit. Sparks flew from where his hand grasped his cane. "I cannot travel the river, and the staff cannot stay here to be taken by the Shadows or, even worse, a Marid."

Grandfather knelt down in front of me and took my arm in his left hand. "Take this," he said, holding out the cane with his right hand.

Stunned, I opened my hand as he placed the cane in my palm. It was the first time I had ever touched it, and I struggle to describe it now. I imagine this would be the feeling if a blind person was given the gift of sight. I felt one with the cane, a part of my own being that had been kept from me was suddenly restored.

As I started to understand and embrace this new feeling—this new life—that was given to me, my senses came alive. I felt a warmth spread from my palm to my arm to my chest and then my entire body. I looked at the cane, and the strange runes looked entirely different than before. I still could not read them, but I sensed a purpose in their patterns.

I held the cane in both hands and closed my eyes. I forgot where I was and just felt the energy of the cane—the magic—

flow through me. When I opened my eyes, I looked upon Mister Ali, his eyes wide and his jaw open, staring at me. My grandfather had a smile on his face.

Grandfather turned to Mister Ali, "You must train him, Ali. You have always known—my fate is to act, not teach."

"But what will you do?" I asked, my voice cracking. My parents were little more than a memory, but they were gone, and I felt their loss every day. I couldn't imagine a life without my grandfather. As much as I complained about him, he was still everything to me.

That my grandfather looked different without the cane only made things worse. What I saw only a day before as making him appear weak as he used it to support his body now made him appear weak in its absence.

"Me?" He stood tall. "I am feared, even by a Marid, and they will not expect me to give up the staff. Indeed, I am sure my presence alone will hold them off for some time, and as long as they know I'm here, you will have more time to escape."

"I will join you as your shield, of course." It was Mister Oz, who looked nearly as fierce as my grandfather.

"No!" Mister Ali sounded distraught, more so than during the whole attack.

"I must, father. They will be suspicious if I am not at the *Pehlivan*'s side."

His father shook his head. "But there is no need!"

A massive explosion shook the entire building. Debris shot through the door from the dining room, tearing away strings of beads, which clattered across the floor. I heard a groan coming from the front. My grandfather looked from me to Mister Ali. "Go! Time is short. I will do what I can to give you more," and he ran through the door into the dining room, Mister Oz right behind.

Mister Ali's eyes shone in the harsh neon light. He paused, looking uncertain for a moment, but then put his arm around my shoulder. "Come, Master Thomas. We have a journey ahead of us." He led me further back into the restaurant. I could hear more explosions from the front when it hit me— my grandfather might die.

"Grandfather!" I turned my head and looked over my shoulder. "Can't I use the staff to protect him?" I took two steps when Mister Ali grabbed my arm.

"Perhaps some day, Master Thomas, but today is not that day," he replied as he pulled me deeper into the restaurant, gently pushing me whenever I hesitated.

We stopped in a room somewhere in the rear of the restaurant. There were no windows, and it was dark, lit only by a single gas lamp. The room was surrounded on three sides by shelves, which were piled high with restaurant décor—rugs, curtains, lamps, candles, and other pieces. As I looked around, Mister Ali bent down and pulled a ring up from the floor.

I hadn't noticed, but the stone floor was interrupted by a huge wooden hatch. It looked like an ancient entryway to a wine or root cellar. Mister Ali grunted and pulled the ring with all his strength. It slowly raised off the floor, revealing stone steps leading down to darkness. Air rushed from the hole, smelling wet and stale. It certainly wasn't a wine cellar.

The hatch stood precariously at a right angle to the floor. Mister Ali walked over and grabbed two torches off a shelf. He lit them in the gas lamp and handed me one. I didn't like how it felt to have both my hands full, one with the cane and the other with the torch, so I dropped the torch onto the floor, held up the cane, and, without even knowing how, lit the top of the cane with a powerful light.

Mister Ali looked at me with wide eyes. He was about to say something when an explosion interrupted him. He pointed toward the staircase. "Come, we must hurry. At the bottom of these steps there is an underground river and a boat. I have not been down here in many many years, but it is our only hope of escape."

The room shook in the aftermath of a muffled explosion. Items on the shelves showered down onto the floor, and the hatch fell back in place with a resounding boom. Crumbling stone fell on our heads. "Hurry, Master Thomas! We must go!"

I watched in surprise as he strained and pulled the heavy hatch open with one hand, while his other held the torch. He was short and stout, but his muscles looked massive. He held the hatch open while the building fell around us. I ran to the steps leading down.

Mister Ali followed right behind me. The building shook again, and the hatch fell downward, barely missing his head. As we both stood still, we could hear the moaning and crashing of immense blocks of stone falling above our head. I cried out, "Grandfather!" and turned to leap up the steps. The light from the cane was blinding.

Mister Ali gripped my shoulder and leaned toward me, his eyes very close to mine. "Master Thomas. Your Grandfather is a powerful and resourceful man. You must trust that he found a way to escape. I do." His kind eyes and smile were too much for me to ignore. I couldn't help but trust him. Still, the sense of loss was overwhelming. Grandfather was all I had left in my life. The thought of his dying staggered me.

Mister Ali grabbed the arm I was using to hold the cane and pulled it up, placing the light between us and above our heads like a beacon. "Be strong, Master Thomas. Your grandfather would expect nothing less. Do not look to the past, we must look now to the future."

I took a deep breath, and in the fetid air and magical light knew that Mister Ali was right. My grandfather wanted me to bear his cane—the staff—and I owed that to him. I wiped my tears even as they continued to flow and turned my head, looking down into the deep darkness which concealed a river somewhere below. "Where does the river lead, Mister Ali?"

He let go of my arm and stood up, the torchlight glinting off his eyes. "I know not, Master Thomas. No one does."

Chapter Four

HRUMPH

Each step left the screams, explosions, and falling stone further behind, while ahead of me lay tomb-like silence. The stillness of the descent reminded me of how alone I was now in the world. I had always dreamed of finally being free and on my own in Manhattan, but it was a bitter thought now. My parents were gone, and now my grandfather was gone, too.

I had only one memory of my parents, waking up on Christmas morning and finding a rocking horse under the tree. I ran to them both and hugged them tight. My father patted my back. My mom kissed my cheek. After they died, there were many times when the memory of those hugs kept me going.

I grasped at that memory, at the warm hugs of my departed parents, but there was a key piece now missing—the knowledge that my Grandfather was at least still with me. I felt empty and numb and scared at the thought that he, too, was now nothing more than a comfort from my past.

Even with the bright light of the cane in my hand illuminating our way, I felt the walls pressing against me. Our steps echoed slightly, and that only made things worse, as it was the only sound I could hear. The presence of the cane—the rough outline of the runes against my hand; the tingling of energy I could sense, even if I couldn't understand it—was calming but also frustrating. I had performed some kind of magic, but it was no different than carrying a torch.

I once again felt useless, and step after step of bare stone and quiet wore on me.

Mister Ali didn't speak, and I couldn't bring myself to break the painful silence. I didn't know how I would have reacted if he had mentioned my grandfather, somewhere in the broken building above me.

Jake Kerr

The staircase was broad and circular. I tried to distract myself and focus on details, but each stone step looked like every other one—hewn from rock and smooth from years of use or erosion. Eventually, my arm tired, and I lowered the cane and tapped it on the ground with each step. At the second tap, Mister Ali stopped and turned. "What are you doing?" His tone was curious, not accusatory.

"My arm was getting tired."

He nodded and replied, "Your grandfather loved the sound of the staff. He would tap the ground with it constantly."

Memories flooded into me: Afternoon walks with my grandfather, his cane tapping the cobblestones, alerting the entire neighborhood to his approach. The school play that started without him in the theater and me devastated at his absence, only for me to hear a tap, tap, tap, down a theater aisle in the middle of the first act. I smiled on stage, knowing he was there.

"I know!" I answered, excited that Mister Ali and I had shared at least one memory of my grandfather. I felt a little less alone.

Mister Ali sighed and sat down on a step. "We should rest for a bit."

I looked up the staircase as I sat down. "Will they follow us?"

"The elementals?" Mister Ali laughed. "Goodness no. They know where this staircase leads."

I was sitting next to Mister Ali, the cane resting on its point between us, the light shining down and lighting our faces from above. Mister Ali smiled, and patted me on the knee. "Don't worry, Master Thomas."

I smiled my bravest smile and decided that the time was right to ask some questions. "Do you think Grandfather is alive?"

He stared at me, the light glinting off his eyes. I felt like he was sizing me up, wondering whether I could handle a hard truth. "Yes," he eventually replied.

A surge of happiness filled me. If Grandfather was alive, that meant he could be saved. I clenched the cane. "I will save him."

Mister Ali put his hand on my shoulder and squeezed. "*We* will save him, but first we must get to safety."

I looked down into the shadows where the staircase led. "Will the river at the bottom take us directly to the ocean, or will it lead us to deeper rivers underground?"

"This is not that kind of river. It is a deep magic from within the Earth, a spirit of reckless impudence that plays games on those that dare to travel upon it."

"It's alive?"

"It is alive in the sense that everything around us is alive, including magic. Your staff is alive, which you will discover in time." I looked at the staff as I ran my fingers over some of the runes. I could feel the power and sense the complexity. It didn't feel alive, but it certainly felt natural in my hand.

"So is the river dangerous? You said it was evil."

"I did not say it was evil, Master Thomas. I said it was impudent. That makes it even more dangerous. Those that enter the river never know where or when they will end up. It is the whim of the river itself that guides us, and it is a spirit with a devious sense of humor."

I tried to understand a river that could play tricks on those that floated upon it. After a short while, I spoke again, "What do you mean 'when?' Can the river take us to other times?"

"It can, but it will not with us. The staff can only exist in one time, and even the river cannot change that. We will end up somewhere in our time, Master Thomas, but whether it is in the midst of our enemies or four thousand miles away, I cannot say."

I loved the idea of time travel, which I had marveled at in H.G. Wells' novel *The Time Machine* and had dreamt about ever since. "But for those without the staff, they could travel through time?"

"Dismiss such thoughts!" Mister Ali stated emphatically. "Such a journey leads only to madness, or worse." Standing up, his face looked troubled, the smile gone. "We should continue," he added, taking a step downward while I scrambled to my feet. Mister Ali walked ahead, while I followed. I couldn't see his face, but I was horrified that I had made him angry. I didn't want to be alone and already missed our conversation.

We walked long enough that Mister Ali's torch began to sputter. After countless turns I had no idea if we were descending for ten minutes or sixty. The only noticeable change was the awful smell getting stronger. It was not just the smell of stale air. Everything smelled of age and decay and lack of movement—the air, the water, even the stone. After a few more minutes Mister Ali stopped in front of me and tossed his torch to the ground.

"Let me rest for a bit, Master Thomas. I am strong, but I am still old." He laughed and sat on a step, his previous anger at me apparently gone. I sat down and dropped the tip of the cane on the floor. The sharp sound of the brass tip hitting the stone couldn't help but make me smile. I felt a surge of emotion for Mister Ali. He was my grandfather's friend. He saved me from the collapse of the restaurant. He could train me in the use of the cane. And, perhaps more than anything, he seemed kind and genuinely concerned about me. Even his anger over my question felt more protective than petty in hindsight.

"Can you please call me Tommy, Mister Ali?" He looked at me and smiled.

"Of course! Declan—your grandfather—always hated titles, too. I believe I cuffed him around the head a few times when we first met and he didn't call me 'Archmage,' but I finally gave up." Mister Ali laughed again, the laughs breaking the deathly silence with a welcome joy.

"Archmage?"

"Ah, Tommy," he smiled as he said my name, "it is a title for those that have borne the staff. In fact, come to think of it, I have been rude—I've been calling you *Master* Thomas when it should now be Archmage Thomas!" He paused, but then added, "But I like 'Tommy' better."

He stood, then stretched. "But enough lounging around. We must be off." His torch was dead, but the light of the cane was easily bright enough to light his way, even with me a step behind.

I stood up and as Mister Ali started again I asked another question. "You had the cane before my grandfather?"

As we walked, his answers echoed lightly off the walls. "For but a short time. His father..." Mister Ali paused. "Well, let me put it this way, his father's talents with the staff were not what the world needed at the time, and he agreed that it would be better that Declan wield it. It was my duty to take it to your grandfather. It was an honor and a burden. I am not meant to bear the staff, and its magic is useless in my hands." He paused, turned, and nodded toward the cane, its light filling the staircase all the way to the turns above and below us.

I was about to ask more questions when I heard what sounded like the lapping of water. Mister Ali paused, and then whispered, "We are close, Tommy." He increased his pace, and after a few more twists of the staircase we arrived at a stone landing.

When Mister Ali had said "underground river" I had expected us to come along the banks of raging waters, flowing through stalagmites and stalactites, but the reality was far different. We emerged in a large room whose floor slanted down to a pool of water that flowed into a large tunnel in the far wall. There was a wooden boat sitting in the water, its prow resting on the slanted floor. It was attached to a stone post by an iron chain. The fetid smell was overpowering.

I couldn't make sense of where the smell could be coming from. The pool in front of us was moving gently and lapping against the stone, as if the water was flowing into the room from another source, but the smell was of stagnation and decay. I covered my mouth, and Mister Ali noticed. "Yes, Tommy. The water hasn't left this room in many many years."

We walked further along the landing. I guess you could call it a landing, but it really seemed more like the room was flooded on the other side. With the dank smell, I couldn't imagine where the river was. Perhaps it was blocked further down the tunnel, fouling the water.

As we walked toward the boat I got a better sense of the room. The floor was solid rock, smooth but uneven, stretching twenty feet beyond the base of the staircase, and it had the appearance of what you would see at the bottom of an ancient natural cavern, worn down not by human hands but rather water erosion over many years. The ceiling was perhaps 20 feet above my head and also smooth. Everything appeared normal, but it all felt strange in some way. I shivered when my foot touched the water.

Our feet got wet as we walked down the slanted rock and approached the boat. The boat and chain were the only things in the room that looked like they were made by human hands. Even that perception proved false, as the stone post the chain was connected to appeared to be an odd-shaped stalagmite on closer inspection. The chain looked like it had been melted into the stone during a volcanic eruption eons ago.

I looked down, expecting to see scummy and brown water staining my khaki pants, but to my surprise the water was crystal clear. Despite the smell and Mister Ali's comment about the water not having moved in many years, it looked clear and refreshing.

Mister Ali climbed into the boat and then took my hand to help me in. It looked like a large rowboat, although there were no oars. The wood was old but in fine shape. There wasn't a drop of water inside. I sat down on a wooden plank near the back that acted as a seat, facing Mister Ali, who sat on a similar plank near the center of the boat. The boat was larger than it first appeared and could have fit two or three more men easily. As I twisted on my seat to make myself more comfortable, I noticed that the boat barely rocked as I moved.

I watched as Mister Ali turned his back to me and started fiddling with the chain. He cursed in Farsi using a word I didn't understand and then turned and sat down with a hrumph. "Tommy, I was going to discuss the staff with you later, but I'm afraid you must free us," he said. He didn't sound happy. "So let this be an exception. Otherwise, the staff is too powerful and you too young to use it." He held out his hand and helped me forward.

I felt both hurt and annoyed at Mister Ali's comment. After all, hadn't I used the cane to light our way, and hadn't my grandfather given it to me for a reason? But these thoughts were fleeting, as the challenge of the chain awaited me.

The chain attaching the boat to the post was connected to an iron ring on the top of the prow. It was a solid chain, with no visible way of removing it. A quick glance showed that it was similarly attached to the post. Without some kind of saw I couldn't think of any way to free us. "Use the staff, Tommy," Mister Ali directed. I shrugged and tapped the chain with the bottom of the cane. Nothing happened. I turned back to look at Mister Ali, not knowing what else to do.

"Tommy, think of how you brought forth the light. You didn't provide the light, the staff did. You cannot hack at the chain as if the staff is a garden tool. You must guide the staff, not simply wield it." Mister Ali smiled and waved at the chain again.

I closed my eyes and gripped the cane tight in my right hand. I sensed the power inside and tried to connect it to the chain. I felt the rough shapes of the runes under my fingers as I imagined the chain falling away at a single touch. Something about what I did was close to the solution, but the actual key was just beyond my grasp. I tried to focus on what I was missing when Mister Ali interrupted. "Tommy, you must communicate with the staff. Find a way to tell it what you want, and it will happen!" He smiled an encouraging smile. "Keep at it. You can do it!"

I paused. I didn't know what to say. Mister Ali was wrong. I knew it instinctively—the entire concept of telling the staff what I wanted made no sense; the connection wasn't like that. I didn't know what to say, however, so I looked at Mister Ali and gave him a nod. He smiled and slapped me on the back.

I turned back to the chain. What was the key? I knew that I couldn't request or command the staff to do my bidding. It wasn't communication. It was something more primal. Yet every thought that filled my mind not only didn't offer a solution but came up completely empty, as if there was no connection to the staff at all. Dissolving the chain, turning it into a mist, breaking a link, breaking the ring connected to the boat—I felt like I was doing little more than daydreaming. But I *knew* there was a solution. It was achingly similar to how I brought forth the light and yet different enough that I couldn't grasp it.

I lowered the staff and just thought about needing to be off and onto the river so I could save Grandfather. And with that thought I felt it. It was so obvious. How could I have not realized it? It was like the time a few years earlier when I was playing baseball with my friends. I was a horrible hitter. Nothing I did improved my batting, and my friends mocked me endlessly. One time I was at bat, and I missed a pitch. My friend Travis, who was pitching, asked me if he should throw underhanded. I angrily swung the bat back in the opposite direction to get in position for the next pitch and experienced an epiphany—swinging the bat from the other direction felt natural. I moved to the other side of the plate and hit left-handed from then on. I became one of the best hitters on my street, solely due to my no longer holding the bat how everyone else did but rather holding it the way that felt natural *to me.*

I moved the cane to my right hand. Not because that was the correct thing to do but because it simply felt more comfortable. I then raised the cane above my head, and, without any additional movement, the chain disappeared. I can't even recall if I thought about it at all. Maybe not thinking about it was part of the solution. It was still quite confusing to me. All I knew was that *something* felt right.

The chain didn't collapse into a pile as if I broke a link. It didn't change into a mist. It didn't even make a sound. The chain was there one moment, and the next it was gone. I looked at the empty ring for a moment, stunned at what I saw, and then turned to sit back down. I could now free a specific boat and create light. I smiled. It wasn't a lot, but it was something.

I looked on the face of a stunned Mister Ali. "How did you do that?" he whispered.

I smiled. "You told me to free us." I felt pleased that I did it, but Mister Ali's response started to make me feel a little uncomfortable that it was so easy. What was I missing? Was Mister Ali alarmed at what I did? What was Mister Ali trying to tell me that I didn't know? Could I end up hurting us by taking short cuts? Despite my success, I considered what I had just done and promised myself to listen to Mister Ali more and my instincts less.

Mister Ali shook his head. His voice was full of awe as he replied, "I expected you to labor over the runes for hours and, even then, I expected us to struggle with nothing more than partially opened links or even a damaged boat." He helped me back to my seat, and I heard him whisper, "I haven't seen such a keen connection to the staff since…" Mister Ali stopped. I had the feeling he wanted to continue but perhaps felt it unwise.

Impressing Mister Ali erased my earlier hesitation. I was a natural! I sat down facing the front of the boat, my back to the tunnel, wondering what else I could do with the staff. Mister Ali faced me from his seat on the plank in the middle. He was quiet, so I asked, "What do we do next?"

"We wait," he said. A moment later, with us both sitting still in the boat, and the sound of nothing but lapping water, the boat moved. There was a slight tug as the boat broke free from the stone landing. It slowly gained speed and headed toward the tunnel that led out of the room.

The boat didn't turn, but floated rear-first toward the tunnel. I looked over my shoulder and squinted into the darkness. I heard a whooshing sound and then the sound of creaking iron, as if a gate was being raised or a heavy door was being opened. A rush of air hit my face. It felt wet and smelled fresh and clean. After being surrounded by the stale air of the room, I felt myself drawn to wherever the breeze came from.

We glided into the tunnel, and the boat sped up. The light from the cane illuminated everything, but the tunnel curved, and I could not see very far ahead. The room behind us fell into darkness as we moved further and further down the tunnel.

The tunnel itself did not appear to be man-made. The water went right up against the walls, which were rough and dry.

Whatever watery erosion had formed them millennia ago had not touched the walls or roof again. The roof was low enough that Mister Ali could have touched it with his hands if he were standing. The river flowed gently, but our boat moved faster and faster.

Mister Ali remained silent as I looked around. He had a calm look on his face, but he was tapping his foot. "Is there a problem, Mister Ali?" I asked.

"No, Tommy. I am just preparing myself for the river."

"This isn't the river?" I looked at the water. Sure, it was probably too small to be considered a river, but we were underground, and I assumed new rules applied. I looked at Mister Ali.

"This is," he paused, as if looking for the right words, "an entrance to the river." He nodded to himself. "This water exists solely to bring someone to the river. It has no other function, and that is why it smelled the way it did. It is not a spring, a tributary, or a stream."

I couldn't quite understand what Mister Ali was saying, but by now I had learned to just file away his explanations and move on. If I asked about everything I didn't understand, we would be buried under stone in the restaurant far above. I looked over my shoulder to see the tunnel the boat was backing its way into. The light from the cane glinted off of something ahead. I noticed the water getting a bit more choppy. Still, the boat didn't jostle at all as it glided forward.

"I see something, Mister Ali. The light reflected off something near that turn ahead."

Mister Ali squinted and then nodded. "It is the gateway to Nar Marratum, the bitter river which will bear us on our journey." I was about to ask why he called the river "bitter," but we were moving quite fast by now, and I focused on the approaching gate. Beyond it the tunnel straightened and continued as far as I could see.

The gate was a large iron portcullis. The bottom spikes hung from the ceiling, and I could see deep grooves down each side of the tunnel which were worn by the raising and lowering of the gate. We were just past the gate when a screech of iron grinding filled my ears. I watched as the gate steadily lowered into the water.

"There is no going back now, my dear Tommy. We are at the river's mercy." He smiled, but there was a grimness to it rather than the mirth I was getting used to.

The water was moving quickly and getting quite violent. The boat remained as stable as if it were on dry ground, and I found the contrast unsettling. "What if we are thrown from the boat! How would we get back in?"

Mister Ali reached forward and took my hand, a comforting smile on his face. "You need not fear violence from the river, Tommy. It is a wicked thing, but it won't drown you." He paused, as if considering his words, and then continued, "Let me explain it this way: The river won't hurt us, but it will deliver us to a spot that very well may be dangerous. As I said earlier, the river will put us where it will cause the most mischief. Sometimes that is in the middle of grave danger. Sometimes it is where it will change our lives in ways that perhaps death would have been preferred. And, sometimes—" Mister Ali paused again. I noticed that he was much more careful with his words than his son. "Sometimes it will put you somewhere that seems innocent enough but will have a great impact on your life later, even years later."

Mister Ali pointed over my shoulder. "And here it is, young Tommy. The mighty Nar Marratum!" I turned around and faced the rear of the boat, which was still moving backward through the water after backing us out of the landing. The boat shot out of the tunnel into an immense body of water. It flowed right past us from my left to my right, but I couldn't see the other side of the river, even in the bright light of the cane.

We continued to move backward across the river rather than along it. The water slammed against the boat, spraying over the side and into our faces. Despite the pounding, the ride remained as gentle as a leaf floating on a serene lake. I looked past Mister Ali toward the way we entered the river, but we had already traveled so far that the tunnel we exited was lost in the darkness. The roar of the river was overwhelming as it echoed within the enclosed chamber. I looked up but couldn't see the roof.

"Are we going to the other side?" I shouted toward Mister Ali. He shook his head.

"We will get to the center and then our travels begin." I turned back toward the rear of the boat and looked into the distance. I marveled at how wide this river must be. We had covered a great distance and apparently weren't even halfway across yet. Mister Ali tapped me on the shoulder.

I turned to see him removing his many-colored robe. He handed it to me, and said, "Cut it in half," making sawing motions with his hands in case I couldn't hear him over the roar of the river. I took the robe but didn't know why I should cut it in half and, for that matter, how to cut it in half. As if reading my mind, Mister Ali pointed and shouted, "Use the staff."

I remembered my grandfather unsheathing the sword from the cane, and I repeated his actions. There was a slight hesitation, and then the sword slid out of the cane easily. I lifted the robe, and began cutting it into two even parts as well as I could. The robe was thick, and I expected quite a bit of hacking at the material, but as the sword touched the cloth it sliced through with ease. It was as if the cloth itself was parting out of respect for the blade.

I handed the pieces to Mister Ali, asking "What are these for?"

He handed one half back and leaned toward my ear. "We need to make the boat comfortable. This may be a very long journey." The boat slowed, and then the prow slid around, facing downstream. After a slight pause, the boat shot down the river.

Mister Ali laid his robe on the bottom of the boat, rolling up one end into a small pile. He took his shoes off and placed them under his seat. He sat on the robe and leaned on the rolled up part. He motioned toward me, pointed toward my feet and said, "Sit."

I placed my portion of the robe on the floor of the boat and sat upon it. The sides of the boat shielded us from the air rushing by, and the river was much quieter as we moved downstream than when we were moving across it, but it was still loud.

Mister Ali didn't say anything. He looked relaxed. Surrounded by the noise of the river and the tumult of the water, the boat remained calm, and for the first time since I walked into the alley with my grandfather, I had the time to consider what was happening.

I thought of the grandfather I knew, sitting in the theater with me and smiling at my delight as Errol Flynn acted the hero. I thought of the grandfather I hadn't known existed, holding off frightening creatures of the dark and smiling as he destroyed others with a wave of his cane. Both of those grandfathers were gone. The thought as to who would raise me entered my head, absurd as it was. Certainly I had more pressing problems than wondering where I was going to live when school was out.

I stifled a laugh for focusing on something so ordinary while I was sitting in a magic boat on a dangerous living river but the suppressed laugh somehow came out a sob. I was embarrassed and tried to hide my fear and sadness. I wiped my eyes so no tears would fall while trying not to bring attention to myself, but Mister Ali was looking right at me. He reached forward and put his hand on my shoulder. He didn't smile, and he didn't say anything. He just squeezed my shoulder.

I turned away and gripped the staff in my fist. Wherever the river took us, I would rescue my grandfather. I was an Archmage, as Mister Ali said, and I could at least make light. That had to mean something against the Shadows. I turned back to face Mister Ali, hoping he could see the determination on my face, but his eyes were closed.

I considered resting, but the light from the staff reflecting off the river caught my attention. It was impossible to tell if the turbulent water was clear or dark, as its surface was impenetrable. I squinted into the distance, but there was nothing but water as far as the light shone. I couldn't see the banks of the river or a roof above us.

I noticed Mister Ali watching me. Without the robe hiding his clothing and body, I could see that he was dressed for battle. The colorful vest that I always took as simply a costume or uniform on the staff of the restaurant was actually reinforced leather, decorated with jewels and stitched with bright thread—but it was still armor. His legs were in the loose fitting clothing that reminded me of the sheiks I saw in the movies, but I was certain that it was hiding leather armor covering his legs, as well.

Mister Ali also looked more impressive without the folds of his robe distracting me. His arms were thick with muscles, and although he was clearly old and a bit stout around the middle, he reminded me of my grandfather—a mighty warrior well past his prime but still a warrior. He nodded, as if reading my thoughts, and leaned close. "There is much to discuss, young Tommy." He sat up and crossed his legs. I did the same.

"So I understand that you have no experience with magic."

I paused. At first I was not sure if I wanted to tell him anything but then I remembered that Grandfather himself trusted Mister Ali. So I answered him truthfully. "Well, that depends."

Mister Ali raised an eyebrow. "Depends upon what?"

"On how you define 'experience.'"

"Why don't you tell me, and we can go from there."

So I did.

Chapter Five

I BATTLE A RIVER

I explained to Mister Ali that Grandfather would take me to Coney Island a few times every Summer, and one time during the previous Summer we passed a street magician. I couldn't remember ever seeing one before.

I quickly found out why. The musicians and dancers were much more popular. Even the fortune-telling gypsies did better than the magician. As we approached I could hear that the magician was being heckled by several boys my age. I heard one boy say, "I'll give you a dime to disappear!" which generated laughter from his friends.

Grandfather changed direction and strode directly to the magician, his cane tapping out the warning of his approach. While Grandfather was often difficult to live with, I knew he was a good man and couldn't stand injustice. I looked forward to him quieting the hecklers with some sharp words or even a thwap from his cane. I had experienced both myself.

He shoved past the boys who quieted in his presence. The magician had a folding table with some glasses on it, and Grandfather smacked his cane onto the tabletop, making the glasses shake. "So what's your game, young man?"

The magician was wiry and looked about college age. He had black curly hair and a small face that fit his small frame. He was dressed in a shabby suit that gave him the look of a struggling poet or other artist.

"My game? I'm a magician, old man." The magician crossed his arms.

"That remains to be seen. Show me." Grandfather lowered his cane directly in front of himself and leaned on it with both hands.

The magician rolled his eyes and grabbed a pitcher of water from behind him and poured it into a glass. He then smiled at my grandfather and made a gesture with his fingers. The clear water turned blue. He moved his fingers again and the water turned red.

I had never seen magic before, and the change was so fast and complete that I found it rather impressive. Grandfather, however, snorted. "An illusionist, eh? But what good is an illusion that science can replicate?" He lifted his cane and pointed it at the young illusionist, who backed up a step. "Sorensen could do that with chemicals." He then stood up straight. "Show me a *real* illusion. One that science hasn't ruined."

"That's the only one I know," the magician replied, anger rising in his voice. "And I don't know who Sorensen is, but these aren't stupid chemicals. This is *magic*."

Grandfather leaned forward, and I could see that he was losing his temper. The magician's audience was enthralled, but it was clear that they were more interested in the old man assaulting the magician than the magician himself. I tugged on my grandfather's sleeve. He looked down at me, and I nodded over my shoulder and said, "Coney Island."

He nodded and tapped the table with his cane. "You are wasting your time." He then turned and started walking.

The magician didn't reply and returned to turning the water into colorful mixtures. I could tell Grandfather was troubled. He muttered about never finding a real magician in America, which surprised me since I didn't think there were any real magicians anywhere. Sure the water thing didn't seem very complicated, but, as magic went, I thought it was pretty neat.

Mister Ali nodded his head as I finished. "Yes, it would not surprise me that Declan would investigate even a hint of magic if it was put in his path. He has seen the decline in magic and I am sure that your experience was not his only disappointment." He folded his hands together. "But he understands that magic is coming to an end. His comment on science spoke volumes."

"But that is not what he said at the restaurant, Mister Ali. He said that magic was needed to defend us against the magical creatures."

"That is not exactly what he said, Tommy. He said the *staff* was needed to protect us. He knows magic is dying. The only difference in opinion is how to handle it." Mister Ali yawned, and that led me to yawn. "Are you tired? Do you need to rest?"

At the mention of rest, a wave of exhaustion hit me, as if it had broken through a barrier and was rushing through to my bones. It couldn't have been more than early evening, but I felt like it was late into the night. The light on the cane dimmed a bit, and my eyes were heavy with drowsiness.

"I feel very tired, Mister Ali, but I want to know more about magic."

Mister Ali shrugged. "I'm afraid there's not much to say. There are powerful magicians in the world, very powerful magicians, but they are incredibly rare and becoming rarer with every generation. The magician you saw is probably not unlike the other magicians across the globe—performing magic to disappointed crowds that know scientists can do better."

I was not surprised at Mister Ali's words. I hadn't mentioned it to him but there was a magic club at my school, Phillips Andover. The members were the unpopular freaks that no one liked. The radio and flying clubs were more popular. Heck, even the physics club was more popular, and none of its members had girlfriends. More than anything, the magic club was an easy target for teasing.

I closed my eyes, and Mister Ali spoke up. "Lie down and rest, Tommy. Let the staff go dark, and I will watch over you." I opened my eyes, and Mister Ali pointed to the floor, where my half of his robe lay folded up.

I didn't even have the energy to reply. I unfolded the robe, curled over a corner for my head, and lay down. The cane went dark as I closed my eyes and loosened my grip. I cradled it in my arms and let sleep overtake me.

I was back at Andover and for some reason I was at a meeting of the magic club. I was in the front of the room giving a lecture on contemporary magic creatures. I was so nervous that I could do no more than stare at my notes and read them. I described fiery Ifrit and flying Djinn, doing my best to describe them using my own experience of seeing them. I glanced up when I got to Shadows and saw that I was alone in the room.

Not a single desk was occupied. On one hand I was relieved, as I had never been comfortable speaking in front of others, but on the other I was embarrassed—the lamest club in the school, and I was presumably the only member. I was unsure of this, however, and spoke up, "Is anyone there?" The lights flickered, and I felt a deep dread.

I was alone, and I had to escape. The certainty of this was absolute. I stumbled down the narrow gap between a row of desks, heading for the door. I stopped as the lights went out. When they came back on they were now candles, and the classroom looked like a stone room in an old castle. The flickering shadows started to congeal and form into magical Shadows. They were all around me, and I pushed aside desks as I looked for a gap to escape.

But there was no escape. I shouted for help, but no one answered. The blackness surrounded me, and I shouted again, screaming for someone, anyone, to help me. A voice, metallic and deep and ominous replied from the depths. "You are alone." Another voice and then another repeated the words. "You are alone." "You are alone." "You are alone."

The blackness was about to overwhelm me when I heard Mister Ali's voice in the distance. "I'm here, Tommy. You aren't alone." I felt someone shaking my shoulder. I opened my eyes, and there was Mister Ali, his entire body illuminated in the blinding light of the cane, which had never shone brighter. "Tommy, you had a nightmare. Everything is fine."

I sat up. Mister Ali watched me, concern filling his face. The dread of the nightmare was still fresh in my mind, but looking upon Mister Ali scared me more. He looked exhausted. His eyes were red, and there were dark circles under them. Even his toothy smile couldn't hide the fact that he had pushed himself close to the limit.

"How long have I been asleep?" I asked. It must have been hours.

"Long enough, Tommy. The staff burns bright, and a nightmare is of little concern to those awake." He smiled, but it appeared forced. "I need but a couple hours to regain my strength, and then we can talk." His eyes closed, and I left Mister Ali alone while the boat sped on through the darkness. The time sped on, as well, for I spent every minute examining the cane—staff, I kept reminding myself, not cane.

There were two forces at work while I examined all of the intricate runes and engravings. The one was the wonderful feeling that I instinctively knew the power of the staff that was revealed to me—light. Light just made perfect sense at a every level. I could not say that I understood *how*, but at least I understood. It was like understanding breathing. You may not know how you breathe, but you know you *can* breathe.

The other force was one of frustration over everything else. I didn't understand how my grandfather blew things up or sent out bolts of destruction. The concept of a shield was equally beyond me. It seemed like mastering the cane was a hopeless goal. I vaguely understood the runes, but it was like memorizing the notes on a piano and expecting to be able to play Rachmaninoff the first time your fingers touch the keys.

Many minutes later, or perhaps even hours, Mister Ali stirred. He stretched his arms and then turned in his seat. As he looked at me, he smiled, but I could see that he hadn't slept well. His face was worn and haggard. He still looked immensely tired. He gracefully swung his legs over his seat and slid next to me.

"My dear Tommy. How are you?"

"I'm a little hungry, but I feel good. I've been working on the cane, and it's challenging."

Mentioning the cane brought a smile to Mister Ali's lips. "Tommy. Of course it is. I would expect no less."

"Could you maybe show me how Grandfather used it? Show me how he held it or what he did?" I lowered my head. "I'm afraid that all I can do is make light."

"Don't be discouraged! Although learning the staff will not be so simple as me showing you how to hold it." At this point Mister Ali touched me lightly on the chest with his finger. "But you can do it, Tommy. I know you can. Remember, in all the world you are the only one who can unravel its power."

For the first time it hit home that I was perhaps special for more than just being one of the people—Archmages—who had carried the staff. The prospect was not a little frightening, and I clutched at a way out, not because I wanted to use it, but because it was reassuring to know it was there. "But you are an Archmage, too. You can take the staff if you want to!"

"Remember, Tommy, I was but a messenger. I carried the staff to your grandfather, nothing more. Even during that short time, I could tell that it was not meant for my hands. I am a Archmage by chance; you are one by nature. So as much as I would love to remove this burden from you, I cannot. No one can, and, as I did for your grandfather, I will do my best to prepare you."

I nodded. "Thank you, Mister Ali. I just can't seem to grasp how to control it."

"Yes. It is unfair that you bear the staff in these circumstances, but it is not to be avoided." Mister Ali added, "A voyage along Nar Marratum is not the best place to teach you about the staff, its history, and the steps to learning how to master it." He motioned beyond the boat. "The magic is too oppressive for me to concentrate." I couldn't sense anything but fast-moving water, but I nodded in agreement anyway. "All I can tell you now is to let the staff guide you as you investigate its power. Its voice is confusing and hard to fathom, but it will be your best guide for now."

I was about to speak, but Mister Ali stood to return to his seat. He smiled, his face again full of weariness, and said, "But let's speak no more of it. The time will come when we can; I will let you know when that time is."

What I wanted to say but kept to myself was that the staff was not confusing or difficult at all. The best way to describe it was that the staff spoke to me in a myriad of voices. What was difficult was that I could understand only one. That voice spoke with complete clarity, but the others were muddled.

I had hoped that Mister Ali could help me translate those other voices. But he described something much different. For the first time as the bearer of the staff, it struck me that I would ultimately be my own teacher.

Mister Ali sat upright, his eyes looking out into the distance. He didn't move, but occasionally his head would nod, and I knew that he was not meditating—he was fighting the urge to rest.

I took to practicing with the staff. I had by now understood how to easily manipulate the magical light of the cane, and I delighted myself by dimming it and making it bright. Mister Ali either didn't notice as he dozed or he didn't care, for he continued to remain still.

Eventually, I learned how to focus the beam of light, and I sent strong beams toward the banks, the ceiling, and into the depths of the water. I focused the light to such intensity that its beam shone far into the distance, but no matter how strong I made the light, I could see nothing but darkness at its end.

When I got bored of peering into the darkness, I created multiple beams of light that shot in all directions. As time wore on I learned to control even these, and I playfully aimed them at the tops of waves in the river, trying to hit as many as I could at one time. I became quite proficient at this and realized that

I was moving the staff around to facilitate my aim. It reminded me of Grandfather using the cane's sword as he reflected the floodlight at the Shadows. I wondered if the light of the cane would be considered artificial light, but then immediately dismissed the idea—if it were then my grandfather would have simply used the cane to disperse the Shadows. The possibility that my grandfather didn't know how to draw light from his own magical cane never crossed my mind.

I tired of playing with the light and closed my eyes as I tried to think of other things I could do with the staff. One of my first disappointments was realizing that I couldn't use the staff to communicate with or observe others. I had tried to focus on my grandfather, to see if he was safe, but the staff remained silent.

I looked at the water churning behind the boat and had a new idea—guiding the boat. I considered the possibility, examining runes and opening my mind to the staff. I focused on utilizing the staff to defeat the river and take us where I wanted to go, but there was simply no answer.

I decided to put the staff in the water and guide the boat that way, and while I realized I had no indication it would work, I couldn't see anything wrong with it, either. I held the staff firmly in both my hands and turned toward the rear of the boat. The water thrashed in front of me as we sped forward.

I turned and faced the river. I knew where I wanted to go. I wanted to go home to New York. I wanted to save my grandfather. I *would* save him. I squeezed tight. It was just me, the river, and the staff itself.

I want to go home, I thought, and plunged the end of the staff into the river.

The boat immediately bucked to the side and then the other. It wasn't enough to toss us into the water, but it woke Mister Ali. "Tommy, what is going on!" he exclaimed as he turned in his seat. I turned to tell him everything was okay, but the boat bucked again spilling Mister Ali onto the floor. The alarm in his face frightened me.

I looked down at the water as it thrashed around the cane, violent and chaotic. The force of the water tugged at my arms, but I held on. *Home*, I thought, focusing all my energy on pushing the boat in that direction, whichever it might be.

The river fought back.

Jake Kerr

The boat rolled left and right. It took all my effort to keep my balance. The water where I had placed the staff was a cauldron of bubbles and white froth. The cane jerked back and forth. I could hear Mister Ali on the edge of my consciousness telling me to stop, but all I was focusing on was keeping my grip on the cane and getting home. The staff started to heat up and I felt myself being pulled forward. I set my feet and tried to hold my ground.

The boat shook more violently, and any thought of controlling it left my mind as I focused solely on stopping and getting the staff back into the boat. I was too weak, and the pull on the staff was too strong. What started as a slow tug turned into my body sliding toward the edge of the boat and the water. I held steady for a moment, and then I felt a horrific wrenching as my body was thrown into the air at the same time the force pulling me toward the water pulled down. I waited for the inevitable splash and rush of water over my head when a hand shot out and grabbed my arm. I looked back and saw Mister Ali, one arm grasping a wooden plank and the other holding my arm, his teeth clenched at the effort.

The pain was horrible as my body was used as the battleground between the river and Mister Ali. I ignored everything

— 95 —

but focusing my thoughts on the staff. I looked for a solution, any solution. The cane was getting hot enough that it started to burn my hands, but I knew I would never lose my grip. And suddenly it hit me—I may not be able to direct the river but perhaps I could hurt it.

The power to control the river didn't exist—that was clear—but the moment I considered whether the river could control or take the staff everything came together. Of course it couldn't. The idea was preposterous. I laughed as instinct took over. If the river wanted to fight, I would fight. I needed to send a painful message, and I knew the staff would deliver it.

The water around the end of the cane turned jet black, and the force pulling me forward suddenly let go. I hurtled back into Mister Ali, scattering us across the bottom of the boat. I pulled myself to my knees as Mister Ali scrambled over to me.

"What have you done!" There was anger in his face as he looked at me.

"I'm sorry, Mister Ali." I lowered my head. I felt stupid for doing something so risky without asking him first. "I thought I could guide us from the river. If I knew it would end this way, I never would have done it."

"How else would it end?" Mister Ali's anger again arose. "To think a child could command the Nar Marratum to do his whim…" Mister Ali stopped and looked at me, and his face softened. His voice was calm as he continued. "Tommy, I apologize. This is my fault. I told you to learn more about the staff." He paused for a moment, and then added, "but it is dangerous to attempt things you don't understand. In the future, let me know what you would like to practice, and I'll give you whatever advice I can."

There were a mass of conflicting emotions in my head. He was right that I had attempted something I didn't understand—I knew that when I began. But I also knew that if I didn't push myself I would never understand. I also trusted Mister Ali. His concern for me was always first and foremost. But I was also disappointed that he still didn't seem to trust me even as he was telling me to trust myself.

I glanced back at the river, angry that I couldn't control it in the end, and gasped. In the aftermath of my fight with the river Mister Ali and I had failed to notice that we were no longer on it. The boat was slowly spinning in a circle on a small placid underwater lake. The light from my cane reflected off of stone walls around us. The sound and violence of the river was gone, and we were surrounded by stillness and quiet. At the end of the cavern was a landing very similar to the one we left when we entered the boat.

"Our journey on the river has ended!" The joy in Mister Ali's voice was clear. I thought back to the respect, if not fear, that was in his voice when we first approached the river, and realized that we could have been in for a much longer voyage. Mister Ali leaned over the edge of the boat and started to row with his hands. I leaned over the other side and did the same.

"Where are we?" I looked around, but could see nothing more than a large pool of water surrounded by stone.

"We won't know until we leave this room. Look, there is our way out." He pointed forward with an arm wet to the shoulder. I looked ahead and saw iron footholds on the far wall rising up from the floor and extending all the way to the ceiling. The footholds became lost in a blot of darkness that could have been a hole or a shadow.

"Those look like the handholds that lead out of a sewer," I noted.

"Sewer… cistern… it could even be the exit from a cellar. The important thing to remember is that once we get out, we won't be able to get back. So whatever we face, retreat is not an option."

The boat made good progress, and it wasn't long before I heard a splash as Mister Ali jumped into the water to guide the boat in. The water came up to his waist, but it quickly fell to his thighs and then to his knees as he pulled the boat up the landing. With a bump, the boat came to a stop, its prow grinding against stone.

Mister Ali took a step toward me and held out his arms. "No sense for both of us to get wet." He smiled. I jumped into his arms, and he easily carried me the few steps to where it was dry.

I thanked him and looked around. "What now?" I looked at the rungs leading up into the darkness.

Mister Ali followed my gaze to the darkness. "The future awaits."

Chapter Six

PILES OF STICKS AND STONES

Mister Ali climbed ahead of me, the occasional squeak of his leather armor leading my way as his soft leather shoes made no sound. The rungs were cold and hard but not unbearable to climb. I was wearing the outfit I normally wore to the theater on Saturdays—khaki pants and a dress shirt. While not convenient for adventuring, it had the benefit of including leather shoes and a leather belt, both which helped in the climb. The shoes protected my feet from the iron rungs, while I tucked the cane into the belt. The only annoyance was that I had to stop often to tug on the belt, as the staff would slowly slip down. The worst part was that we had to climb in utter darkness, as the cane's light extinguished the moment I took my hands off it.

"I see a light!" Mister Ali exclaimed. I looked up and saw a slight glow far above. "We must be careful. I am sure the river was not in a good mood when it decided where to leave us."

I felt differently. As I wrenched the staff from the river, I felt that the river was as happy to have me gone as I was to leave. It was a battle to a draw—at least it felt like a battle to a draw—and I didn't think the river had any conscious say on where we were deposited other than a spot where we wouldn't be able to get back easily.

The dull light above slowly grew stronger, pushing back the frightening darkness. The rungs came up to a ledge and as Mister Ali looked over the lip, he described what he saw. "It's the end of a mine shaft. There are rail tracks and electric lighting."

He pulled himself up and then turned and pulled me up with ease. The moment I was on my feet, Mister Ali turned to the other direction and dropped into a crouched position. He looked ready to fight.

"We must be careful," he whispered. "Our enemies could be anywhere."

I looked around, and saw nothing but shadows. But they weren't the Shadows that attacked my grandfather and me, just the darkness hidden from the electric lights. I pulled out the staff and held it up. Light sprung from the end and lit up the whole corridor. It was a small tunnel, hewn from solid rock. We were at the end of a rail line that led up the tunnel. It disappeared in a curve that started about twenty-five yards away. The corridor echoed with the clanging sound of a generator in the distance.

I turned to see if anything might have followed us and where there was once a ledge with a ladder leading down was now a solid wall of rock. I tested it with the staff, but all it did was make a small tap. "Mister Ali…"

He turned and nodded. He didn't seem surprised. "Onward then. I will lead."

I fell into step a few paces behind Mister Ali. I couldn't see his face, but he was constantly murmuring and wringing his hands. Every once in a while he would stop and then wave a hand to the left or right. It all seemed very odd to me.

We had traveled around the first turn when Mister Ali stopped and turned to me. "There is magic here, so we must be careful" He waved his arms around the tunnel. "And I don't believe it to be a threat. Still, we don't know why the river chose this destination, so we should be careful. The exit is ahead, and I would like us to be prepared for anything." He continued forward.

His eyes glinted in the light of the cane—he appeared to rarely blink as he continuously surveyed the tunnel around us. As we had moved further along our journey the jovial Mister Ali receded further and further back, as the warrior Mister Ali came to the fore.

We passed the generator that powered the lights, and approached the entrance to the mine. A bright light shone, and I realized that I had lost all sense of time on the river. At least now I knew it was daytime. We were near the entrance when Mister Ali held out his hand. I stopped as Mister Ali turned around and held a finger to his lips. He pointed to me and held up his palm.

Mister Ali emerged from the mine and slowly proceeded forward, stopping every so often to crouch down and squint into the distance. The mine faced flatlands that extended to the horizon. I couldn't see a living thing.

As he proceeded forward, I tried to look for danger outside the mine. The landscape was completely alien to me, and I wondered if, like John Carter, we had perhaps been transported to Mars. The ground was arid, with large stones protruding from the dirt in random spots. The vegetation was sparse and looked half-dead. It was also hot. The temperature had risen so gradually as we traveled along the mine that I hadn't noticed the scorching heat until it was overpowering.

The good news was that we were on a hill, which made sense since we were in a mine. This presented us with a very good view moving forward. It would be tough to surprise us, and—I noted happily, it was bright enough that I didn't think I would have to worry about being surprised by Shadows.

There was a wide path cleared in the dirt that led downward. It avoided some of the steep drops that marked the hill but was still uneven. Mister Ali was on the path standing tall, staring at the plains ahead of us. I noticed him nod his head, and then he turned and gave me the all clear.

I had taken about five steps out of the cave when I saw a dark shape fly over my head toward Mister Ali. To my horror,

Mister Ali fell in a heap. Two more shapes flew toward him, but they clattered against the ground nearby. Mister Ali slowly turned, and I heard him yell, "Tommy! Run back to the mine!" when I felt an excruciating pain in my right hip. My leg gave out, and I dropped the staff as I braced for the fall.

The attack seemed to increase in intensity the moment the staff fell out of my hand. I watched as more projectiles shot toward Mister Ali, who was now rolling around and avoiding them with a feline grace. A blow hit me in the thigh. Scrambling to my knees, a cloud of dust exploded next to me, leaving a track in the dirt. It was from a rock. *A rock?* Who attacks someone with rocks?

I turned to crawl behind a boulder for cover when I noticed the staff. I grabbed it with no other thought in my mind than I needed it. I wasn't pulling it to safety. I wasn't keeping it from an attacker. I clung to it like I clung to my grandfather's sleeve, and like my grandfather the staff led the way.

I stood tall and held up the staff. From somewhere behind me I heard Mister Ali scream "No!"

Another rock hit me, this time glancing off my foot, but I barely felt it as I looked up at our attackers. A projectile flew toward me, and I swung up with the staff. There was a "thunk!" and the stone flew off into the distance. Two more rock whistled toward me, and with a spin a knocked them to the ground. Thud. Thud.

It was me, but it wasn't me hitting the rocks. I swung with the skill of Ted Williams hitting baseballs, but the staff was assisting me in some way. The rocks were flying so fast that the staff moved in my hands like a blur.

"Flee, Tommy!" Mister Ali yelled out. I looked up and saw a path to the top of the hill above the entrance to the mine. I continued to effortlessly knock away stones as I considered Mister Ali's words and then disregarded them. No. I wouldn't flee. The world was stripping away everyone from my life, while I sat by and did nothing. My parents. My Grandfather. Even Mister Ali, who I had just met, was now in danger. I strode toward the path.

I scrambled up the hill, barely paying attention to the rocks as I warded them off with the staff in one hand. At the top was a large outcropping of stone directly over the mine entrance. It was the perfect spot for an ambush, and standing behind it were three figures made of rocks and sticks. They had arms and legs but otherwise had little semblance to a human. I watched as one of them grabbed a rock with an hand made of a broken branches. It twirled and the rock flew at me. I swung the staff, and the rock flew at one of the other figures, hitting it square in what looked like a chest. It exploded into a cloud of dust.

The other two figures paused as they turned toward me. They were alien and horrific looking. Where their eyes would be were dark holes between intertwined sticks. Rocks filled gaps between the tree limbs and sapling trunks that made up the body, and it all came together in a human-like shape. However horrifying they looked, I wasn't afraid. I was hot and angry and, more than anything, ready to finally no longer live a life alone in a secluded townhouse or a private school. I was Errol Flynn! I was the bearer of the staff! I twirled it in my hand and walked toward them.

I knocked away a stone and swung the staff at the second figure, and it also exploded into dust as the end of the staff pounded into its side. The third figure got off a throw, but I was too close, and while I didn't knock it away, it glanced off my side to little effect. Shortly afterward it was also little more than a pile of sticks and rocks.

I looked over the promontory but couldn't see Mister Ali. Just then I felt a hand on my shoulder, and there he was standing behind me. His face was covered in blood, and he was bleeding from various other locations where the rocks had hit him. In his right hand he held a knife. The hilt was colorful and decorated with gems, but the blade was all business, curved and sharp and shiny from many sharpenings.

"Well done, Tommy. Your facility with the staff was unexpected." He looked at the heap of sticks and rocks next to us. "I think I understand." He leaned down and examined it more closely. As he held up and peered at a stick, I noticed that one of the boulders near the edge of the outcropping had indentations all over it. It looked like someone had taken an ice cream scooper and had pulled out hand-sized scoops of rock.

Mister Ali stood up and kicked the heap, sending dirt and twigs flying. "It is as I expected. They were golems created out of the material around here." He waved his arms around the clearing. "I'm guessing that all of the known exits from the river have similar golems guarding them."

"Golems?" It was a creature I was only vaguely familiar with.

"Yes. Magical animations. They are simple-minded but can be mighty opponents if made of the right material. Luckily, these were made of sticks, dirt, and rocks." He nudged the pile with his foot.

I nodded. "At least we are safe now." I was disappointed that Mister Ali didn't say anything about the battle. I had beaten the golems and was hoping for more acknowledgement than "well done."

Mister Ali walked over to the ledge and looked out to the horizon, nothing but harsh sun, dry rocky plains, and half-dead vegetation as far as the eye could see. "I'm afraid not, Tommy. While the golems did an admirable job for their master in hurting us, their primary role was to raise the alarm. Right now, I'm sure that whoever is after us knows exactly where we are and is preparing to send something a lot more dangerous than a pile of sticks."

Mister Ali limped away from the outcropping, and as I went to follow him, I realized I was injured more than I had thought. My hip hurt badly, and I had to limp, too. I found it depressing that a stupid creature made of sticks doing nothing more than throwing stones had nearly defeated the duo of a mighty magician like Mister Ali and me, the Archmage. Defeating them didn't seem quite so special anymore.

I winced, and Mister Ali twirled to look at me, alarm on his face. "You are hurt." He shook his head. "I'm afraid we are in very poor circumstances—we are injured; we don't know where we are, and we have no way to get to either safety or healing." Mister Ali sheathed his knife and looked at me. "Do you have any ideas?"

In other circumstances I would have been honored at Mister Ali asking me for assistance, but I ignored him and stared at the top of the hill. A sliver of smoke rose up in the distance.

Chapter Seven

I MEET NAOMI, WHO HATES ME

"There is smoke in the distance," I stated, pointing over Mister Ali's shoulder.

He turned, and after a glance spun back to me, his grim visage replaced with a broad smile. "Perhaps a fireplace or a stove!" He turned and limped a few steps while waving me forward. "Come, we must reach it as soon as possible!"

Mister Ali sounded excited but looked concerned. I wasn't sure, however. Between my bruised leg and the heat I had little energy to do more than worry about walking without falling. The cane was helpful, but not in its magic. It was a much needed support as I climbed the hill. In fact, ever since the attack the cane seemed particularly normal in my hand. Granted, I didn't think much of using it for light or any other kind of assistance, but it still felt too normal.

I decided to see if I could connect again with the cane while also helping myself. I lifted the cane as we climbed, and focused my mind on a single thought: Heal my hip and leg. I strained, but the staff remained silent.

Mister Ali glanced back at me and asked what was wrong. "Nothing. I'm sorry, I was just trying to see if the staff could heal me." I lowered the cane to the ground and leaned on it.

Mister Ali nodded, walked back, and held my elbow as we continued up the hill. "Alas, Tommy, that is a rare talent with the staff, indeed. There have been Archmages who were mighty healers, their skill at a level to bring someone from even the brink of death back to health." Mister Ali shrugged. "Perhaps someday."

We reached the top of the hill and paused at the crest. I looked down, focusing on the source of the smoke. It floated up from the chimney of a building at the base of the hill. It appeared to be some kind of rail station, as it stood alone next to a rail line. There weren't any other buildings. Not even roads. In fact, it looked like this wasn't a town at all but little more than a railroad maintenance stop.

Mister Ali stared at the building next to the rail line with a broad smile on his face. "We have the luck of Aladdin, Tommy!" I had no idea what Mister Ali was talking about, and it must have shown as when Mister Ali looked back at me he quickly added, "A train! It is the fastest magical transport we have."

Mister Ali started walking, a new jump in his step brought on by enthusiasm. "I will tell you more once we board the train. But this is great news! We will find shelter and safety soon!"

Despite his injuries, Mister Ali set a vigorous pace down the other side of the hill. I had to stop a few times when the pain in my hip became too great. Mister Ali would walk back to me, concern in his voice and face, but I could tell that he was nervous and wanted me to keep moving.

"Can we pause for a moment, Mister Ali?" I asked at one point. My leg and hip were hurting. By now we were on flat ground, but the rugged descent and our pace was too much for me.

"Of course. Do you need to sit down?"

"No, I just need to rest my leg a bit." I didn't dare sit down. I didn't think I would be able to get up again, and the thought of an old man like Mister Ali carrying me was too embarrassing to bear. I still wanted to impress him, and I really wanted to grit my teeth and barrel through this short journey to the rail house. So I leaned on the cane and did my best to stretch and massage my leg.

Mister Ali leaned back into a mighty stretch. He let out a loud grunt of "Ahhhhhh," but it got cut short when he jerked himself back up to his full height. His sudden stop and the intent look in his eyes caught my attention. He was staring where the rail line disappeared into the hills in the distance. I turned to follow his gaze.

"Do you see that, Tommy?" I squinted into the harsh light, and after a moment I saw what I thought was a dot on the horizon.

"I'm not sure. Is it smoke?"

"It's not smoke." Mister Ali continued to stare.

I did my best to look, but all I could see was the dark spot. It was perhaps a bit more visible now but still tiny. "A zeppelin?" Mister Ali shook his head. "A flock of birds?"

He continued to stare in the distance, but grabbed my arm and tugged me gently forward. "Tommy, we need to get to the rail station as soon as possible." He started to walk briskly toward the house, half supporting me, half pulling me. I could tell something was worrying him, as he would glance over his shoulder and then push the pace even more. By the time we got to the house, we were half running, half stumbling.

He pounded on the door, which was locked. As he shouted, "Waymaster! Unlock the door now!" I was finally able to look back. The dot had turned into a dark cloud of black that spread across a large swath of the horizon. I had no idea what it could be, but it was clearly not good.

A woman opened the door. She was dressed in khaki coveralls and had flowing dark hair with a white streak on one side. She looked unhappy. "Who are you and why are you here?"

"Shut up, woman. I need to see the Waymaster," Mister Ali replied. He started to push his way past the woman when she gave him a firm shove that sent him flying backward.

"I'm the Waymaster." She held up a pistol and pointed at Mister Ali and me. "And who are you?"

Mister Ali looked shocked. As he regained his balance, he looked up at the Waymaster angrily. "That's not important right now. Look!" He pointed in the distance. The Waymaster glanced over, and her eyes went wide.

"What is that?" I looked back to the direction that Mister Ali indicated. The black cloud was clearly visible on the horizon.

"Djinn!" Mister Ali's anger disappeared and was replaced with urgency. "And it looks like dozens, perhaps even hundreds of them." He turned to me and put his hand on my shoulder. "They are after the staff, Tommy. I'm afraid I did not have the opportunity to discuss this with you on Nar Marratum, but perhaps it is time to give the magical creatures the staff and return it from whence it came."

I looked at Mister Ali, aghast. "No! Grandfather risked his life for me to keep the staff safe." Mister Ali's face fell, and I immediately felt bad for dismissing his idea out-of-hand. But I was also confused. He and Grandfather had argued about this at the restaurant, and my grandfather strongly disagreed with Mister Ali. Was he perhaps trying to use my ignorance and youth to get his way? I didn't want to feel that way. Mister Ali was Grandfather's friend and was looking out for me. So I replied, "I mean, I understand that it will put me in danger, and I understand that there is much that I don't know about magic, so perhaps this is foolish of me, but *I can't.*"

Mister Ali nodded. "Of course, Tommy. It was unfair of me to ask." He turned to the Waymaster. "We will have time to discuss this later, but I have no choice but to trust you and you to trust me. You see what we are facing."

The woman nodded. "There are no trains near, but I can summon one." She turned and strode into the building. I glanced back at what was now a black stain spreading across the horizon before following Mister Ali and the Waymaster in.

I shut the door and almost ran into Mister Ali. The Waymaster was stabbing him in the chest with her finger. "I heard you mention the staff. Is the Archmage with you? I will not summon a train if the Archmage is here. Are you playing some game?"

Mister Ali sighed. "Here is the *new* Archmage." He moved out of the way and nodded toward me." I saw a dawning comprehension on the Waymaster's face as she looked at me and then the cane and then back at me.

"There's a new Archmage?" Mister Ali nodded, as he adjusted his armor. "His powers...?"

"He can make light," was Mister Ali's succinct reply. "Now I ask you again, *Waymaster*, as our lives are probably in the balance. Can you get a train here quickly?"

The question pushed the Waymaster to action. "Yes. Yes, of course." She ran over to a box that was on a work table in the corner and started tapping on it. It was a telegraph machine, and as she tapped on the small metal arm I heard her mutter, "Light!" loudly under her breath, sounding disgusted.

Mister Ali didn't say anything else, but sat in the middle of the floor and began chanting in Farsi. He would occasionally move his arms in precise movements. At one point he winced, as his bruised arm acted up, and a stream of curses came out of his mouth. He immediately began again, however, his face a mask of calm.

"We should reinforce the doors and windows while he casts his shield." It was the Waymaster. She was standing beside me.

"Okay. I'll do whatever I can to help." I took in my surroundings. The station was long and thin, and we were in the center. On the far end in front of us was a plain closed door. Behind me was an open area that contained a waist-high solid wood divider with a swinging door at the end. Beyond it was a large area that looked like it was a mess of random train-related materials. There were wooden boxes, some closed, some open. There was equipment of every size and shape, from a large wheel that must have weighed hundreds of pounds to a pile of railroad spikes that looked freshly cast. On the near side of the divider was a long wooden table with loose papers, folders, and mugs with pens and pencils in them. It also contained packages waiting to be delivered. Dominating the center of the room opposite the door we entered was a pair of huge metal doors that faced the rail line. They were latched closed and looked like the doors you see on a freight car. It was clearly the point where things were moved to and from the building and the trains.

The Waymaster pointed at the front door. "We need to defend that." She then pointed to the double doors that led to the track. "And we need to clear that. Our only hope is to get on the train and then get moving. That means we need to defend ourselves for a long time and then when the train arrives battle our way out to it "I am Waymaster Bergeron," the woman added as we started to stack wooden crates and chairs in front of the door and windows.

"Tommy," I replied, grunting as I pulled a desk along the floor, "and that is Mister Ali, my teacher and protector."

"So the new Archmage needs a protector?" She snorted.

She was about the age of my English teacher at Andover, and I knew I should treat her with respect, but her attitude bothered me. "I am new, but you should not underestimate me! It is foolish to judge others on their size and age."

The Waymaster paused and looked at me. "You, a *child*, are going to presume to tell me not to judge? I bound the Marid Prince Aafez and my reward was this." She spat out the words. "A shack that is barely a Way Station. And do you know why?" I shook my head. "Because I am a woman." I thought to Mister Ali's comment at the door, asking the woman to take him to the Waymaster. "So please, *Archmage*, tell me about judging others based on something other than ability."

I was about to stammer a reply when Mister Ali opened his eyes. "Is a train coming?"

"It is about five hundred miles away." The Waymaster returned to piling things in front of the windows.

Mister Ali stood up gingerly. "Five hundred miles? How long will that take to arrive?"

"An hour, give or take."

"My shields won't last a portion of that. What defenses do you have?"

Waymaster Bergeron shrugged. "This is an outpost, barely a Way Station. There are elementary shield spells, but nothing intended to hold off Djinn." She walked over and looked out the front window, which I was in the process of blocking with stools and chairs. "They are maybe twenty minutes away at most."

She then turned to me. "What of you Archmage? Do you have any ideas?" Mister Ali and Waymaster Bergeron stared at me; was it hope in their faces? Concern? Sadness? Perhaps it was all of those things.

"I'm afraid not, Waymaster Bergeron." I looked at the staff, which I held tightly in my right hand. I added apologetically, "I still have a lot to learn." The Waymaster sighed and turned, probably as disgusted with me as I was with myself.

"Bergeron." Mister Ali stated. "You are the daughter of Oliver."

"What of it?"

"He oversaw the London trains during the Great War."

"I know." She kept stacking things.

"Is he here? Is he the Waymaster?" Mister Ali sounded hopeful.

Waymaster Bergeron spun around and marched over to Mister Ali. "He died you old fool. *I'm* the Waymaster of this dusty shed. Not King's Cross. Not Union Station. Not Grand Central. This pathetic station, a station so small it doesn't even have a name. Just a number. Is that so hard to accept?" She stood toe-to-toe with Mister Ali. "And how long *will* your shield last?"

Mister Ali looked down. "I'm not sure they can withstand this many Djinn."

The Waymaster shook her head and then yelled out, "Naomi!" She turned, grabbed a chair, and walked toward a window, looking a combination of annoyed and concerned. "She is young, as well, but she at least knows some spells!" The sound of disdain was clear in her voice, and I was about to object when all thoughts left my mind—the wooden door at the end of the room opened, and a blond-haired girl my age entered. Her hair was long, and fell across her face. She wore dusty dungarees with a roughspun white shirt designed for heavy work. She wore brown leather boots, the kind cowboys wore in the movies.

I couldn't take my eyes off her as she approached. She had the high cheekbones and arched eyebrows that, combined with her long wavy hair, would have been at home on the screen at the Ziegfeld Theater, but she had a hard and serious look to her. She had none of the giggly shallowness of the schoolgirls from nearby Abbot Academy in Andover, and none of the austerity of those at our church. She looked practical, tough, and beautiful.

She approached with steady and nonchalant steps, pointedly ignoring me and Mister Ali as she stopped near the Waymaster. It was only then that she looked me up and down, as if assessing a horse on the auction block. Before I could say anything she turned away to face Waymaster Bergeron. "Yes, mother?"

She was maddening. Did she like me? Was she dismissing me by turning away? I was worried more about her opinion than the approach of magical creatures on the wind.

"We are about to be attacked by scores of Djinn." Naomi didn't flinch, but raised an eyebrow.

"We are? Why are they attacking us? We're barely a Way Station."

"They are after the Archmage."

At the mention of the Archmage, Naomi's attitude shifted dramatically. "The Archmage is here!?" She looked at Mister Ali and me. "Where is he? It will be an honor to watch him in battle!" It sounded like she could barely contain her excitement.

"Naomi," her mother said with a sigh, "That's the Archmage." She pointed at me.

She turned to face me, and the disappointment on her face was obvious. "Him?"

"Yes, and he can even make light." I caught the sarcasm in her voice and looked to Mister Ali to defend me, but Mister Ali looked shocked at the presence of Naomi. "Now enough dawdling. What level of shield spell have you mastered that can cover this room?"

Naomi shrugged and replied breezily, "I could summon the Mantle of Anaitis."

Waymaster Bergeron was about to speak when Mister Ali interrupted her, "Ridiculous! That's a master level spell, and you expect me to believe this girl can cast it? We don't have time for schoolyard exaggeration, Miss Bergeron!"

Naomi didn't look at Mister Ali, nor did she flinch. In fact, she didn't even register his presence. She looked at her mother and stood quietly. Waymaster Bergeron glanced at Mister Ali quickly but didn't respond. She knelt down in front of Naomi and took her hands. "How long can you sustain it?"

"Thirty minutes at most. It is a difficult spell." The Waymaster nodded, as Naomi added, "Is help coming? How much time do we have?"

The Djinn are 20 minutes away, and a train will arrive in an hour," she replied flatly. If Naomi waited to start the shield until the last possible moment, it still left ten minutes of unremitting Djinn attacks, which didn't sound like it would turn out well for us.

"I'll do my best, mother." Naomi knelt and spread her arms out straight at her side. She then proceeded to embark on the beautifully fluid and complex number of body movements, focusing on minute changes in the positions of her fingers and hands. Some of the movements she made with her fingers appeared impossible. I looked at Mister Ali, who stared in shock.

I wandered over and whispered to him, "Is she doing it?" He nodded but didn't say anything.

"It's *Waymaster* Bergeron," the Waymaster said to Mister Ali. "You called me 'Miss,'" she added.

"Yes. Yes. I understand," Mister Ali muttered. He was staring at Naomi. "Where has she trained?"

"She is self-taught." The pride in her voice was obvious. "She has the standard texts and the trains deliver and take away new ones as fast as she can devour them." I looked at the Waymaster, who was smiling. "Which is fast." I looked at Naomi, spellbound at the fluidity of her movements.

Mister Ali turned and picked up a box. "You were foolish to support this. Magic is too difficult and too dangerous for girls." He walked the box over and stacked it near the front door.

I looked at the Waymaster. I could see her jaw clenching, but she didn't say anything. After a moment she turned and went back to the telegraph machine. The silence was difficult for me. I owed so much to Mister Ali, but I felt that it was unfair of him to dismiss Naomi's efforts. I glanced at her. I didn't know what she was doing, but I was certain it would be helpful. Why couldn't Mister Ali see that?

Naomi was still casting her spell when the Djinn arrived. The slight light that could be seen from the windows darkened, and you could hear the dull thud of pounding from outside. There were no explosions, just the sound of arms, legs, and bodies pounding against Mister Ali's shield.

"Your shield is holding, Ali," the Waymaster said.

"I'm afraid it won't last long," he replied. I was glad they were talking, at least.

Moments later, a glow started in Naomi's hands and slowly spread out across the room. As it passed through me I noticed that it only glowed outward. Once it was past me, I could barely see it. As it penetrated the walls, the sounds from outside grew muffled.

"We have 30 minutes," Naomi stated. She then stretched out on the floor, her hands behind her head. We stacked a few more things, but by then pretty much anything that could block a door or window was pressed against them.

"Perhaps you should thank the *girl*, Ali," Waymaster Bergeron stated, her voice full of bitterness.

"She did well," Mister Ali replied, but there wasn't much enthusiasm in his voice.

We waited, the only noise the muffled sounds coming from beyond Naomi's shield. After a few minutes Mister Ali flexed his fingers and pulled the vicious knife out from its sheath on his thigh. Naomi continued to rest on the floor, her blond hair spread around her head like a halo, her hands folded on her chest. She may even have been asleep.

Suddenly, Naomi's eyes shot open, and she said in a clear calm voice, "The shield is weakening." I heard the sound of screaming, although it remained muffled. The sound was awful, like a mixture of shrieks and high winds. It reminded me of the attack on the restaurant. I must have looked scared, as Mister Ali put his hand on my shoulder.

"Stay behind me." He smiled at me and then turned toward the door.

Just then several things happened in short order one after the other. Naomi stated, "The shield is gone." The screaming increased to a painful intensity. The front door blew in with an explosion of air, barely missing Mister Ali and bouncing off the double doors behind us. Naomi leapt to her feet. And, finally, the Djinn were upon us.

Mister Ali crouched in front of the door, launching himself against Djinn as they entered. One after the other they approached only to be struck down by a slash from Mister

Ali's knife. As they were mortally struck, the Djinn would completely disappear into a puff of air. The door was small and Mister Ali was relentless, but there were just too many. Soon, Mister Ali was fighting two Djinn, while barely holding more off at the door.

It was at that point when the window blasted open.

The chairs protected us from the glass, and delayed the entry of any Djinn, but the barricade immediately began to fall to the strength of the creatures. At the first appearance of a clear opening, a bright ball of fire flew toward it from my right. The Djinn in the frame of the window burst into nothingness. I looked over to see Naomi on the balls of her feet, her hands and fingers moving in a blur. After a few seconds of movement, she would throw her hands forward and a ball of flame would shoot from them.

She glanced at me and smiled wickedly. "Detonations!" She turned back to face the window but added in an amused voice, "I'm not allowed to do them." She launched another one toward the window. But she couldn't perform the spell fast enough and Djinn were slowly making their way along the wall, using our own barricade as a shield.

"We have five minutes!" It was the Waymaster who was at the telegraph, tapping away.

I looked at one of the Djinn. They were the color of a dark stone with a tinge of green. They were heavily muscled and about the size of a large man, with long arms and sharp claws. Massive wings were folded tightly against their backs, allowing them to move easily, if clumsily, in the tight spaces amidst the barricade. Their faces were human only in that they had eyes, nose, and a mouth. They didn't appear to have hair, and there were folds to their face that gave the appearance of melting or having been windblown. As one turned to squeeze behind a large cabinet I saw a glimpse of long sharp teeth, as well. They didn't have any clothes or weapons, just those claws and teeth.

I gripped the staff, wanting to do something. Mister Ali held off three Djinn. At least four others were pushing through the barricade of the window. I backed against the double doors and held the staff up with my hand, preparing to help either Mister Ali or Naomi. For the first time I heard the noise from the double iron doors, which had been drowned out by the screams of Djinn. It was a pounding and scraping, and I realized that even if the train did come in time, we would have to fight through the Djinn waiting on the other side of those mighty doors.

A claw struck Mister Ali's shoulder, and he staggered back. I ran up holding the staff in front of me. I remembered how the staff had destroyed the golems by barely touching them, and I hoped that would work here. I thrust the staff into the side of a Djinn on Mister Ali's left. It turned to me, but before it could strike, Mister Ali stabbed it, and it disappeared into a puff of air.

"Get back, Tommy! I can hold them," Mister Ali yelled. He was bleeding from his shoulder, yet swinging his knife and spinning like a dervish.

I ignored his words, and went up and swung the staff like a cudgel, bringing it down on the shoulder of a Djinn. The Djinn grunted in pain, and I felt the vibration of the impact through my arms, but the Djinn wasn't slowed. I backed up as Mister Ali spun and sliced through another Djinn.

I looked over at Naomi. Two Djinn approached her with leering smiles, sharp teeth clearly visible. She gave up any pretension of casting another spell and started to backpedal. She had moments before she would be cut to ribbons, and I turned around looking if someone could help, but Mister Ali was in a mortal fight, and Waymaster Bergeron was furiously tapping on the telegraph. One of the Djinn raised his arm for a slicing blow to Naomi.

I clenched the cane, thinking of nothing other than my desperate need to stop the Djinn and help Naomi. A brilliant light burst forth, filling the room with such brightness that everything looked pale and colorless. The effect was so astounding that I imagined that everyone was moving in slow motion. I blinked, and opened my eyes to screams of pain from the Djinn, rather than their piercing shrieks. The two in front of Naomi were clutching at their eyes. Naomi quickly shot off her detonations, destroying them. Mister Ali easily dispatched his blinded opponents.

Naomi looked at me, her eyes wide. She smiled, and then crouched again, preparing to cast detonations at the Djinn still pushing in the doorway and the window.

The Djinn continued, relentless in their attack, but I was full of joy. I had stopped them. Me! The incompetent Archmage had stopped them. I was thinking of ways of getting from the building to the train with dozens of Djinn between the two when the pounding on the iron doors stopped. They were replaced by a distant sound that I knew well from the newsreels I watched in the Ziegfeld Theater: Machine guns. The rata-tat-tat grew louder, and Waymaster Bergeron slid her seat back, stood, and yelled out over the persistent shrieking noise, "The train is here!"

She ran right past me and up to the doors and started to unlatch them. I was about to warn her about the scores of Djinn outside when, with a grunt, she pulled the door open. There was a gap of about 10 yards between the building and the train engine, which filled my vision. The sky was dark with countless Djinn, but they were being held off by furious machine gun fire by two men standing on the ground next to the engine.

The scene was remarkable. Magical creatures held at bay by tommy guns. A few Djinn made it close through the hail of bullets, but they eventually fell to the deadly weapons. The opening of the doors caught the Djinn's attention, and they turned and immediately set themselves on Waymaster Bergeron and me.

I thought I was dead for sure. A huge Djinn let out an unearthly wail and spread its wings as it leapt toward me. I instinctively brought up the staff to defend myself. All I could see was a claw swinging through the air and a sneering mouth full of vicious teeth. The claw hit the staff and the force threw me to the ground. At the same time, the staff sent some kind of force up the Djinn's arm. It disintegrated.

An arm grabbed me by the shoulder and dragged me to my feet. "Get to the train, Tommy!" It was Mister Ali, and he practically threw me toward the two men guarding the engine.

As I stumbled toward the train, I watched the bizarre scene of deadly hails of bullets erasing entire portions of the dark sky. One of the men pointed into the engine and yelled "Up there. Now!"

There must have been a powerful shield spell around the train itself, because Djinn hovered around it, rage in their faces, but unable to get close. I watched as their claws slashed at air, bouncing off an invisible barrier.

I scrambled into a room at the front of the train, which was open but small. There was a window facing the track ahead and plenty of gauges and levers. I leaned against the rear wall and held my hand against my chest, breathing deeply. A few moments later Mister Ali limped in. He had a bad gash on his shoulder, and countless scrapes and cuts elsewhere. His colorful armor was shorn away at points, and he was covered in sweat and dirt. When he saw me, he smiled weakly but didn't say anything. He patted me on the shoulder, but I noticed him wince when he did so.

I was about to ask how he was when one of the men from the train arrived. He was half supporting/half dragging Naomi into the compartment. She was screaming and using all her force to break free and head back outside. The man's grip was like a vise, but his face was full of sadness and sympathy. "It is too late, miss. The best thing you can do for her is save yourself." She fell to the floor and sat with her back against a wall. She pulled her knees up tight to her chest and sobbed.

The other man with the machine gun climbed up into the compartment. "We are safe on the train for now, but we need to get going. It would be bad if a Marid showed up. *Really* bad."

Mister Ali walked past me to the rear of the compartment, grabbed a handle, and slid open a door that revealed a large and comfortable room. "Come, let us rest and allow the engineer to do his job."

We all moved into the room, which looked like a combination of a living room and study. It was paneled in dark wood. I walked over to a plush reading chair and sat down for the first time since we had entered the mine. I set the cane across my lap and watched as Mister Ali walked in with Naomi. She shot me a murderous glance.

"This is your fault!" she screamed at me. Mister Ali whispered something in her ear and turned her away, leading her to a sofa. He touched his hand to her forehead and she closed her eyes, her head slowly falling onto the plush arm.

Mister Ali approached me, leaned down, put his hand on my forehead, and whispered, "I owe you many answers Tommy, even though you are too modest or respectful to ask the questions. You will have them, but right now you must rest."

At that moment the pain in my body suddenly hit me. My leg hurt, but not as bad as my hip, which took the initial rock throw from the golems in what felt like something that happened ages before but actually had occurred less than two hours previously. I leaned back, and I could vaguely hear Mister Ali saying something in Farsi, but it quickly got lost in a haze. Somewhere in the distance I heard a train whistle. The wail of the whistle was worse than that of the Djinn. It was otherworldly and painful in a way I couldn't describe. But it stopped as suddenly as it started, and I felt Mister Ali's hand on my shoulder. "We will heal you when you wake." Then all was dark and blessedly quiet.

Chapter Eight

I FAIL AT MAGIC

I awoke in so much pain I was afraid to move. As I opened my eyes, Mister Ali came forward. His shoulder was bandaged; his armor was still damaged but clean. All in all, he looked much better. "Tommy, there is a lot we need to talk about, but we must heal you first. Do you understand?"

"Healing me would be good," I replied. I winced as I stretched my leg.

Mister Ali nodded. "I want you to be quiet and relax as much as possible while I do a small healing spell."

"Will it hurt?"

"No, but don't expect much. You will still be sore."

"I can live with sore." I smiled. I wanted to appear brave to Naomi, but when I glanced over she appeared to be asleep.

Mister Ali put his hand on my head again. He said a few words in Farsi, and I felt a warmth flow from my head down to my toes. I felt more relaxed and, although the pain didn't go away, it felt more bearable. He repeated the process three times, and each time the pain felt slightly better.

"You have been very brave, Tommy," Mister Ali whispered. He walked over and pulled a chair over to mine. He sat down, leaned forward, and folded his hands between his knees. "Are you okay?"

I nodded, although I didn't feel okay at all.

"That's good. We are finally safe on this train, and there is a lot you should know. We have about two hours before we reach our destination, and I want to answer any questions you have and tell you about things that you need to know. Is now a good time or would you like your healing to progress some more?"

As I focused on my hip I realized that most of the pain was gone. It was replaced by a throbbing ache and even a slight numbness.

Without looking up, I whispered, "Now is good."

There was a pause, and then Mister Ali sighed. "Very well." His voice regained its former strength, if not its joyful lilt, and he continued. "Before I begin, Tommy, is there anything you would like to ask me first?"

I looked up at him, and without thinking and without knowing why the words came to my lips, I asked, "Is Grandfather dead?"

Mister Ali's face looked pained, but he quickly regained his composure. "I don't know the answer to that question, Tommy. I asked the engineer, who knew nothing, and I didn't have time to ask the Waymaster to find out." At the mention of Naomi's mother, I quickly glanced at her. She was staring at us and clearly eavesdropping, but her face was blank.

"I'm glad you mentioned your grandfather, as that is as good a place to start as any. He may be alive—"

"He is alive." I stated it with firmness. As a fact. I knew it was true. It had to be true.

Mister Ali paused and then nodded. "Yes, he is a mighty warrior and one of the greatest Archmages in history. He very well may be alive. So let me tell you about him. We do not have time for me to tell you his entire history, but he was marked from his youth for greatness."

My awareness of my surroundings started to fade as I focused on Mister Ali describing my grandfather in ways I would never have considered mere days before. The man who I defined by his gruff affection and the tapping of his cane as he hobbled along behind it was actually a mighty warrior.

"As you will find out as you progress in your learning, Tommy, each Archmage wields the staff in different ways. As I mentioned, some have been healers. Others have had power over nature. Still others have been great creators, building things like the Great Pyramids with little more than the movement of the staff. This process takes time, but your grandfather immediately knew his calling, which was to make peace within the magical realm by the force of his terrible power with the staff."

"Terrible power?"

"This is difficult to describe to one so young, and it will sound like evil, but I assure you it is not—your grandfather was a great master of destruction. When he was wielding the staff, whole armies would be torn asunder. It is forever to his credit that he always used his power to defeat evil and to bring peace, but he was never afraid to use his power to its greatest limits. In a very short time, through nothing more than his efforts, age-old rivalries and wars were stopped, the rivals too afraid of your grandfather's wrath to raise arms against each other. He defended the English from the Germans, and yet helped my people by forcing the English to leave Persia. Your grandfather aligned himself with no one."

Mister Ali paused, but I didn't say anything. I had nothing to say—all I wanted was to hear more. As if deciding on whether to go on, Mister Ali stammered over the next few words. "Except... except for the Shadows."

"The Shadows that attacked us?" I asked breathlessly.

"Yes," he answered. "The Shadows are creatures of pure magic. They are both incredibly weak and immensely powerful. They are weak because they can easily be stopped by magical or artificial light, as you saw. Despite that, they are strong because they can absorb anything into their darkness—living, dead, mineral, vegetable. Nothing can resist them.

"This led to great fear, as you might imagine. Every culture has stories about monsters waiting in the dark, and all these stories emanate from a fear of the Shadows." I nodded. It all made sense. "But the Shadows are misunderstood, Tommy. They just want to be left alone."

"But they attacked Grandfather and me." I thought of the attack in the alley. Fear of the Shadows didn't seem unreasonable.

"Ah, yes. That." Mister Ali sighed. "To understand that, let me point out one thing that has changed in the last forty years or so: electric light."

"The Shadows are being hurt by the invention and spread of electric light?"

"Very good, Tommy," Ali replied. "Yes. The Shadows have been driven from the cities due to Edison's creation of an efficient light bulb." He turned back to me. "But that did not bother them. It was a concerted effort in Europe to destroy them. After millennia of powerlessness and irrational fear, the world now had a weapon to destroy the Shadows, and they used that power relentlessly. Your grandfather saw the truth and used his own powers to stop the massacres."

I looked at the staff and immediately saw the hole in Mister Ali's story. "But the world *did* have a weapon: magical light!"

Chuckling, Mister Ali replied, "This may be hard to believe, Tommy, as it was the first skill you have learned, but magical light is immensely difficult to create. Your grandfather, who could conjure explosions that would level a city, could not create even a spark of light. Such is true for nearly everyone, and even those that can create a minor glow must work tremendously hard and spend years of study to do so."

I turned in my chair and winced. "How is your leg?" Mister Ali asked.

I stretched my leg. "It's sore." I made myself comfortable on the chair and then asked, "So Grandfather defended the Shadows?"

"Indeed. The story is more complicated than that, of course. Thirty years ago a great leader in Europe approached the Shadows about joining his army to conquer the world, and when they refused, he swore to destroy them. As everyone hated the Shadows, they had no one to help them.

"Declan—your grandfather—did what he always does. He defended the powerless, despite the fear that everyone had of them. In the end, he helped defeat the armies amassed against the world and the forces amassed against the Shadows.

Vingrosh, their leader, owes the existence of his people to your grandfather."

"But he is the one who attacked us!"

"Yes, he is." Mister Ali fell silent.

"But why?"

There was a long pause. I looked at Mister Ali, his face lost in thought. There was no dawning comprehension, no sudden insight. He just looked at me and replied, "I have an idea, but I am not sure."

I didn't know what to say. It all sounded rather ominous. Friends of my grandfather attacking him and me. I was not stupid. I knew that Mister Ali was talking about the Great War, but I was taught the war was about German aggression, not magical creatures. How much didn't I know? I had read the news about what was currently happening in Germany and Europe. Was it related to the Shadows again? Was it more of the same or was it different?

One thing I did know was that it was much more personal than I had ever known. My family was part of these horrific world events. I found it overwhelming, but I have to admit that I felt it thrilling, as well. My grandfather had defeated armies, and he did it with the staff that I now had in my hands. Perhaps someday I could defeat armies, too.

With another gap in the conversation, Naomi suddenly spoke up. "So the Archmage is dead?" Her voice was choked with emotion. I don't know what her connection was to my grandfather, but she was clearly distraught. Her blank face had turned into one twisted with incredulity and sadness.

"Certainly not, miss Naomi. He stands here in front of you." Mister Ali bowed his head in my direction.

"Him!?" She practically spat the words. "He is hardly an Archmage. He couldn't even defeat a room full of Djinn! He's not a warrior. He's... He's... a streetlight!" Mister Ali looked shocked. I'm not sure he knew how to deal with the combination of a young lady of some magical skill and a voice of impudence and disrespect.

She stood up and walked over to us. I straightened in my chair, not knowing what was going to happen. Naomi looked glorious and terrible as she stood, her hands shaking, facing me and Mister Ali. "The Archmage would have wiped the skies of Djinn in moments. He—" She stabbed her finger in the direction of my face. "—allowed my mother to die."

With the quickness of a cat she swung her palm at my face, but Mister Ali was quicker. His hand shot out and grabbed Naomi's arm, stopping it inches from my cheek. He gently but forcefully moved her hand down to her side. He stood up, put his arm around her shoulders, and gently turned her away from me.

"Your anger is justified but misplaced." He squeezed her shoulder and led her back to her seat. "We all owe you great apologies. You have been through a trauma even greater than Tommy's leg, and yet we left you all alone, ignoring your pain." Mister Ali was going to say something else when Naomi violently pulled herself away from him

"I don't need your pity or your calming spells! I'm used to being alone. I have my own spells." She sat down and glared at me. She started making movements with her hands that looked oddly familiar.

Mister Ali immediately raised his voice and moved between Naomi and me. "Don't be foolish. I can only excuse so much."

I couldn't see her but her voice was cold, "I was just practicing. At least one of us should be useful if we are attacked."

His head shaking, Mister Ali turned and walked back to me. He pulled his chair closer, sat down, and put his head near mine. In clipped tones he whispered, "She is in shock. We must excuse her behavior. She doesn't mean it." I looked over at her. Her chest was heaving, her body barely containing her anger. She certainly looked like she hated me, and that she meant it with every bit of her being.

The thing is, I knew how she felt finding herself alone. I had lost my parents. My grandfather, for how much I loved him, kept me alone in his townhouse. Even boarding school was a lonely experience. Mister Ali must have noticed me looking at Naomi, as he raised his voice from his whisper. "This is not the time for anger but for learning." He left a meaningful pause and then continued, "Tommy, we don't have much time, and we still need to discuss the staff, but I would like to answer any other questions you may have."

My mind was a blank, but I knew that I had countless questions. My eyesight drifted out the window to the terrain zooming by, and the obvious question came to me. "Where are we going?"

"Ah, I forgot that you were asleep when we discussed our travels. We are going to London." Mister Ali's voice was flat, as if he wasn't happy about our destination. "It is a great center of magic, and we will be safe there. We can use the time to talk, train, and plan what to do next with the master magicians who are there."

"Can they help me find Grandfather?"

Mister Ali paused and then replied, "Perhaps. Regardless, they will need to hear about the attack on the fortress in New York and can perhaps give us information about what machinations are behind these strange events."

I couldn't help but wonder why Mister Ali wasn't excited about going to a center of magic. Wouldn't that be the best place for me to learn? Wouldn't those be the people who would best help me save my grandfather? I looked out the window, thinking about the uncertain future that was ahead me, when it hit me—we were on a train.

"How can we be going to London? We are on a train, Mister Ali!"

Mister Ali smiled. "Ah, I'm glad you asked, Tommy. This brings our lesson full circle. You understand about technology and science?" I nodded yes. "And you understand about magic?" I didn't know much about magic, but I didn't want to interrupt Mister Ali so I nodded yes again. "Well, the two disciplines are nearly always in conflict. Yet, some-times—rarely—the two can be combined to create some-thing amazing that independently can't be done by one or the other.

"The modern locomotive is a great example of that. Deliv-ering such a great vehicle with magic alone would be near im-possible. Similarly, reaching the speeds this train does and its ability to skim over water is an impossibility for technology. Isn't it wonderful?"

"It's amazing!"

Mister Ali shook his head. "But here's the thing, Tommy. This train is a rarity. Magic is dying in the world because tech-nology has proven more powerful. This magical locomotive is even now barely better than an airplane. Someday it will not be. Remember our discussion of the Shadows? They see this. All magical creatures see this. I neglected to say it earlier, but this is why I believe the Shadows attacked you and your grand-father—they want magic to leave the world, for the world to forget them, to forget magic, to allow them their own valleys, their own lands. It will provide them peace."

I thought back to the conversation Grandfather had with Mister Ali in the restaurant. "So getting rid of the staff will accelerate the disappearance of magic?" I thought back to the news reels and the motion pictures at the Ziegfeld Theater. Magic was nowhere to be seen. I knew of magic being used in the war, but it was considered a small part, an important part but a small part, like cryptography and spying.

"Yes, and if we are honest with ourselves this is a good thing. Magic has rarely been used for good in our history."

Mister Ali was about to continue his thought but Naomi interrupted. "That is a lie." She leaned forward in her chair. "Magic has been an undeniable force for good. It has saved millions of lives. It has defeated tyrants. It has united countries." It sounded like she was reciting some pledge from school, but I found the passion and the words powerful. I couldn't help but agree with her.

I didn't want to disagree openly with Mister Ali, but I thought that maybe Naomi would think better of me for doing so, and, after all, I did actually agree with her. "Naomi is right. How can a force be evil or good? You could say the same of technology. Is electricity evil or good?"

"You are too young to understand," Mister Ali replied, calmly.

"And you are old and cynical." Naomi squinted her eyes at Mister Ali. Part of me admired her ability to just confront anyone. I doubted I could ever be like that. I glanced at Mister Ali. His face was turning red, and he was clenching his teeth.

I wanted to stop her from fighting with Mister Ali, so I interjected, "Mister Ali. You said you would teach me about the staff." The words came out awkward, and I felt stupid, but Mister Ali turned to me and smiled.

"Ah yes, Tommy. I am not so cynical that I would avoid teaching you of the staff." He shot a glance at Naomi and then pulled his chair closer to mine. "We run low on time, so I can't tell you much of its history, but we have time for me to let you know how to unlock its secrets. Perhaps some of those secrets will even be revealed to you. That is my hope, at least."

And for the next ninety minutes Mister Ali went into great detail explaining things that made no sense to me. Worse, he was telling me things that I knew to be patently false. He talked about understanding the runes that lined the staff, but I knew that they had nothing to do with speaking to it or understanding it. I didn't want to hurt Mister Ali's feelings so I listened closely and worked through his exercises.

He set me numerous tasks. I failed at everything, but I kept trying. It would have been easy to get discouraged by my lack of progress, but I knew that this wasn't even the correct process. So I soldiered on to make Mister Ali happy. The worst part was knowing Naomi was watching.

At one point I tried to lift a coffee mug with the staff, and—to my shock—it began to rise. Mister Ali was thrilled and gave me a hearty "good job!" but I knew that it wasn't me. I quickly dropped the end of the staff and the mug dropped to the table. I glanced over at Naomi in time to see her stretching her fingers and smiling. I wanted to think that she was trying to help me, but I knew that it was just her subtle way of mocking my incompetence. I slammed the base of the staff to the floor.

"Tommy, I know you are frustrated at the difficulty of learning these rune movements, but trust me, you are doing fantastic! You may even be able to do lower level magic consistently in a year or two, and precious few Archmages are able to learn the inner workings of the staff that quickly." I glanced at Naomi, who rolled her eyes.

Our conversation was interrupted by the train's whistle. Mister Ali stood and clapped his hands. "We have arrived in London! Wait here. We will disembark shortly." He walked through to the front of the train, closing the door behind him.

Naomi looked at me, her face unreadable. I tapped the staff on the floor nervously. Finally, I spoke up. "I know what it's like being alone." She didn't say anything in response. The train brakes squealed as we slowed down, and I braced my feet and glanced at her again. It may have been the momentum of the train, but I swore I saw her nod her head in response.

Chapter Nine

I LIGHT UP A ROOM

The front door opened and Mister Ali came through with a tall thin man. He looked on edge. His eyes darted around the room, and his steps were short and jerky. I recognized him as one of the engineers due to his uniform, but I remembered him most as one of the men who was firing machine guns at the Djinn as we made our escape to the train. His skin was taut on his face, and as he smiled a toothy smile, he looked almost skeletal. "Hello passengers. I'm Frank Wilcox, your engineer. Welcome to King's Cross station." He spoke in clipped sentences, which only underscored the impression of nervousness he exuded. He spread his arms out and nodded toward each window.

"This was an unscheduled stop. So you must depart immediately. Jeremiah and I were glad to be of help, but we cannot dawdle. You will be safe here. There are friends waiting for you." He smiled his parchment smile and then motioned to the front with his arm. "Off you go!"

As I passed him, he grabbed my arm and leaned close to my face. I cringed, but he only whispered, "It was an absolute honor having you on my train." He then loosened his death grip, and looked away before I could respond. I walked into the front of the train and saw the engineer Mister Wilcox called Jeremiah leaning against a complex array of switches and levers.

I thanked him as I passed. He didn't say anything, just smiled and tapped his forehead with a finger. I followed Mister Ali, who led us down the steep train steps to the platform. We were about ten feet onto the platform when I turned to wait for Naomi to exit. I was immediately distracted by the train, however.

What was a shiny and new sleek passenger train in the dusty foothills was an old beaten up English steam train here. I looked up and down and couldn't see a hint of the train I boarded. Mister Ali noticed my wandering eye and whispered in my ear, "It is an illusion spell. The train itself doesn't change, but how we perceive it does."

I nodded and whispered to Mister Ali over my shoulder, "The whole train seems magic. It not only travels incredibly fast, that small engine car has that magical room inside!"

Mister Ali looked around and then smiled. Patting me on the shoulder he whispered, "That is just further illusion. We cannot use magic to create space where it doesn't exist or to create room where there is none. The engine car is actually quite long and has multiple rooms, but the illusion that emanates and is shaped from the source in the engine makes it look like a standard train."

I nodded and looked down the train. What other secrets did the train hold that I could not see due to illusion? For that matter, what secrets did the world hold that were hidden from my view? I thought of the Persian Garden, which I saw as a restaurant but which was a magical fortress. That illusion worked and there wasn't even magic involved. I followed Mister Ali as he turned toward the station, swearing to myself that I would work extra hard to see if the true nature of other things was being hidden from me.

Random people walked to and fro on the various platforms while others stood waiting. There were other trains, all similar to the one we came in on. Mister Ali paused, looking at something near the large archway exit and then said, "Very good. He understands the gravity of our situation."

"Who does?" I replied.

"Cain. He is a powerful magician here in England. He sent three masters to meet us." Before I could ask anything else, Mister Ali added, "Don't say anything from here on out, Tommy. You'll learn everything soon enough."

We approached three men who were dressed identically. They wore black suits with black bowler hats. Each of them had a large walking stick in their right hand, and stood as still as statues. Despite Mister Ali's warning, I couldn't help myself and blurted to the two on the right, "You are Persian!" They reminded me of the kind staff of the Persian Garden, and I felt immediately at ease.

The two masters didn't say anything. They just stood still and looked at us. Mister Ali leaned down and whispered, "Yes,

Tommy. Magic was born in my homeland, and it is the home of the most powerful magicians."

I was disappointed that they didn't share the jovial nature of Mister Oz or Mister Ali. I guess I expected all Persian people to be jolly and act like those I knew from the Persian Garden, but of course that was silly. The masters looked stern and serious, like undertakers waiting for some poor souls who were being transported in their coffins via the train. They didn't look evil, but there was a coldness about them.

The English one on the left pulled a watch from his pocket, and I noted that they all had similar accouterments, with pocket watch chains and shiny silvery buttons. The one who looked at his watch spoke up, "You made very good time." He had a British accent, and his tone was very business-like.

Mister Ali bowed. "We did indeed, Richard. I am glad you came, as strange things are afoot. Have you searched the station?"

The one Mister Ali called Richard ignored his question and looked at me. "I recognize the staff, so this must be the new Archmage, but who is this other? We were not informed that there would be more than you and the boy."

Before Mister Ali could say anything Naomi stepped forward. "I am Naomi Bergeron. I'm a magician." Mister Ali's eyes opened wide, and I got the impression that he was not only surprised that Naomi was there but that her stated reason was unexpected and not very welcome.

"You brought a domestic mage for the trip, Ali?" The man smiled for the first time.

"*Domestic* mage?" Naomi started to move her hands. Richard and and the other two mages raised their hands and lowered their bodies slightly to a crouch.

"Stop this foolishness!" Ali's voice boomed. "She was to return with the train. I'm not sure why she is here, but we will make arrangements."

Naomi took two brisk steps forward and looked up at all three of the masters. "I am here to avenge my mother. Tell me where I can find Djinn. That is the only arrangement you need to make." Her face was fierce, but her voice was in complete control and measured.

Mister Ali looked mortified, while all three masters looked down at Naomi in silence. I didn't know what was going to be said next, but I was horribly afraid that they would send

Naomi away, so I spoke up. "I am the Archmage, and she is with me."

I tried to speak in a firm voice, but the response indicated that I did anything but. All three masters, even the two stone-faced ones, burst out in laughter. One of the formerly quiet masters spoke up. "Let the boy bring his girlfriend. It makes no difference to us."

I was about to object, and I heard Naomi stammer, but Ali's voice again boomed out. "Enough! You will not speak this way to the Archmage. I may not be a master, but I am a Lord of Persepolis."

The demeanor of the men in the black suits immediately changed. The one named Richard bowed his head to him and replied, "Of course, Ali. We mean no disrespect. The youthful enthusiasm of the Archmage is," he paused and then continued, "refreshing."

I glanced over my shoulder at Naomi. She was oblivious to the conversation, staring at me. Our eyes met, but she didn't react at all. I wish I could have read her mind at that moment, but her thoughts were a mystery to me.

Mister Ali relaxed a bit and stated, "We should go."

The master on the right nodded, and all three of the men in dark suits turned and started through the arch toward the exit. Mister Ali walked behind the three of them, with me next to him. Naomi tagged along behind, and I kept looking back to make sure she was still with us. I seemed to be the only one who cared.

We were in the middle of the station when Mister Ali stopped and said, "Something is wrong."

Immediately, the three masters fell back around us. I had become familiar enough with magic by now to know that all three were doing something magical. I had seen magic done before, but this was something else. The master next to me was moving his arms and hands so quickly I could barely see his fingers. While the movements were purely physical, the fluidity and speed looked otherworldly. It reminded me of Naomi in the train station.

The one at the front said in a calm voice, "Djinn are here." Mister Ali nodded and slid his knife out of its sheathe. I looked around and noticed that the people in the building were quickly leaving. Some had left belongings behind.

"This works for me," Naomi muttered. She was bouncing on the balls of her feet and stretching her fingers, a smile on her face.

One of the Persian masters stretched his fingers. Speaking to us, he said, "I will shield us. It is foolish for them to send Djinn, but that fact alone worries me." He began mumbling to himself while he performed the shield spell.

Mister Ali sheathed his knife and knelt down, facing me. "Tommy, Djinn are mighty creatures as you've seen, but an army of them are no match for three masters. This is very open, so it is more difficult than defending a single door, but please don't be afraid, you are safe."

And with that Djinn swarmed into the building. They came in from every direction, and I couldn't possibly see how we would survive. It was one thing to defend a door, as Mister Ali had said, and it was another thing to defend a swath of land between a building and a train with two machine guns, but this was a huge chamber and we were being assaulted from all sides.

While one master continued to create a shield, the other two stood quietly, crouched down, their hands still and extended in front of them. The Djinn flooded in yet approached tentatively. I could see claws extended toward us as a group approached on the ground. Others took to the air and flew around us, keeping their distance.

There was a flash of fire, and in the distance a Djinn disappeared in a puff of air. Naomi turned to me. "Warning shots are so much more effective when you kill something with them." She winked, and I caught my breath. She was beautiful but grim. Her attitude reminded me of Grandfather, his wild hair framing a terrible smile as he destroyed creature after creature.

Richard turned and scowled at Naomi. "Be patient. Simin's illusion may be enough."

Mister Ali put his hand on Naomi's shoulder and whispered, "Simin has created an illusion that may frighten off the Djinn." She rolled her eyes but didn't object.

The Djinn approached, but they seemed cautious and even frightened. I looked again at the masters. The unnamed master's shield was unlike the one that Naomi created and visibly glowed around us. It also didn't muffle the sound. He continued his magical movements, while the master that was named Simin presumably was maintaining an illusion. The master named Richard stood at the ready.

The illusion failed as a horrendous screech filled the now empty chamber. Another joined in, and like that the Djinn attacked. I suddenly realized part of the danger of Djinn—their voices. In a closed chamber full of them, the volume and harshness of their screams was painful. I covered my ears with both of my hands as I watched the three masters at work.

Master Richard finally jumped into action, and it was extraordinary how fast he moved. He was casting the same spell that Naomi cast, but at a much higher speed and with a wider effect. Each detonation took out three or four Djinn. He would unleash a spell, and I felt a slight breeze through my hair. It would project out like a ripple in a pond, and every Djinn it hit would disappear in the vacuum of air I learned meant that they had been destroyed. Three of the spells in succession cleared whole sections of approaching Djinn.

I felt a whoosh from behind me, and I turned to see Naomi launch spells at Djinn approaching from behind. The three masters all turned and looked back at Naomi, shock on their faces.

The shield spell was clearly powerful, as the Djinn could not get closer than its iridescent shine about twenty yards beyond us. They clawed and bit at the shield, but it held. Meanwhile the unnamed master and Naomi decimated them. As long as the shield spell held I couldn't see how the Djinn had a prayer of doing anything other than dying.

Mister Ali glanced at me and then placed his mouth next to my ear and spoke through the wails, "Remember this, Tommy. The power you are seeing here is trivial compared to the might of your grandfather when he wielded the staff." He nodded toward the staff I held in my hand against my head as I covered my ears. I certainly didn't feel mighty at that moment.

Naomi continued to relentlessly attack Djinn. As far as I could tell she was doing more than the illusionist master, who was looking around the room but not casting spells. I forgot about the danger, the screams in my ears, the teeth and claws. I forgot about everything but Naomi. She spun around, moving with a devastating grace, her hair flowing out as if she were dancing at the Savoy Ballroom. She glanced at me, and I turned away, embarrassed.

The attacks must have had an effect because the room wasn't as full as it was before. More Djinn were flying, however. I couldn't understand what they had in mind, as they didn't attack and the detonations eventually destroyed them. There was a screech that sounded like otherworldly joy. This was followed by the sound of a huge chandelier that crashed to the floor about twenty yards from us. Several Djinn had loosened it from the ceiling and dropped it to the ground. I couldn't understand their goal, however. The glass didn't block any exits, and it wasn't close enough to hurt us as it fell. It did achieve one effect, however. It led to the Djinn fleeing the room.

After the painful screams, the silence was somehow even more ominous. I couldn't hear any Djinn nearby, either by the scratching of their claws or their screaming. The masters stood at the ready, their bodies not moving but their heads scanning the chamber. Mister Ali grabbed my shoulder and as I looked up at him, he closed his eyes tight and put his thumb and forefinger to the bridge of his nose. I was about to ask him what was wrong when his eyes shot open, and he exclaimed, "Shadows approach!"

The masters stood upright and all three reached into their suits and pulled out flashlights like I had never seen before. They were cylindrical and much smaller than the boxy flashlights I was used to. They still had a large light at the end, however. They flipped switches, and the ends glowed yellow.

Mister Ali shouted, "They approach from the corners. Everyone, form a tight group. The masters can defend us with their light!" I looked out and the memory of the encounter in the alley filled me with a paralyzing dread. From the distance, black flowed toward us like spilled oil. I took a step closer to Mister Ali. Naomi backed up to us, as well. She looked terrified.

We stood together, the masters surrounding us, moving on the balls of their feet and swinging their arms around, sending light out in one direction after another. They had given up any pretense of magic and were simply waving the flashlights around to cover as much ground as possible. It was a hopeless task. The masters could swing their light around, but there was too much open space.

The Shadows seemed to be biding their time, testing our defenses. They would flow in and then out as the masters' lights would swoop toward them. By now the entire room was oozing black, along the walls, the floor, and even up the walls. In fact, I was the only one that noticed that the Shadows were flowing along the ceiling. I had remembered how they had congealed up into stalagmites in the alley, now Shadows started to slowly flow down from the ceiling toward us, like stalactites above our heads.

I stammered out a "look up!" but the masters ignored me as they darted their lights around the room, desperately trying to stop the flow of black toward us. As much as I missed my mom and dad, I really wanted my grandfather. He had faced down the Shadows once before with such cleverness and agility. He was the mightiest Archmage ever. He could save us.

Naomi was smiling as she looked directly at me, her eyes glinting in the ambient light of the moving flashlights. "We need a streetlight." She emphasized the word "streetlight," and just as I was feeling thoroughly useless in her eyes I finally understood.

I stood up and grasped the staff with a sure hand. I was still but a novice in understanding the complexities of the staff, but this—the language of light—I was fluent in. I took one look around. The masters were frantic, swinging their arms wildly trying to get the light to cover more ground than was possible. The entire room was black as pitch, and the ceiling looked like it was oozing black paint, which was slowly dripping down upon us.

Mister Ali had felt me pull away from him, but he immediately knew what I had planned the moment he saw me extend the staff upward like a beacon. "Of course! What a fool I have been. Tommy, you can use the light that lit our way to keep the Shadows at bay. Then we can make our way out to safety!"

I closed my eyes, and all the frustration from Mister Ali trying to train me in the staff fell away. I was one with the magic coursing inside it. I called forth light, pure and bright as the sun. It was so clear and so simple. I smiled, and without a word or motion I made it so.

It was almost as if the staff knew I was eradicating Shadows and delivered a different light than the one I had used to blind the Djinn back in the Way Station. From the top of the staff a pure light filled the entire room, every crevice, every crack, every corner. If it was the light from any other source we all would have been blinded, but it didn't affect us. One moment the Shadows filled the enormous room, seconds from destroying us, and the next they were utterly gone.

I returned the light to the normal beacon that led Mister Ali and me on the staircase, the river, and the mine.

"Not bad, streetlight," Naomi said, but she turned away before I could smile at her.

Mister Ali slapped me on the back and shouted, "All hail the Archmage!"

The masters stared at me, their mouths wide open. Richard then spoke. "We can't dawdle. This was an attack meant to destroy any possible defenses we had. We can't afford to enjoy our luck. We need to get to the Citadel immediately." He reached down, picked up his walking stick, straightened the bowler on his head, and strode briskly toward the exit, the other two falling in step behind them.

I heard Mister Ali mumbling about "luck," but he didn't argue. We fell in behind the masters as they led us onward.

Masses of people were gathered outside as we exited. Several of them pointed to us and shook their head. Some had hands over their mouths in shock. All of them appeared concerned about what had happened inside. As we passed one group, I heard someone say, "How did they survive the gas leak? They say it still isn't safe to enter!"

The masters arranged themselves around us. They handed their walking sticks to Mister Ali, who took them without complaint. As we walked forward, I watched as they stretched their hands and scanned the ground and skies. I clenched the staff and looked for shadows, prepared to pierce them with light. Naomi walked next to me, flexing and unflexing her fingers.

I turned back to Mister Ali. "Where are we going? They called it a citadel. Isn't that like a castle?"

Mister Ali replied, "A citadel is a fortress that guards a city. We are going to the Citadel of London. It is one of the greatest fortresses in the world, although few even know it exists."

We reached a limousine. A stranger stood guarding the open doors. He bowed his head as I approached and swung his arm toward the open door. Everyone stood still, waiting for me to get in. I felt awkward, as these were my friends and I didn't think it appropriate that I was receiving special treatment. Still, I entered the car and slid along a huge seat to the opposite end.

This was obviously another illusion, the black limousine was probably the size of a bus, and as we all gathered inside, there was plenty of room for more people.

The moment everyone was still, Mister Ali turned to the master named Simin. "That was a stunning illusion, Simin." The master looked annoyed.

"You noticed that?"

"Yes, but it was some of the most complex magic I've ever seen, and you did it while walking. Even your gait seemed normal."

The master grunted. "Not normal enough apparently."

"What illusion?" I asked.

"Now that's what I was looking for!" The master laughed.

Mister Ali smiled. "Master Simin here created multiple illusions of us leaving the station. Someone looking for us would have had a hard time choosing which group was the real one. Or even knowing there was an illusion at all. That alone is extraordinary, but he also excluded us from the illusion, which is something very few magicians can do."

"Parlor tricks," Naomi noted. She was sitting across from me, her legs were stretched out in front of her, crossed at the ankles. She looked immensely pleased with herself.

"Respect, young lady!" Mister Ali replied, anger in his voice.

"Respect?" Naomi pulled her legs in and pointed at Master Simin. "He didn't help at all while I was saving us. At least his friends did something."

"Naomi!" Mister Ali's voice filled the limousine.

Master Simin raised his hand at Mister Ali. "It's okay Ali." He stared at Naomi for a moment and then made a few movements with his hand. Naomi screamed and grabbed her throat. An enormous snake was curled her neck.

"Get it off me!" Her hands grasped at her neck, her fingernails scratching and clawing at the snake.

"Enough, Simin!" Mister Ali again raised his voice.

I looked at the master, and he smiled and shrugged. "Just a parlor trick."

The snake was gone, and Naomi was taking deep breaths, her eyes wide as she tried to regain her composure. She looked at me, and I saw something in her eyes. Was it a plea for help? Embarrassment?

"You will never do that again." I tried to sound confident and powerful. I must have succeeded because Master Simin looked at me.

"Excuse me?"

"You are not to cast spells on another in my presence unless they request it." My voice was steadier, but it took an effort to keep my gaze on the face of the master. His stare was intimidating.

There was a long pause, and then Simin replied, "As you wish, Archmage." He then turned away and dropped his hands to his side.

I looked at Naomi, who was rubbing her neck with her left hand. "You could try to be nicer," I added, although I was certain I sounded much less confident in my comment to her.

"As you wish, streetlight." I thought I saw the corner of her mouth turn up, and the rest of the ride was a blur.

Chapter Ten

NAOMI PASSES A TEST

"Not far now," Mister Ali said, although all I could see through the windows was English countryside.

Naomi spoke up. "So what do we do once we get to the Citadel?"

Master Richard replied, "I don't know what *you* will be doing, but *we* will present the new Archmage to Cain. He will decide on what to do next."

Naomi fumed but didn't say anything else. I decided to ask my own questions. "Who is Cain, and will he help me find my grandfather?"

Mister Ali replied before Master Richard could speak, "Cain is the greatest master in the world. He has achieved heights in magic not seen in centuries. His guidance will be invaluable."

"Archmage." It was the master whose name I still didn't know.

"What was that?" Mister Ali replied.

"Archmage Cain. He accepted the Archmage title recently."

Mister Ali's face was frozen in shock. He recovered quickly, however, and raised his voice. "Such arrogance! Such disrespect! There is and can only be one Archmage, and he sits with us right here." He crossed his arms, looking defiant.

Master Richard shrugged. "You can take it up with him." He seemed amused at the prospect.

We rode in silence, and I considered the circumstances. The masters were truly impressive, but they didn't seem very pleasant or even welcoming. I was worried about Mister Ali. He appeared out of his element. He was clearly impressed with the presence of the three masters, but they didn't treat him with a corresponding respect. I looked over at him, and he had the furrowed brow and pinched face of someone holding in their anger and unhappiness.

Naomi ignored us all. She was making rhythmic movements with her hands, which I understood to be some kind of magical manipulation. She was focusing her attention on some imaginary point in the distance while she repeated the motion over and over again.

I stared at her. The focus in her blue eyes and the sharp angles of her face gave her a serious and intense look, but I found it made her even more beautiful, like a lion or tiger. Despite her dusty dungarees and her dirty and wrinkled shirt, there was nobility in her, a nobility of purpose and a nobility of stature. I thought back and wondered if I did the right thing in confronting Master Simin. She seemed thankful, but were my actions actually insulting? She didn't need me to save her. She didn't need anyone to save her.

She made some small error in movement, something I didn't notice, something I couldn't notice, and dropped her hands, shaking them in annoyance. She looked up and caught me staring at her. I turned away, embarrassed, but my heart leapt at what I perceived to be a slight smile out of the corner of my eye.

I looked out and noticed we were far from the city. It suddenly occurred to me that perhaps these masters weren't to be trusted. "I thought we were going to the Citadel?"

"We are." It was the nameless master.

"Then why are we heading away from the city?" After being attacked three times in quick succession I was nervous and not very trusting, even though it appeared that the masters had helped save us.

The nameless master sighed and answered as if he was tutoring a student who hadn't done his homework. "Just because it protects the city, doesn't mean it needs to be in the city." Mister Ali tried to break in, but the master waved him off with a hand. "It is called Fort Belvedere, and it has been the center of magic for over five hundred years."

I had heard of Fort Belvedere. It was the home of the recent king of England who had abdicated his throne. I wondered if the former king was also Cain. With Mister Ali's talk of my grandfather being involved in great battles and evil leaders, it struck me as a reasonable. The prospect thrilled and intrigued me.

The concrete turned into dirt and before long we turned onto a driveway leading to a large estate. It was cobblestone and in much better shape than the primary road that led to it. The main house looked nothing like a fort and more like a mansion. There was a massive stone wall in front, but it appeared to be useless against any real attack, as it contained windows and was not very tall.

"This is an illusion," I stated.

"Very good, Tommy," Mister Ali replied. "This is a folly, which is a building designed to look like something, even though it isn't intended to actually be used for that purpose. In this case, there is a wonderful irony at play. You are looking at something meant to look like a fort, yet commonly known to be useless as one. However, the reality is that it is a mighty fort, indeed."

The limousine drove through a small opening in the defensive wall, despite the fact that we were in a large vehicle. The opening changed even as I watched it. It was now a large gated entry big enough to allow us to pass. We entered a courtyard. It appeared cramped between the wall and the mansion behind it. There was a fountain, around which went the stone road from the gate to the steps leading to the house. The limousine stopped in front of the steps, where a small group of uniformed men were waiting for us.

One of the men opened the doors to the limousine. The three masters exited first and went off to talk to a man to the left. An imposing man stood facing us. Mister Ali shouted "John!" and went up and hugged him.

"Ali! So glad to see you safe." The man Ali called John patted him on the back and then pulled away.

Mister Ali turned to us. "This is Lord Gort, Knight Commander of the Army Council."

"Wonderful to meet you, Knight Commander," I replied.

Lord Gort was older with thin short-cropped grey hair and angular features. His eyes had a sorrowful look that struck me as distinctly unmilitary. Despite my perception, his uniform was covered with medals, and he looked very serious. He didn't frown, and he didn't look angry, but he wasn't smiling either. More than anything, he looked like he was in the midst of a difficult and painful mission, and his calm was all that stood between loss and victory. He nodded to me and said "Archmage." His voice was even but short, like wasting a single syllable would pain him. I immediately liked him, despite his reserve.

Mister Ali returned to my side. "We weren't expecting a group, Ali, but it is understandable. Details were in short supply after the disaster in New York." Lord Gort looked at me. "At least you have the staff and the new Archmage with you."

"He is a worthy heir, John. Tommy used the staff to destroy a cavernous room, black with Shadows!" There was great pride in Mister Ali's voice. Lord Gort looked unsurprised. I couldn't help but feel proud. I had experienced the terror of the Shadows and knowing I defeated them was probably the greatest thing I had ever done in my life.

"And who is the girl?" He didn't sound pleased as he asked the question.

Mister Ali looked surprised that Naomi was still with us. "This is Naomi. She is an apprentice Waymaster. Her mother perished defending us from the Djinn. We will need to—" Mister Ali paused and then continued, "find her a home."

Naomi stepped forward and addressed Lord Gort. She completely ignored everyone else. "Excuse me, sir. My mother trained me to be a master magician, not a Waymaster."

"Mother? A female Waymaster?" Lord Gort seemed intrigued more than judgmental.

Before Naomi could reply, Mister Ali broke in. "Her grand-father was Waymaster Bergeron."

Lord Gort's face lit up. "Your grandfather was Alexander? What an amazing coincidence we have here. The granddaughter of our greatest Waymaster, and the grandson of our greatest Archmage." He looked at Naomi. "So, how can I help you Miss Bergeron?"

Naomi stood tall. "I have decided that I would like to conclude my studies here." I marveled at her. She was more polite and re-spectful than I had ever seen her, but she was just as demanding as ever. She looked a combination of charming and confident.

For the first time the Knight Commander looked amused. "You wish to conclude your studies, do you? Well, I have no need of domestic magic. However—" Lord Gort paused and then smiled. It was the smile of someone preparing to tell a hi-larious joke at your expense. Not of one who is happy in your company. "Duncan, come over here!"

The man with the medals that was talking to the Masters looked at us and walked over. "Sir?"

"What is that accursed spell that the senior Journeyman are always complaining to Cain about being on the exam? The one that none of them can do."

Jake Kerr

"Do you mean Arachne's Ladder?" Duncan replied.

"That's the one!" Lord Gort turned to Naomi. "If you could show me Arachne's Ladder perhaps we may have a place for you." It was as if time had stopped. We all stared at the two of them facing each other, the chiseled member of the Army Council and the young girl with the cowboy boots, dungarees, and defiant eyes.

Naomi stood up straight, and pulled her sleeves up to the elbow. She placed her palms flat against each other and then began manipulating her fingers with such speed that it looked like she was weaving something with her wrists shackled. A moment later she moved her palms slightly apart. Her fingers continued to move and every few seconds she would edge her palms outward. I caught a glimpse of something shiny between her hands, and as they moved further and further apart, it became clearer. Soon, her hands were about a foot apart, and a glowing mesh of material was spread between them. It looked like a tightly knit web of glowing thread. I looked at Naomi's face, and there was perspiration dripping down her forehead. She stared at her hands.

She stopped, a look of defiance on her face. All told it had taken her about five minutes. She shoved her hands toward Lord Gort. "It would be stronger if I had more time." I looked around. Mister Ali's jaw was dropped open. Duncan was frowning. One of the masters was shaking his head.

"No doubt." He smiled for a moment and then it was gone. He turned to Duncan. "Finally, someone with potential." He let his comment sink in and then continued. "Find comfortable lodgings for the Archmage and Ali. And take this young one," he looked directly at Naomi, "to the Academy."

"My Lord!" I expected the surprised response, but I was saddened that it came not just from Duncan but also from Mister Ali. For some reason girls weren't considered as magician material, but I had seen Naomi, and it was clear that she was not just skilled, she was nearly as accomplished as the masters.

Duncan continued, "She is but a girl." He nodded toward Naomi, as if perhaps the man who seemed to run the Citadel had somehow missed that fact.

"General Duncan, how many of our current senior journeymen can do that spell at all, let alone using nothing but their hands?"

"None, but they are all quite young, sir." Duncan sounded defensive.

"Nonsense." And with that the conversation was over. Lord Gort turned and walked away, without a wave or a goodbye. Over his shoulder he added, "Follow me, Ali. Cain wants to speak with us, and I'd rather get that annoyance out of the way." It suddenly struck me that I was going to be without Mister Ali for the first time in—what could it have been—days? Longer? Being without him concerned me, even though we were finally in a safe place.

"Couldn't I come with you, sir?" I blurted out. Mister Ali leaned down and put his arm around me and smiled warmly.

"It is okay, Tommy. Your time to speak will come. In the mean time, you should get some rest. This has been a most difficult journey, and you need a soft bed."

I whispered "Okay," and hugged Mister Ali. He stood, patted me on the back, and then pulled away, turned, and hurried after Lord Gort.

As Mister Ali retreated, Duncan turned to us, disgust on his face.

"Corporal, take our guests to the living quarters," He addressed a soldier that was standing by the limousine. "And take that one to the academy." He waved toward Naomi with his hand.

The corporal nodded and walked toward us. He looked to be only a few years older than me, and when he reached us, his voice was very respectful. "If you would please follow me this way, Lord Ainsley can attend to your needs. Your quarters are not far from there." He pointed to a long wing off the main building, with three stories and lots of windowed rooms that overlooked the entrance. There were three doors along its length, all of which looked identical.

We all walked along quietly. I looked around the Citadel, trying to take in what was illusion and what was real. What struck me the most was that even when you knew you were looking at an illusion, it was still difficult to see through it. Occasionally, I would get a glimpse of turrets and men manning them in place of what looked like a slate roof, but such images always slipped back into the reality as I perceived it—the former King's country retreat with the appearance of a fortress.

As we walked along the gravel path that fronted the mansion, its immense size became clearer despite the illusion. It was as if we were taking three steps for every step that it looked like it would take to get to our destination. After longer than I ever thought it would take, we reached the first door. The Corporal stopped and pointed at it.

"These are the guest quarters. They border the main house and are adjacent to the apprentice wing, which starts at that door." He pointed at the second door. "The training area and classrooms begin down at the end." He then pointed to the third door. "Young lady, that is the Academy and you will be spending your time down there." He looked at Naomi, and then turned back to me. "But our first stop is here."

He walked up and grabbed a large iron door knocker shaped like a frog. He rapped the door three times, which rang out much louder than I thought it would. Immediately, there was a click and the door slid smoothly outward. The door was massive, at least four inches thick and made of iron bound solid wood, but it moved as if it was as light as a feather. Was it actually a light door and an illusion made it look massive? Or was the door actually this massive and so well designed that it moved smoothly in the frame? By now I was losing track of what was and wasn't real.

A girl about my age stood in the door frame as the door swung fully outward. "Hello, Felice. We need lodgings for the new Archmage." He waved an arm toward me.

"Yes, sir. And for the young lady?"

"I am taking her to Mister Sagan." Felice's eyes went wide, and she stared at Naomi. Before Felice could say anything more, the corporal added, "I know. Perhaps they can find a room on the floor above the dormitories." He turned to me. "Felice will escort you from here."

I thanked the corporal and followed Felice into the building. I looked back over my shoulder, but Naomi was already gone, heading off to her new life as a future master. I wondered when I would see her again.

Chapter Eleven

A WALL CONFUSES ME

I was ushered through the entryway into a large sitting room. Felice told me to make myself comfortable as she exited through an arch to the right, which led to an open room with a marble floor.

The room we were in was cavernous, with a ceiling that was probably twenty feet above my head. It was dark and lit by candles, as there were no windows. There were bookshelves against the wall to my left, while there were large wingback chairs in each corner with a reading lamp and side table next to each. One table had a book on it and a pipe resting in an ashtray, smoke curling up from its bowl. All of the walls were paneled in a deep reddish wood, with the far wall covered with portraits and various landscapes. The wall to the right was paneled and broken up by the arched doorway, which must have been at least twenty feet wide and appeared to be some kind of antechamber.

Dominating the room was a huge painting on the far wall. It was of a fierce man with black flowing hair holding a staff above his head. He stood at the front of an army dressed in bright colors on a huge grassy plain. In front of him was another army, this one dressed in drab grey. The staff shot lightning bolts and fire out toward the opposing army, spreading disorder and injury. I looked more closely at the painting, and the detail on the faces of the soldiers' was magnificent. The looks of terror were realistic enough to make me shiver. I immediately recognized the face of the man holding the staff. It was my grandfather, and perhaps even more disturbing than the faces of the army he was defeating was the look of joy on his face. That joy, juxtaposed with the terror of the soldiers, made my grandfather look almost evil.

"Does anything in the painting look familiar?" I looked over to see Felice standing near the door she left through.

"That's my grandfather," I stated.

"Yes. But I was talking about that." She pointed at the staff. I took a step closer to the painting and examined the staff. It was my grandfather's cane. I looked at the cane in my hand and then back at the painting. The cane in the painting was missing the brass tip at the bottom, but it was undoubtedly the same one. I held up the staff toward Felice, and she smiled.

I looked back up at the painting. "That's a battle from the Great War. You can see the trenches in the background. I've never seen depictions of the battles with anything other than guns and cannons."

"Guns and cannons, ha!" I turned to face a man stooped with age. Unlike everyone else in the Citadel, he actually looked like a magician. He had a small beard that came to a point just beyond his chin. His white hair was slicked back on his head, and he wore a black robe that contained some odd designs in the depths of the shadows that drew your eye but were frustratingly difficult to make out. He was extremely thin, and his bones were a mass of sharp angles beneath his skin. His eyes were so dark as to be black. He walked through the archway, and although his spine forced him to lean forward, he didn't use a cane. Felice walked over and remained a respectful distance behind.

"What use were guns and cannons against the *Pehlivan*?" The old man chuckled. "They melted at his glance and exploded against their own at his command. No, young man, the Hindenburg Line fell as fast as the *Pehlivan* could walk along it."

I had not seen my grandfather melt anything with the staff, and the painting showed nothing of guns and cannons, so I couldn't help but doubt the entirety of the old man's story, but he clearly had great admiration for my grandfather, so I overlooked it.

Felice stepped forward. "This is the new Archmage." She looked embarrassed, and it struck me that she couldn't remember my name.

"You can call me Tommy," I volunteered.

"This is Lord Ainsley," Felice interjected. "He is the master of the Citadel. He oversees the buildings, grounds, and rooms and has for many years." She bowed and stepped into the background.

Jake Kerr

"Tommy, eh?" Lord Ainsley walked up to me and stared right into my eyes. "Declan is your grandfather?"

"Yes, sir."

"Expected as much. I thought he'd go to the grave with the staff in his hands. At least he didn't wait to pass it along to his great grandson." He laughed a loud wheezy laugh. "You came here alone?"

"No sir. I came with Mister Ali and a student named Naomi."

"Ali is here?" The mention of Mister Ali brightened Lord Ainsley's face. "You must tell him to stop by. He is an old friend of mine. Ha! He couldn't perform magic to fool a sideshow, but he has the eye." He tapped his forehead with a finger. "Could see through even Cain's illusions. Is young Baraz here, as well? There were many a day I took care of that boy while his dad and the *Pehlivan* were off together."

I was struck with a sudden sadness, as I thought back to my grandfather and Mister Ali's son, whom I had known for a long time as the maitre d of the Persian Garden. In a soft voice I added, "I'm afraid he is missing. He and my grandfather were left behind in the attack on his restaurant in New York. They

— 199 —

are feared dead." I felt sick saying the words "left behind" as much as I did saying the words "feared dead."

Lord Ainsley paused and then looked at me. "The *Pehlivan* dead? Well, I find that hard to believe. And young Baraz was almost as good with the sight as his father. He'd be a slippery one to catch. The two of them together? I find it more likely that your grandfather hatched some foolishly dangerous plan and that he'll succeed in it after we have all given up hope." He must have seen the sadness in my face because he gave me a tentative smile and patted me on the shoulder. "Have more faith."

And with a clap of his hands, he broke the somber mood. "Now, let me give you the partial tour as I take you to your room. This is the reading room. There are popular books on the shelf back there, but the actual library is through that door in the back. If you would like access to books, please let me know, and I'll make arrangements with Felice and the librarian."

He then led us through the wide archway into what looked like an antechamber. The marble floors were polished to such a sheen that they were almost mirrors. To the left through the archway was a majestic stone staircase at the back that led up to the second floor. Opposite the archway was a set of double wooden doors that were closed. To the right was a stone wall that matched the décor of the room but that seemed out of place. In fact, I was thinking that the layout of the building was wrong. This room should have been the entryway, and the sitting room should have opened only to internal rooms, not the outside.

Lord Ainsley was looking at me strangely. "Is there something wrong?"

I didn't know how to answer, so I was honest. "That wall shouldn't be there. That should be a door. And these two rooms are in the wrong spots." I pointed back to the library.

"Very good. Did the staff tell you that?"

"No sir, it just seemed like it made sense."

He nodded. "Tell me then, which room is easier to defend upon attack?"

"This one. The stone walls seem more durable, and there is not easy way in from the outside. Plus, you can defend the stairs from a height."

"Very good, but wrong. The other room is much easier to defend for reasons I shall not go into right now. Suffice to say that the oddness of this room and what you have observed are by design. Many things in this Citadel will look odd or feel wrong. They *are* odd, and they are wrong, but always remember that they are that way for a reason.

"But enough lessons for today!" Lord Ainsley pointed up the staircase. "Your lodgings are upstairs, the first door to your left."

"Thank you, Lord Ainsley."

He waved his hand in response. "Felice, bring our young Archmage some food and drink. From the looks of him he could use some fresh clothes, as well. See the quartermaster. He'll complain, but tell him I requested it. He'll complain some more, but he'll give them to you." Lord Ainsley laughed.

"Thank you!" I was growing very fond of the old man who seemed to know my grandfather and was looking out for me.

The old man waved his hand in a dismissive fashion and turned away, which I was learning was his general response to anything that he didn't want to bother with. "Ring the bell if you need anything," he said as he walked back toward the archway and into the sitting room. "Oh, and don't leave the building."

"Follow me," Felice stated. She led me up the marble steps, which were smooth and free of wear and dust. They looked like they hadn't been used since they were laid. At the top, there was a wide landing that overlooked the antechamber, and there was a hallway that extended back from the stairs. We were on the second floor, and the staircase continued up on the left, the third floor lost to my view. The hallway was dark wood with a long rug that ran down its center. The rug was a deep red with swirls and designs of bright colors. It looked very regal to me. I assumed my eyes were playing tricks on me, for the hallway extended as far as I could see, reaching a point somewhere in the distance. It must have been hundreds of yards long.

I looked back at Felice, who was smiling. "It is impressive, yes? Cain created this illusion himself. The hall extends down about ten rooms on each side, when you reach the end it slowly curves around then turns you around and you continue back in this direction, where the illusion continues. It does not take long before you wonder where the staircase came from or how far you've been walking. She opened the door to my room at that moment. "I recommend you keep your bearings."

I entered the room behind Felice. She pointed at a hand bell on the nightstand next to the bed. "Ring that if you need anything. It need not be loud." She then turned and walked out of the room. Before I could respond she had closed the door. The room was small but comfortable. Like the hallway, the floor was hardwood but mostly covered by a large rug. It was of the Persian variety and very thick. The bed was an old four poster, with a reddish stained wood. It appeared very solid and was thick with white linens and blankets. There were several brightly colored pillows on it. Across from the bed was a tall standing mirror.

I looked in the mirror and could barely recognize myself. I was encrusted with dirt, and the fine clothes I wore to the theater with my grandfather were torn and stained with blood, dirt, and sweat. My hair was a tangle. But what struck me the most was the cane I held in my right hand. I had never seen it in my hand before, and the effect was shocking. I had spent so many years watching my grandfather hold, twist, swing, and walk with the cane, that seeing it in my hand for the first time created an odd connection to him in me.

Jake Kerr

I stared at my face and then my fist gripping the cane tightly. I looked weary, and I looked mighty. For the first time since I was on the boat on the great underground river I realized that there was more to the cane and more to me than anyone had expected. More than anything I felt humbled.

I noticed the bed in the mirror and turned. I had not slept in a bed in, what, three days, four days? I had lost count. Thoughts of anything but sleep displaced everything else. A great weariness descended upon me, and as I sat on the edge of the bed to remove my shoes I let myself fall backward just to feel the cushion of the soft blankets. I doubt I felt my head hit the mattress before I was asleep.

Chapter Twelve

THE QUARTERMASTER GIVES ME SPECTACLES

I awoke curled near the pillows. I had somehow bur-
rowed under a blanket, but other than that I was
exactly as I was when I climbed onto the bed. Light
shone through a large window in the wall to my left, and,
to my horror, my shoes were still on and the light illuminated every bit of dried mud and dirt that I had ground
into the linens and blankets as I slept.

I leapt off the bed and furiously slapped at the linens,
using my hands to push the bits of dirt onto the floor. I realized that I was just getting the floor dirty in the process,

so I started to try and sweep the dirt into my left hand with my right. I looked around for a wastebasket, but there was none. I shoved the bits of dirt into my pockets and then continued to clean the bed. I did my best, but it was a lost cause. The bottom of the bed looked like someone had danced on it with dirty shoes.

It was not how I wanted to present myself to Duncan or Lord Gort or Lord Ainsley. I felt rather intimidated by their importance and sophistication. I had never been outside of New York, and their accents made me think I was talking with royalty.

I stood up and looked around the room. There were two nightstands on either side of the bed, each with an electric lamp of ornate design. They sat upon white lace that covered the entire surface. Other than the hand bell on the table nearest the door, there was nothing else on them. They both had drawers, which proved to be empty. Across from the doorway stood the window, and next to the window was a reading chair. It was navy blue with golden accents. A floor lamp stood between the chair and a small reading table. Upon the table was a book, *Elementary Illusion.*

Jake Kerr

It was very worn and, as I looked through it, every page appeared to have handwritten notes. Some were crossed out with newer notes written underneath. They all referred to the subject matter, which was creating basic illusions, such as making a single item look like two items or (later in the book) making a room look bigger than it was. Each chapter was full of finger and body manipulations that were illustrated down to minute distances. There were images meant to be visualized and recitations, as well, but these seemed secondary to the physical element of each spell. The first illusion was one where you were to use a page of writing on the textbook and make its mirror image appear on the previous open page, which was blank. I attempted the first few finger movements but immediately gave up. My thumb couldn't move in the way illustrated in the book.

I put the book down and looked out the window. I blinked and looked again. There was a huge wall in the distance across the courtyard. When we entered the Citadel, there appeared to be a small decorative wall, but this wall was at least forty feet high, and I could see armaments atop it at regular intervals. To my right I could see the building extend out for what must have been 50 yards or more. I got my bearings and realized that that must have been the where the hall extended out. The courtyard was drab and covered in brown grass that looked like it was dying. There was a path that led to large wooden doors in the far wall. Closer to the building, the path turned and extended to the training wing, where it ended in a circle. In the center of the circle was a working fountain, with a statue of some figure sending water from his scepter into the pool.

My stomach grumbled, and I had to use the bathroom. As there was no bathroom and no food, I went to ring the bell. Before I did, however, I rearranged the linens and blankets so that they hid the dirt left by my shoes. The wait staff may know that I was uncouth, but no one else had to know. I rang the bell, which had the tinny sound of a bell designed to call attention, not make music. I waited.

After a few minutes I rang the bell again. I waited a few more minutes, and as I considered leaving the room to look for someone or ringing the bell a third time, there was a knock at my door. I opened it, and Felice was standing there, holding a tray of food. "You know, a little patience doesn't hurt. You only needed to ring the bell once."

I stammered out an apology as Felice walked in and placed the tray on a trunk that I hadn't noticed at the end of the bed. Was it covered in linens? I was wondering how I missed it when Felice said, "I have your clothes outside. Give me a moment."

I looked at the food—it was cold meats, cheeses, and some bread, along with a pitcher of water—and marveled again at the trunk. It stood there clear as day. Felice re-entered with a pile of clothes, which she placed on the reading chair. "You'll need to see the quartermaster for shoes."

I thanked her as she began to walk toward the door and then blurted out, "Is there a washroom or perhaps an outhouse nearby?" I was embarrassed to ask, but my need was great.

She laughed, "Right there," and she pointed to the wall next to the mirror. All I saw was a wall.

"I'm sorry. I don't see anything but a wall." She turned and walked toward it.

"Why, it's clear as day. You can't see this door?" She rapped on the wall, but it sounded like wood, and then I started to see the blurry outline of a door. "Wait a moment, there is a slight illusion on this." She squinted at the door, then turned and squinted at me. "You honestly can't see the door?"

I shook my head. "It's becoming clearer now," I added sheepishly.

She chuckled. "You have no sight at all. This illusion wouldn't fool a mouse. Heck, I can barely even tell there's an illusion that's been cast on the door." She turned the knob and opened the door. "Better?"

"Yes!"

"Well, whoever lived in this room before you must have been practicing illusions. From the looks of this they weren't very good at all, and normally I'd say not to worry, but for you," she paused, "I would…" She paused. "Well, I'm not sure what I'd do. Maybe we can switch rooms." She shook her head and walked toward the door.

"After you are washed, full, and dressed, ring the bell. Quite a few people want to meet you."

"I will. Thank you, Felice."

She turned and smiled. "Anything for the Archmage!" She closed the door behind her, and I sprinted toward the previously hidden door. I couldn't believe I had missed it. I opened the door and found a modern bathroom. After using it and washing my hands, I went back and devoured the food on the trunk. The trunk. I hadn't told Felice, but apparently the trunk was covered in some illusion, as well. I opened it, but it only held more linens and blankets. It didn't fade from view, so I was thankful that I was able to at least see through this illusion.

I took another look at the illusions book, but it had no advice on seeing through illusions, only casting them. I placed the book back on the table and decided to wash and change. Remembering the bed, I went into the bathroom to remove my clothes and shoes, not wanting to soil the carpet.

The water was cold but refreshing. For the first time I could see the damage that I had sustained in the various attacks. There was a deep purplish bruise on my hip, and my shoulder had a scrape with bruises around it. I had various cuts and smaller bruises pretty much all over. I looked like someone had knocked me down a few times and pummeled me.

The water turned so dark with grime that I had to empty it and draw a second bath. When I was done, however, I felt better than I had since we had left the Persian Garden. I went back into the room and examined my new clothes. It was a military uniform, but unlike the one I had seen on Lord Gort. The pants were a thick canvas-like material in a khaki color and matched the shirt, which was starched and rough against the skin. The socks were thick wool and reminded me of winter back in New York. Where I would have expected epaulets or insignia were blank folds of cloth. I looked at myself in the mirror, and I looked like a raw army recruit, the folds of cloth absent any medals illustrating nothing but mere potential.

I was clean, rested, clothed, and full. I had many questions to ask, and I felt that now was the time to find the answers. I was convinced my grandfather was alive as Lord Ainsley implied, and that was my immediate goal. To find him and help save him.

In the short run, however, I looked forward to seeing Mister Ali and Naomi again. Naomi seemed to finally accept me. I wanted to compare notes with her and see if I could somehow convince her to delay her studies to help me find my grandfather.

But I pushed all these things aside when I noticed the staff lying on the bed. I had not been alone with it since my time on the boat when I thought that Mister Ali was asleep. What was I missing? Light came so naturally. Focused light, brilliant light that filled a cavernous room, soft light to guide our way in darkness—all these things came easily to me. But everything else seemed impossible. I wanted to make Naomi gasp as I destroyed our enemies with terrible bolts of magic, but that was beyond me. I was the *streetlight*.

I walked over, sat on the bed, and took the staff in both my hands. I closed my eyes and, instead of looking for something new, I let myself think of what I had done with the staff and what that meant. I thought of light, a magic of such difficulty that the luminescence of a candle was considered a great accomplishment by masters. Perhaps its purity was the key. But if that was the case, why was my Grandfather, clearly one of the greatest Archmages in history, completely unable to create light with the staff? I could not figure it out.

I thought about how I had freed the boat, but to my mind that was an accident. I couldn't even remember what I did to make it happen. I thought of my assault on the river. I had not shared the experience with anyone, but it was clear to me that the staff had almost taken on a life of its own. I felt its joy at battling an equal.

Had it won? I could not tell, but the magic of that moment was beyond me. It appeared that the staff did some things on its own. I twirled the cane in my hand and closed my eyes.

Mastering the staff was a challenge I could meet. It would just take time. The fact that until then I would be of little use to anyone just made me even more committed to succeeding. Further thought was interrupted by a knock on the door. I opened the door to an angry Felice.

"Why didn't you ring the bell? They have been waiting for you!"

I shrugged but said nothing. I felt the delay had been worth it, and I didn't want to start an argument or sound impolite by responding truthfully. My foot slipped a little on the hardwood floor near the door, and I used that as an opportunity to change the subject. "I still need shoes."

Felice looked exasperated. "I know! Which only adds to our delay. You do realize you are to meet with Cain, don't you? Making him wait is not advisable."

I replied rather sheepishly, "I haven't been told much of anything."

Felice shook her head and walked out the door, adding, "Well, I'm afraid I can't be of much help on that count, but

I'll do my best. We'll have a bit of time while we get you some shoes."

I followed her out the door and was once again struck by the enormous length of the hall. We walked to the marble steps, and my foot slid out from under me on the shiny marble. I caught myself by grabbing a decorative pillar at the top.

"Please be careful!" Felice looked annoyed again. "The last thing I need is for the Archmage to break his neck on my watch." She slowly led me down the staircase as I gripped the balustrade.

We went through the doors that led to what I assumed was the training wing, the direction where they took Naomi. I had expected a hallway that led to rooms, but we entered a single room that took up the entire width of this wing of the building. The ceiling was at least two stories above us. There were just the standard smaller room windows in the front, and they stood at ground level and near the ceiling, which made me think that this was probably an area where a large number of rooms were removed to make space for this larger one. The décor here was decidedly more utilitarian. There were no carpets, and the floors, while still marble, were worn and dull. It was brightly lit by harsh electric lights that hung from the ceiling. The room was open and contained little furniture. Dozens of men could have gathered there without difficulty.

Directly across from us was another set of double doors, which led further down the wing, while to my left, against the far back wall was a long wooden table with a man behind it. He was moving clothes from piles on the floor onto the table. They were uniforms, much like I wore, and the man was organizing them on the table by size. As we approached, a young man in a uniform came in from a small door to the right, carrying more clothing. He dropped them on the floor and was walking away as we reached the table.

"Hi, Captain. Sorry for the delay, but the Archmage is here for his shoes."

"Ah, this is the *Pehlivan*'s grandson!" There was a broad smile on the man's face, and his hands were clasped together across his chest, as if Felice had just brought him a delightful present. He was in a uniform like mine, only his was marked by shiny buttons and a number of ribbons and awards. He had stripes on his shoulder, which I assume marked him as a captain. He was thin, as was his face, and he had a pencil-type mustache. It was the same color as his hair, which was as black as oil. He wore circular glasses that were small but looked large in the midst of his narrow features. More than anything I was struck by how little he looked like a soldier. He reminded me of the bookish boys in my school.

I felt guilty at my thoughts and decided to use courtesy as my penance. I shoved my hand forward and announced, "I'm Tommy, it's wonderful to meet you, Captain!"

"Well, well, young man, I applaud your enthusiasm! And you look quite dashing in that uniform."

Felice quickly cut in, "This is Captain Rechin, he is the quartermaster for the Citadel."

Captain Rechin stood up straight and held out his arms over the various articles of clothing around him. "It is an honor to outfit our boys." He stopped and looked at Felice. "Which reminds me, Felice. When will the recruits be coming? I'm not quite prepared for them, and I would hate to have them milling about the room when they could be doing something more useful."

"Lord Ainsley said they won't be here until dinner, Captain."

"Ah, very good." He turned back to me. "So, about your shoes." He walked around the table and approached me from my right.

"Do you need to measure my feet? Or perhaps you would like me to get my old shoes from upstairs, they fit me quite well," I stated, trying to be helpful. The quartermaster shook his head.

"No, no, that's not necessary. One doesn't outfit hundreds of young men without learning how to size shoes quickly and efficiently." He paused and leaned down, looking at my feet. "Now you are obviously younger than our usual recruits, but you're still a good size. He reached toward my right foot and then jerked his hand back. "No need. No need," he muttered to himself. He walked back to his table and over to a pile of shoes. "In fact, I have the correct pair right here."

He turned back to me, a pair of black shiny leather boots in his hand. He walked over and made to hand them to me, but he jerked his hands back again as I reached for them. He peered at me closely through his lenses. "How do your clothes fit? Don't lie!"

"Very well, sir," I answered.

He then handed the shoes to me and stated, "Then these will, as well."

I thanked him for the shoes, and not seeing a stool around, sat down on the stone floor and put my boots on. They fit perfectly. I stood up and noticed that while I was putting my shoes on the quartermaster had left.

"Where'd Captain Rechin go?" I asked Felice.

She shrugged. "He left while you were putting your shoes on."

"Should we go or wait for him?"

"Well, that would mean making Cain wait even longer." She paused, and then added, "I highly recommend we leave."

I tested the shoes—they gripped the floor well, even though it was a smooth stone—and then replied, "Okay, let's go."

We were halfway across the hall when the quartermaster's voice rang out. "Wait! I am not done outfitting the Archmage!" We stopped, turned, and watched as Captain Rechin ran up to us. When he arrived he awkwardly stopped and bowed in the same motion. I didn't have the remotest idea as to how to respond.

"I was but a young assistant when the former quartermaster outfitted the *Pehlivan* for his first assault on the dark magician on the continent. He lamented for weeks afterward that our arsenal had been bare of gifts to help the *Pehlivan* in his battle. To him it was the greatest failure he could have conceived—a quartermaster unprepared for his duty." Captain Rechin looked intense. "Our stores do not carry the magical items they had in the past. Indeed, such items are fast disappearing from the world and we have little hope of seeing them replenished." He then smiled and held out his hand, which was holding something. "But we do have this, which I humbly pray will be of use to you."

I reached out and took a pair of spectacles from his hand. Captain Rechin looked at me expectantly but said nothing. They were identical to the glasses on the quartermaster's face, and not knowing what else to do I put them on my face, even though my vision was perfect. Captain Rechin smiled as I looked around the room. Nothing looked different.

I looked at Felice, but she seemed as nonplussed as I was. I felt incredibly foolish and not a little embarrassed for the quartermaster but could think of nothing else to do, so I asked, "What… do they do?"

The quartermaster answered, "They are glasses. They sharpen your vision." Before I could respond, he added, "You are very welcome, Archmage." I couldn't help but notice that we looked eerily similar with our dark hair, uniforms, and now, identical spectacles. "Wear them for your meeting with Cain," he added, winking at me.

I nodded and gave as sincere a "thank you" as I could. We shook hands, and then Felice and I turned and continued our journey out of the hall. At the door, I looked back with the spectacles on my face, but nothing appeared out-of-the-ordinary. The quartermaster had left and the room was empty. I quickly took the lenses off and slid them into my shirt pocket, wondering if I'd ever find a use for them.

Chapter Thirteen

CAIN

"We are *so* late," Felice said.

"Is that bad?" I replied, as she briskly led me through the antechamber and into the reading room.

"You are going to meet Cain." The tone of her voice answered the question. It sounded like she was glad I was the one meeting Cain and not her.

"Where is Mister Ali? I thought I was going to rejoin him?"

"I don't know. I'm just supposed to take you to Cain."

She led me though the front door, and the bright light

blinded me. I was tempted to put the lenses on, but they weren't sunglasses, and I figured it would do little more than make me look strange.

I stopped. "Maybe I can ask Lord Ainsley where Mister Ali is." I turned back to go inside when Felice grabbed my arm.

"It's too late, and maybe he'll be meeting you there." She looked almost scared. "Please… I don't want to be any later than we are."

"Okay," I responded, and Felice immediately took off along the large building that comprised the bulk of the Citadel. There was a lot of activity on this side of the building, with groups of men in uniforms marching to and fro. They looked like they were heading in specific directions, but the layout of the Citadel was so simple that I couldn't understand what they could be doing other than moving from one end of the building to the other. None of them seemed to be engaging in any kind of exercises or practice in the yard. In the distance I was able to regularly hear gunshots ringing out, but I couldn't tell if the noise was coming from the other side of the wall, the other side of the building, or in some distant corner of the large courtyard that faced the building.

As I looked around the courtyard I felt a little dizzy. When I would look in one direction I would see a huge expanse of grass, but if I looked in a slightly different direction the horizon did not match with my original perception. It was all very strange, and I decided to just focus on the back of Felice's shoulders to avoid getting a headache.

She set a brisk pace. We walked past the drive where we had been dropped off the night before and where I saw Lord Gort enter the main Citadel building with Mister Ali. We continued past the large doors that stood at the center of the building and continued on down the other wing. "Is it much farther?" I asked.

"We are going to the end of the building. Depending on how the illusions affect you, it will either be a much longer or much shorter walk than you expect," Felice replied over her shoulder. She then added, "So for you it will be much longer than you expect." She chuckled.

"It doesn't look too far. I can see the end of the building and the last staircase leading up to the small door. It's—" I paused, figuring out the distance and our pace, "about another one or two minute walk before we get there."

Felice laughed. "In about two minutes, we'll be about a third of the way there."

"That's ridiculous," I exclaimed. "There's no way this building is that big!"

Felice stopped and turned to face me. "Even those who have been here for years are still figuring out the actual dimensions and nooks and crannies in this place. This building is actually three different buildings, each of immense size. What you see is a single impressive country house with two large wings. It is dramatically larger than that. And the whole grounds—" Felice waved her arms around, "cover miles."

She must have seen the disbelief in my face, because her look softened. She leaned toward me and continued in a conspiratorial tone. "Cain is probably the greatest illusionist in history. Much of the enchantments around the Citadel are his work. It is difficult for a master to have a static illusion sustain itself for more than a few weeks. Some of the Citadel enchantments were created by Cain years ago and are still holding."

When I didn't show any reaction, Felice looked angry. "Look, Tommy, I'm trying to help you! You must understand what I'm telling you. You can't trust anything you see around here." She waved her arms in a broad circle. "And Cain is not just a powerful magician, he knows he is a powerful magician. As a result, he doesn't suffer fools or ineptitude gladly."

I nodded and replied, "I understand."

She turned and began walking, once again speaking to me without looking at me, "Good." She took a few steps and then added, "You should fear him." She didn't explain what she meant, and I didn't ask as I thought it was clear enough. At the same time I didn't understand her comment at all. Weren't we all on the same side? Why would I fear someone who was going to work with me to learn how to use the staff or who was going to help rescue my grandfather?

Also, deep inside me a small ember of pride, created when I discovered the greatness of my grandfather and then stoked when I was able to use the staff myself, was blown just a little brighter by Felice's comments. It was not accomplishment or acknowledgement this time but rather challenge and lack of respect. I knew there was much I didn't know, but at the same time, however, I was not blind to the fact that I had already mastered making light. I may not have been able to make a great fortress look like a country estate, but I had already seen firsthand that there were things I could do that masters—and even this mysterious Cain—would never be able to do.

So as we approached what looked like a simple wooden door and my appointment with Cain, I was feeling both fear and confidence. We climbed the stone steps and entered through the door. A small entryway that looked like it could have been the side entrance to the main quarters of a large house or even the servants' entrance greeted us. There was room perhaps for four people to stand without crowding. The floor was tightly laid brick and the walls were wood paneling, but not the elegant paneling that I saw in the reading room earlier. This was purely utilitarian, with hooks for jackets and coats and a distinct lack of decoration. To the left was a closed wooden door. Facing the entrance was a larger but still nondescript door. To the right was an entryway that took up almost the entire wall. Beyond it was a room that looked drab and grey. The floor was concrete and upon it was a number of wooden chairs. Cubbies lined one wall, but they were open and most were empty. More than anything it looked like the locker room at Andover. My attention was drawn from the room by a familiar face walking toward us from inside it.

"Master Behnam, so sorry we are late!" Felice grabbed my arm and pulled me toward the master. It was the quiet master from earlier at the train station who had created the shield. He was dressed the same as before—a black suit and bowler hat. His walking stick, however, was nowhere to be seen.

"It matters not to me. Cain may not quite agree, however. Regardless, I'll take our new Archmage to him now. You may return to your duties, Felice." Felice thanked him and practically sprinted back out the door. She didn't say goodbye, and with an unspoken goodbye on my lips I turned back to the Master. "Follow me," he said, his voice emotionless.

"Is Mister Ali already here?"

"Ali has been here for some time." He pushed the door across from the entrance, stopping only when he saw I wasn't following.

"Can we call for him?"

"No." He continued walking, and I followed.

After the long walk from my room and then the standing still for a few minutes the pain in my hip returned, although it felt much better after the night's rest. Still, it throbbed, so I took the cane in my left hand and used it for its lowliest purpose—assisting my walking.

The doorway opened to a massive corridor that must have been a hundred yards long. The floor was shiny marble, lined on both sides by marble columns. The arched ceiling was thirty or so feet high, and the walls were covered with tapestries that featured everything from medieval battles to pastoral scenes. There were dozens and dozens of them the length of the corridor, and the only consistent thing was that they were all huge. There wasn't a single window. It was very majestic and reminded me of how ancient Greek or Roman palaces were described in my favorite adventure novels. The effect was partially ruined by the lighting; in the place of torches, each column had multiple bare electric bulbs that were very bright and illuminated the room from floor to ceiling.

As I used the cane a tap echoed with each step throughout the cavernous room. Each tap of the cane on the marble filled me with wonderful memories of my grandfather and the ever-present background noise of his cane—our walks on my street, in the museum, and even the many trips from the Ziegfeld

Theater to the Persian Garden. The tap, tap, tap accompanied us everywhere.

"What are you doing?" Master Behnam had stopped and looked alarmed as he stared at me with what almost looked like fear in his eyes. I asked him what he meant. "The staff. You are using it like a cane and… tapping it on the stone."

"I injured my leg. I am using the cane for support."

"Does it have to make such an infernal racket?" I raised the end of the cane and moved it toward Master Behnam's face to show him that it was bound in brass and that I couldn't do much about the noise. But as I raised the cane toward him, he flinched and backed up a step.

"It's brass…" I said tentatively.

"Never mind," he said in a strained voice. He turned and started again at a faster pace. I rushed to catch up, doing my best to be quiet, but the tap tap tap of the cane followed us as we walked.

Master Behnam didn't say anything the rest of our journey down the long hall. At the end were two large bronze or brass doors that were at least ten feet high. They weren't very shiny, and there wasn't a doorknob or handle to be found. As I watched, Master Behnam walked up and put his right palm on the right door. After a moment the door swung open.

Before I could even glance through the crack of the opening door the sound of angry voices could be heard. Two men were arguing. I heard Mister Ali's raised voice say, "This is foolish!" and then silence as the doors opened fully. Master Behnam walked through them, and I followed close behind. The transition from the long cavernous and marble hallway to the room it led to was mind boggling. I looked around and couldn't believe what I saw—a small office that looked like it belonged to a detective in a police station.

"I've brought the boy, Cain." Master Behnam moved to the side and I walked forward. Mister Ali was sitting in a wooden chair across from a sparse wooden desk. He had a kind smile on his face as he looked at me, but he remained quiet. There was an empty chair next to him, but what drew my attention was the man sitting behind the desk.

He had thin and straight dark hair that was was short, slicked back, and parted on the side. He looked like Howard Hughes, only without the mustache. Like the masters I had met, he was very thin, but while two of them were Persian, Cain was English. His face was square and angular, with an aquiline nose and pronounced brows and cheekbones. He smiled, but it wasn't the bright smile of Mister Ali or the intimidating smile of my grandfather; it was a patronizing smile, one of amusement. He wore a grey suit that looked like it had just been pressed. His hands rested on the desk, and they twitched and moved in a way that was disconcerting.

It was the twitching that struck me more than anything. He appeared to have an odd neurological disorder, because his eyebrows, his eyes, his lips, and even his ears would twitch at odd moments. As if this weren't enough, his body would jerk every so often, as well—a shoulder would suddenly shoot up, an arm elbow would strike outward.

"Ah, our new Archmage!" Cain stated. He didn't stand up. "Please, have a seat." He motioned for me to sit in the chair next to Mister Ali. He then looked over my shoulder and said, "Thank you, Behnam. You may return to your post." The Master didn't say anything but turned and walked out the doorway. I noticed the massive doors closing behind him when Mister Ali finally spoke.

"You look wonderful, Tommy! You got enough rest, I hope?" His words came tumbling out, and the tone was a mixture of relief and happiness. I could see both Mister Ali and Cain, and the difference in their appearance was striking. Mister Ali was old, kind, and relaxed. Cain looked annoyed, pained even. It took me a moment before I realized that Cain was annoyed at Mister Ali, but Mister Ali couldn't tell as he was looking at me.

I did my best to diffuse the current tension, which was perhaps still in the air from what they had been arguing about earlier. "Yes, Mister Ali! Everyone has been wonderful." I turned to Cain. "And Mister Cain, thank you for helping me and for your hospitality."

He waved a hand. "No thanks are necessary. You are the rightful Archmage, and we'll do whatever we can to help you. And please just call me Cain. No 'mister,' no 'sir,' or anything like that."

"Thank you, sir," I replied, which drew a sharp look from him. "Thank you, Cain."

"Very good." Cain stared at me and didn't say anything else. The silence was awkward, and I noticed Mister Ali opening his mouth to speak when Cain abruptly said, "Shut up, Ali."

I was a respectful young man, but I was also loyal to a fault, and while I understood that Cain was powerful and important, his treatment of Mister Ali angered me. I slammed the staff to the ground where it let out not a tap but a larger noise, like a small clap of thunder, and said, "You should treat Mister Ali with more respect. He is an Archmage, too, you know!"

Cain looked at me with wide eyes for a moment and then laughed loudly. "I don't know what is more humorous, Ali. That this child is threatening me or that I should consider you an Archmage."

Mister Ali's face reddened, but before he could say anything, I blurted out, "He carried the staff to my grandfather. He is an Archmage." Mister Ali looked at me and shook his head slightly. Cain also shook his head, but he rolled his eyes as he did it.

"Set the boy straight, Ali," Cain said.

Mister Ali turned to Cain. I fully expected him to hit him or cast a spell at him or something. I wanted him to do so. Instead, Mister Ali replied, "Cain, I fully admit that I did not earn the Archmage title. I have yet to hear you admit the same."

For the first time Cain's body was still. Through gritted teeth he said, "Do you doubt my power, Ali? Even now?"

As the tension increased, Mister Ali looked more and more relaxed. He leaned back in his chair and replied, "I do not. It would be foolish to do so," and after a pause for effect, he added, "but I do doubt your claim to a title that has been reserved for the bearer of the staff."

Cain stared at Mister Ali for a moment and then leaned back and put his arms behind his head. "Your opinion does not matter." Cain looked over to me, but before he could say anything I spoke.

To this day, I don't know why I said what I did. It was not arrogance, certainly. Perhaps it was the opposite—a great humility in the face of what I knew my grandfather had accomplished as Archmage. But I do know that what I said was important, and while very foolish, it was my duty to say it. "I am the Archmage, and I will not allow you to use the title. I know my Grandfather would have objected and, therefore, so do I."

It must have looked silly for such words to come from the mouth of a fourteen year old boy, but both Mister Ali and Cain had the stunned look on their faces as if they had taken my pronouncement very seriously indeed. Mister Ali spoke first. His voice was strained and he sounded frightened, "Tommy, it's okay. It is but a title."

Cain immediately added, "Yes, Tommy, it is but a title, but in my case the title actually means something. For you it means that your grandfather handed you a piece of wood." Mister Ali stood up.

"This is going too far, Cain!"

"I agree, Ali. The boy clearly needs to learn a lesson." Mister Ali blanched and reached for his curved knife. A man moved around from behind me and placed a hand on Mister Ali's shoulder. Mister Ali froze. It was Master Behnam, whom I hadn't even seen or heard re-enter the room.

"This has always been your problem, Ali. You are too quick to anger and too slow to understand. Now you will sit down." Benham pressed down with his arm, and Mister Ali slid down into his chair, staring at Cain the whole time. Cain had the look of someone dealing with an unruly child.

He turned to me. "Now, Archmage, do you see the glass of water on my desk?" I glanced down and there was a tall glass of water, with beads of condensation, sitting right in front of me. I could have sworn it wasn't there when we came in. In fact, I could have sworn it hadn't been there a moment earlier. I nodded. "Good. Now pick it up and throw the water at Mister Ali." Cain smiled.

I picked up the glass. It was very cold and slippery from the condensation. I looked at Mister Ali and paused. Cain noticed my hesitation and interjected, "Or throw it at Behnam. Throw it at me for all I care. Just throw the water at something."

I tossed the water toward Master Behnam, and it hit him full in the face. The top of his suit was soaked in water, and water dripped from the tip of his nose and chin. He looked at me, but did no more than blink. I looked back at Cain. "What was that for?"

"What was what for?" Cain asked back. For some reason the glass was no longer in my hand. I looked around, and it was nowhere to be seen. As I glanced around I noticed Master Behnam, and he looked completely normal. There wasn't a drop of water on him. I looked back at Cain, who waved his hand in dismissal.

"If you stop at the glass, it is but a parlor trick, common to any traveling magician of any repute. But add more senses to the illusion, and it becomes significantly more difficult." Cain suddenly motioned toward me. He had a glass in his own hand and tossed the contents at me. I shielded my eyes with my hand, but it did little good. I was drenched with water. It dripped from my hair and clothing.

"You didn't need to do that," I said to Cain, as I patted my wet uniform shirt.

"Do what?" And the moment Cain said the words, I realized I was completely dry.

I stared at Cain, but he still wasn't smiling. "Motion, multiple senses, maintaining the illusion over time, even removing the illusion—all of those things are immensely difficult. Something as simple as throwing water at someone is a master-level illusion." I nodded, starting to understand Cain's power.

"There is more." Cain leaned forward, his elbows on the table, and his hands folded in front of him. He looked me right in the eye. "I am going to hold up my index finger. Flames will burn from its end. I will not be burned, and you will know very clearly that it is but an illusion. I will reach forward and touch your arm with this flame. It will catch your sleeve on fire, and you will know that this is but an illusion, as well. To make it clear this is an illusion, I will have the flames spread down your sleeve toward your wrist in a straight line. It will look completely unreal, and your mind will clearly see it is an illusion. Do you understand?"

I nodded. "You are going to create the illusion of fire and try to apply it to my sleeve."

"Try," Cain chuckled. "Yes, I guess I'll do my best." He laughed again. "Your job is very simple, Archmage. All you have to do is see through my illusion. It is unreal, after all. So watch me," he paused, "*try*, while you feel no pain and know that you aren't really on fire." Cain leaned back.

"I understand," I replied.

"Sorry, but I don't think you do or you would be taking this much more seriously. I will not repeat this again: This is an illusion. I am telling you it is an illusion. You know this is an illusion. I want you to see through this illusion, and I want you to see the reality and not the illusion." Cain held up his forefinger, and a three inch flame flickered above it. "Do you understand?"

I looked over at Mister Ali. His jaw was clenched, but he said nothing. Master Behnam still held him tight. "I do."

Cain leaned forward and touched my sleeve near my elbow. It immediately caught on fire, and I could smell the fibers burning.

I could feel the heat on my arm. The flames moved down my arm toward my wrist in a perfect circle. It looked impossible, but I barely noticed—the heat became intensely painful. The fabric charred, and I could see my skin burning. I could *feel* my skin burning. The pain was horrible. I tried to focus and just think that this was an illusion. It didn't work. I started to wave my arm to put out the flame, but that only made it worse. Despite the pain, I stared at the flame and focused on the knowledge that it wasn't real, but it again did no good. I cried out in pain, my arm burning, and the smell of charred flesh entering my nose. Tears poured down my face and just when I thought I was about to faint, I was sitting in my chair swinging my arm in the air with no flames, no pain, and no smell.

I touched my arm, but it felt entirely normal. My shirt was unharmed, and I wiped the tears from my face with it. I looked up, and Cain had a pistol pointed at me. When he noticed he had my attention, he turned it in his hand and held it toward me, handle-first. I took it and held it in my hand. "Why are you giving me this?"

"It is an illusion. Examine it closely. Not a single part of that gun exists. The bullets, the handle, the trigger—they are all part of your mind right now. I looked over the gun, and every single part looked and felt real. "Now shoot me with it."

I knew this was a test, and I knew that Cain would never put himself in jeopardy, so I turned the pistol to Cain and shot him right in the chest. The recoil of the shot knocked my arm into the air, and the sound of the shot rang in my ears. I could smell the gunpowder. Of course nothing happened to Cain. He sat in his chair with a big smile on his face. "You seemed a bit too enthusiastic in doing that." The gun in my hand was a little warmer and smoke came out of the barrel.

"Now here is the final exam for this short lesson I have given you. I want you to ponder the answer when you leave, and then when you come back we can perhaps be more productive. Do you understand?" I nodded, intimidated and awestruck.

"Here is your question: What do you think would happen if you took that gun in your hand, the one that is a pure illusion and doesn't exist, the one that had absolutely no effect when you fired it at me, and you shot yourself?"

My immediate instinct was to say that nothing would happen. It was entirely an illusion, but part of me was certain that was wrong. I thought back to the pain I felt from the flames on my arm, and I answered emphatically, "I would die."

Cain nodded gravely. "Yes, *Archmage*. If you were to take that non-existent gun in your hand and shoot yourself with its non-existent bullets, you would die." Before my eyes and with no warning the gun turned into a bunch of wildflowers.

Cain stood up. "Behnam, please remove the enchantment on Mister Ali and escort the two of them back to their quarters."

Master Behnam let go of Mister Ali's shoulder, and he slumped in his chair before pulling himself back up. He looked exhausted and was taking long and labored breaths. He must have noticed the alarm on my face, because he held up his hand and said, "It's… okay… Tommy. Just give… me a second."

I stood up and gave Mister Ali my arm. He used it for support to pull himself up. He looked back at Cain with what looked like hate in his eyes. "We will talk again, Cain."

"Of course," Cain replied, holding out his hands palms up.

As I turned to look for the huge double doors, I realized they were gone. We were in a small office with a standard wooden door. Master Behnam reached for the knob, opened it, and suddenly it was a double door pushing outward into the great hallway. We exited and must have looked a sorry sight. I was limping on my leg and using the cane, while Mister Ali had trouble keeping the strength to walk more than a few steps at a time. Master Behnam was silent behind us, offering no help.

As we limped down that long hallway I thought about Cain's final question. The implication was so obvious that it filled me with awe and dread. Cain's illusions were useless against him, but they could affect and even kill others. With the complexity of Cain's illusions it became frighteningly clear just how powerful he was. It was almost as if he could warp reality.

The cane tapped alongside me, echoing off the ceiling and floor, but it didn't provide me with any connection to the might of my grandfather. I felt defeated. In the face of such powerful illusions, the power of the staff seemed minor in comparison. I was nothing more than a streetlight. I had entered the hallway thinking that I was the Archmage and Cain was the pretender. I exited wondering if perhaps the opposite were true.

Chapter Fourteen

A BETRAYAL

aster Behnam left us at the door, and when we got to the bottom of the steps, Mister Ali stopped, leaned over, and took several deep breaths. They didn't happen often, but it was at moments like this where I was reminded that Mister Ali was quite old. I would never have described him as frail, but he sometimes looked it. I asked him if he was okay, and he nodded and replied, "I'm fine, Tommy. I just need some rest." He looked over to me and then patted me on the back. "We have much to talk about."

"Cain doesn't seem like he wants to help us." We walked back the way we came.

"That's part of what we need to talk about," Mister Ali replied but didn't elaborate further. The courtyard, which appeared larger than it did when I was last outside, was full of soldiers, moving in various formations. They carried normal weapons, and in the distance I could hear machine gun and rifle fire.

"Who are these soldiers?" I asked. "They don't look like magicians."

Mister Ali smiled. "That's because they aren't magicians. They are part of the British army. This is the Citadel of London, Tommy. Most of the people here are soldiers or officials who work with the armed forces. But there is magic here. Powerful magic." Mister Ali didn't say anything else.

We were about to pass another one of the generic and numerous entrances that led into the building when Mister Ali stopped us. "Let's stop here, Tommy. I fear our situation has changed, and I have some questions I want to ask Lord Gort. It would be good for you to listen in." The two of us hobbled up the short flight of stairs to the door, which was made of

---

Jake Kerr

wood and looked identical to the outside door that opened to the long hall to Cain's office.

Mister Ali didn't knock but rather just pulled the door open and walked in. I followed behind him. Inside looked like the reception area of a busy office. To the left were three wooden chairs, two of which were occupied by young men in British army uniforms. To the right was a bare wall with a bulletin board on it. The items seemed bureaucratic, and the information was not very revealing. Across from us was a wooden desk, featureless and worn. Behind it sat a woman in a uniform. She was young and pretty, with auburn hair and black glasses. She was writing something on a piece of paper when she looked up and noticed us.

"Can I help you?" She placed the pen down and folded her hands together, all her attention on us. She glanced at my cane, but its meaning didn't seem to register.

"I would like to speak with Lord Gort."

She looked down again and picked up her pen. "I'm afraid that's impossible. He is very busy."

"Perhaps he is not too busy to speak with the new Archmage." Mister Ali nodded toward me. I tapped the cane on the

— 249 —

floor and then leaned on it. The woman looked at the staff and then at me, and then sighed. She seemed unimpressed.

"Fine." She pushed her seat back and stood up. "Have a seat, I'll have to go find him." Mister Ali thanked her, and she left through a door behind her desk. We turned toward the chairs, where the two soldiers were staring at us.

Mister Ali bowed slightly to the two men and sat down in the empty chair. He held his head, and I was alarmed. He looked terrible. "Are you okay, Mister Ali?"

"I'm fine, Tommy. Fine. I just haven't had a constriction placed on me in a long time." He frowned.

I was going to ask what a constriction was when Lord Gort walked through the door with the receptionist. He stared at both of us with his intimidating gaze and then spoke up. "You both look horrible."

"A meeting with Cain will do that to you," Mister Ali replied. Lord Gort nodded.

"Well, I can't say I'm surprised." He turned to the receptionist, "Corporal, I am not to be disturbed." He then turned back to us. "Let's go to my office." And without waiting for a reply he went through the door leading further into the building. We scrambled to catch up. Luckily, unlike the other parts of the building, the hallway was simple, direct, and seemed to make sense.

Eventually we stopped in front of a simple wooden door. Lord Gort turned the tarnished doorknob and we found ourselves in a large office, with bookshelves and a reading area to the right, and a small round conference table with four chairs around it to the left. Facing us was a beautiful carved mahogany desk. There was a large map of Europe on the wall behind the desk, and a thick Persian rug on the floor. The whole office looked decidedly more elegant than anything I had seen in the Citadel other than perhaps the reading room in the residence wing. The general sat down behind his desk and waved us into two large wingback chairs that faced it.

To my shock he stretched back, put his feet on his desk, and his arms behind his head. "So how did Cain offend you this time, Ali?" I was annoyed that everyone seemed to treat Mister Ali with disdain, and although Lord Gort appeared to be sincere, the question sounded like a veiled insult. Mister Ali, however, seemed relaxed and appeared not to mind.

"It was nothing like that, John." Mister Ali also leaned back and crossed his legs. The two seemed comfortable and at ease with each other. Mister Ali tapped his finger on his leg and then went on, "I expected Cain to show off to the new Archmage, but this was different." Mister Ali thought for a moment and then continued. "It appeared that he wanted to scare him."

"Interesting," Lord Gort replied. "What did he do exactly?"

"He had Behnam put a constriction on me, and then he used a fire illusion to set the Archmage on fire to show how powerless he was against his illusions. I expected the show, but not the assault on both of us." Mister Ali gestured to me.

Lord Gort dropped his feet to the floor and leaned forward. He picked up a pipe from a tray on his desk and started to fill it. "Well, I had hoped he would use tact, but I guess I should have expected that his first inclination would be to use intimidation."

"To what goal?"

"He wants the staff, of course."

"What? Impossible." Mister Ali shook his head. "He can't even use it."

"He knows more of magic than anyone, and he clearly believes he can." Lord Gort used some instrument to pack down the tobacco in his pipe and continued talking without looking at either of us. "I would tend to think that he's probably right. How much do you *really* know about the staff, Ali?"

"As much as anyone!" Mister Ali dropped his leg to the floor and straightened in the chair.

Lord Gort didn't say anything but struck a match. He lit his pipe and finally looked up at us as he sucked in the air, the pipe's glow giving his face a tinge of red. He took a big puff and leaned back again. The smell of cherry and smoke filled my nose.

"Regardless, he feels he knows more and that he can use the staff." He inhaled on his pipe again. Lord Gort answered and exhaled at the same time, his words filled with the scent of cherry. "With what's happening in Germany, I can't say I blame him for wanting to try. So where do things stand? I like you Ali, but I want to remind you that I find all this magic a distraction."

Mister Ali didn't say anything, and it struck me as odd. A distraction? Magic—my grandfather's magic—saved every-one in the Great War, and now it was a distraction? I cleared my throat, and both Mister Ali and Lord Gort looked at me.

"Excuse me, sir, but how can magic be a distraction? This entire Citadel is a center of magic! Magic won the Great War."

I was respectful, but I had a hard time hiding my enthusiasm. I had just learned about the importance of magic, and to hear anyone—even a member of the Army Council—disparage it bothered me.

Lord Gort laughed so hard, smoke came out of his nostrils and mouth.

"Did you say this Citadel is a center of magic?" He stared at me so intently that I shrunk in my chair. I nodded in response. He turned to Ali. "I guess it's technically the truth, but tell me, Ali, how many magicians are there in the Citadel right now who could be of any help in the case of war?"

"Well, the masters and Cain, of course." Mister Ali looked uncomfortable as he answered. "There are a number of journeyman that I'm sure would be of benefit."

"Nonsense." Lord Gort held out his pipe and stabbed it in the air as he talked, tendrils of smoke underscoring his points. "Any five of the boys in the practice fields with machine guns and a competent sergeant would be of more value to me than Cain's masters." His arm moved faster as my question appeared to have opened an old wound. "And the journeyman? I'd rather give them a rifle and a canteen and be done with it. They won't amount to anything." He finally turned to me. "Young man, the only magician worth anything on this island is Cain." He took a puff of his pipe and then added, "Him, I value."

I was shocked. It was the Citadel of Magic. Mister Ali told me so. I looked at Mister Ali and was surprised not only that he didn't object but that he looked chastened. Not only chastened—he appeared weary, as if he had been caught in a lie he had been carrying for a long time but wasn't quite ready to let go.

"But what of the German magician, John?" Mister Ali leaned forward. "This Hitler is dangerous."

"We don't even know if he *is* a magician, Ali. Even if he is, it is some kind of new magic, a magic of the voice that bends wills. At least that's what Cain is saying, but to be honest, I don't much buy that either. Cain is just trying to spread his influence."

Mister Ali didn't object to this line of thought, so I spoke up, hoping that he was just being polite in not disagreeing with Lord Gort. "But what about the staff? What about magic in the Great War? I thought this was a center of magic? Certainly the staff can help now with magical defense. Even Cain seems to think so!"

Mister Ali sighed, "You are correct about the staff, Tommy. And you are right that this is the center of magic in England." He looked at me and had a sympathetic smile on his face. "I told you that magic was dying. I just didn't tell you how much. It is almost gone. And—again—I must reinforce to both of you—" Mister Ali looked at Lord Gort. "—that the staff is indeed powerful. Tommy, your grandfather *did* do great things in the Great War, but I was perhaps exaggerating when I said he won it for us." Mister Ali lowered his head and looked at the floor.

Lord Gort snorted. "He did a good job at Marne. I'll give him that."

I was in shock. I slumped in my chair. Magic was nearly gone in the world. I couldn't quite grasp the enormity of that thought. I had seen magicians create shields, shoot detonations, and create illusions. I had seen a magic train. I had fought a magic river. I had seen so many amazing and wondrous and terrible things. Magic couldn't be dying. It just couldn't be.

"You mentioned the staff, Ali…" Lord Gort was speaking, but I could barely pay attention to his words.

"John, now is not the time." I was considering the reality that the three masters I had met along with Cain were the only real magicians in England. How many more were there in the world? Dozens? Fewer?

"Nonsense. I need to know what happened in New York. I thought we had agreed that Declan would give the staff to Vingrosh, and we could move ahead without that risk…" What did this mean to me? Was I that much more important now that magic was so rare? Or was I less important? "…I'm disappointed that things went so wrong. There were deaths."

Wait. What had I just heard? I looked over at Mister Ali, but he was looking at Lord Gort and avoided my gaze. "We can discuss that later, John." Mister Ali's words came out in a rush. "We need to do something about Cain. He is letting his power go to his head!" Mister Ali glanced at me, nervously. My hands started to shake, and I felt the muscles of my stomach tighten. It was similar to the feeling I had to when I found out my parents had died. My life and everything I had held onto had abandoned me.

Mister Ali had planned the attack on my grandfather.

"Vingrosh…" I stammered in a whisper. I wasn't sure anyone heard me.

"We have plenty of time to discuss Cain. I want to know about New York. Why all the violence? We had Vingrosh calling in Djinn. Did he really think he could force Declan to do anything he didn't want to do? And the deaths—" He shook his head. "This was handled very poorly, Ali, and now Cain is all ready to be the savior, which helps none of us, least of all me. I have a war to prepare for." Mister Ali glanced at me, his face white.

"You betrayed Grandfather!" I shouted the words, or I assume I shouted them. I was dazed, and could barely think. I was standing, and the heavy chair was on its side on the ground.

"Tommy, listen to me. It is not like that. He was to give up the staff voluntarily—"

"He was your friend. You had him attacked!" The end of the staff glowed slightly.

"Now, now, young man. Settle down," Lord Gort replied.

"I had no idea Vingrosh was going to attack him, Tommy. They were just to talk and your grandfather was to hand him the staff. I didn't know that Vingrosh would try to take the staff by force. I swear!"

"Why didn't you tell him that! You lied to him the whole time! And what about the attack? You casually cooked while

Grandfather was trying to save our lives? Did you expect him to die quietly since he wouldn't listen to reason?" I shouted the last words, using Mister Ali's own words against him.

The tears flowed down my face. My protector. The man who was to teach me how to use the staff. The man my own grandfather had chosen to help me. He was the one who had betrayed us.

"It's not like that, Tommy." He tried to reach out toward me, but I shoved his arms aside with the cane and ran to the door. I needed to think, to mourn, to figure out what was going on. I was confused, betrayed, and, more than anything, I needed to find out who my friends were.

"Ali, let him go." It was Lord Gort. "He'll understand in time" were the last words I heard as I slammed the door behind me.

Chapter Fifteen

PLANS ARE MADE

I didn't remember leaving the building. Maybe I passed people. Maybe I didn't. Maybe people talked to me. Maybe they didn't. All I wanted was to find Naomi and tell her what happened. I didn't know what she would say, but I had no other options. The people in the Citadel didn't care about me. They wanted the staff. Mister Ali didn't care about me, either. He just wanted to destroy the staff. I didn't know why, and I didn't care. All

I knew was that the only person I could count on was Naomi, and even she possibly still hated me.

I stumbled around, cursing the illusions that were placed on everything. I finally found the door to my quarters. The Academy was further down. I ran to the next door, and it still took longer than I expected. I tried the handle, and it opened.

I walked in and found myself in another antechamber like the one that had the staircase to my quarters. The floor was dusty and worn, however, and the staircase was marked by chips in the balustrade and damaged steps. To the right was a large door that was closed. To the left were double doors that were held open by doorstops. Beyond them was a long hallway filled with wooden doors with frosted windows. Young men in the same uniform I was wearing wandered here and there. Some had a few medals or stripes, but most were unadorned. They paid me no mind.

I remembered the Corporal mentioning that they would find room for Naomi in the floor above the dormitories, so I climbed the stairway, which was mostly empty. The top was again similar to my quarters in the other part of the building. I started walking toward the hallway that led to what I hoped were the rooms over the dormitories when a young man exited the hallway.

He looked at me and squinted. "You shouldn't be up here. Who are you, and who is your Floor Captain?"

I nervously tapped the cane on the floor. The young man, who looked about five or six years older than me, crossed his arms. I considered my options and realized I had only one. I was alone. My family was dead, and my friend betrayed me. The only one I could rely on was myself. I stopped tapping the cane and held it up.

"I'm the Archmage, and I'm looking for Naomi, a student of the Academy. Is she housed on this floor?"

The young man glanced at the cane, and then looked at my face. "You aren't the Archmage."

I had enough. No one respected me. No one cared for me. I squeezed the staff in my fist, and a dazzling light shone forth. The young soldier shaded his eyes. I didn't care if I blinded him. "I am the Archmage, and if you don't help me I will be forced to go to Lord Ainsley and drag him here to help me instead." The young man stepped back, still shielding his eyes. "I can assure you that Lord Ainsley will *not* be happy."

"I'm sorry, Archmage!" He looked down, avoiding the glare of the staff. "She's down the hall. Third door on the right."

I snuffed out the light, and the soldier looked back at me. His eyes were watering. "Do you know if she's in her room?"

"Yes, she is. I was just delivering her the schedule for her disciplinary duties." He inched toward the steps.

"Disciplinary duties?"

"Yes, she left her class this morning without permission. She has kitchen duty as punishment."

"Punishment?" He nodded. I pictured Naomi being told to clean dishes and laughed. "I will discuss this with her," I added, trying to sound solemn, although I couldn't get the picture of Naomi hurling detonations at piles of dishes out of my mind.

"Can I leave, sir?" The soldier had made his way to the top of the stairway and looked like all he wanted to do was sprint downstairs. I nodded, and he did so.

I knocked on Naomi's door. I waited, and as I was just about to knock again the door flew open and there was Naomi, wearing the same uniform as me, her golden hair disheveled and half covering her face, her eyes bloodshot. The snarl on her face fell as she recognized me. "Tommy!"

"I need your help," I replied, unable to think of anything charming or witty to say. She grabbed my arm, pulled me into the room, and slammed the door.

The room was small, maybe ten foot square. There was a cot in the corner, a chest at its end, and a wooden chair next to a small desk. That was it. Naomi slid her hair behind her ears and sat on the cot. "So what's the problem, streetlight?" She motioned to the chair, and I sat down.

"It's a long story," I replied.

"Well, I have nothing but time. I'm leaving this place as soon as I can. Do you know what my first class was this morning?"

"Elementary illusion?" It was the first thing that came to mind after my meeting with Cain.

"Introduction to domestic magic." She practically spat the words. "Do you know how many other magicians were in the class with me?"

"None?"

"You got it." I couldn't quite believe what I was hearing. She was already practically at master level, and they had her working on magic to do chores? It made no sense. "So what's your story? They have plans for you to illuminate Big Ben for tourists?"

"Eleven years ago my parents died in a subway crash in New York."

Naomi sat up straight, stared at me for a moment, and then lowered her head. "Oh, Tommy. I'm so sorry."

"My grandfather raised me."

"The *pehlivan*."

"Yes, but I didn't know that. I barely knew about magic at all until days ago."

"But you're the Archmage. How could you not know?" Naomi stared at me, fully engaged in my story.

I then outlined the events of the past week. I described the attack from the Shadows, the attack on the restaurant, and how my grandfather had given me the staff and how Mister Ali was to protect me as we escaped. I described the river, the golems, and finding ourselves at the Way Station. Through it all I outlined the underlying story of my grandfather wanting to keep the staff and Mister Ali wanting to get rid of it.

"You mentioned that on the train," she replied, and I nodded.

I then outlined my meeting with Cain. Her jaw dropped as I described his illusions. "Illusion is not my speciality, although I can perform a few of them." This did not surprise me at all. In fact it wouldn't have surprised me if her few illusions were near master level. "So let me assure you that what he did sounds impossible. No one could be that skilled with magic. Illusions are simply too complicated to do what you describe. The coordinated body control it would take…"

I thought back to Cain's spastic body movements and wondered if that was related to his abilities. Was his entire body prepping spells while I watched? I thought back to the pain of my arm on fire and replied, "I assure you he is that skilled."

I then discussed how Mister Ali and I went to meet with Lord Gort. I then described the conversation, ending with Mister Ali's betrayal. I clenched the staff in my hand. "I don't know what to do."

Naomi stared at me. "How could he betray his friend like that?"

"I don't know." I looked at Naomi, and the sympathy and concern on her face removed any doubts I had. She cared about me. I didn't know what to say, and the silence lingered. I considered what she had gone through as well, and I realized that all we had was each other. I lowered my head and whispered, "I'm sorry about your mother. She sounds like she was an amazing woman." It felt right to say it.

Naomi didn't reply, and I glanced up to see if she was perhaps mad at me. She was crying, so I looked away. She cleared her throat and then whispered, "Thank you." I glanced at her, and she was wiping her eyes. She looked at me, smiled, and added, "We're both alone now."

I nodded. "The domestic mage and the streetlight."

Grinning, Naomi replied, "So what do we do?"

"We will save my grandfather." I said the words with an unexpected force.

"Absolutely." Naomi nodded. "He'll be able to use the staff to make everything right." As soon as she said the words, I could tell she felt bad. She covered her mouth with her hand and added, "I'm sorry, Tommy. I didn't mean it that way."

I smiled. "It's okay. I know he's more powerful than I am. I'm kind of useless, actually. I just don't want to be alone anymore." And as soon as I said it I felt bad. She had just lost her mother. Could I be any more insensitive? I broke the awkward silence that followed by saying, "But first we have to get out of here. We can perhaps get beyond the walls, but then were do we go? You can be sure that someone will be chasing us."

Naomi smiled and stood up. "You forget that I'm the grand-daughter of a legendary Waymaster. I know all the train stops in England. Once we get our bearings, I'll find a stop and we can flee on a train."

"Will that work?"

"Trust me," she replied.

I stood up and for some reason Errol Flynn popped into my head. "The grandchildren of legends. Alone without family. Unwanted despite our power." I meant to be inspirational and said the words as if I were narrating a motion picture. I smiled and held out my hand. "We make a good team!"

Naomi looked at me quizzically and hesitantly took my hand. It was the hesitation that killed me. As soon as I shook her hand I realized how stupid it was. She was beautiful and powerful and smart and we were about to travel alone together and I pretend we're in a movie, and, even worse, *I shook her hand?* Who does that?

I quickly pulled my hand away. My heart was racing from anger at myself, and I knew that if I didn't get away for at least a little bit I would die of embarrassment.

"I need to get my old shoes. These boots don't fit," I lied. "I'll meet you here after I go grab them from my room."

"Uh, Okay," she replied. She tucked her hair behind her ears again, and I turned away. Did she have to be so pretty?

I walked out the door and down the steps. I tried to forget the handshake, but I couldn't. All I could think about was that her hand was warm and soft and that she had gripped my hand tight.

Chapter Sixteen

PLAN C

I alternated between trying to focus on hiding myself and making sense of how I could deal with Naomi. I would dodge a group of soldiers and then nearly run into another group while imagining that when I wasn't annoying Naomi I was embarrassing myself in front of her. I somehow made it to my quarters without being seen and opened the door only to run right into Felice. Her eyes went wide.

"Did your meeting with Cain go okay?" She practically whispered the question.

"Well, he questioned my ability to wield the staff, and then he lit my arm on fire, which was intensely painful. Other than that, it went great."

Felice nodded, as if she expected my response. "That's not so bad. I'm sure he won't light you on fire next time." I almost laughed, but she was serious. *Not so bad.* The thought made me even more desperate to leave the Citadel. I thanked Felice for her concern and made my way up the stairs to my room.

I opened the door, planning on switching from the boots to my shoes and then rushing back to Naomi so we could escape. I took one step into my room and stopped cold. There was an old man sitting in the reading chair looking over the illusion textbook.

He looked up at me. "Is this yours? A waste of time if you ask me." He tossed the book on the floor. He was ancient. The small amount of hair he had was white and slicked back in an attempt at style. He had grey eyes, and as they peered at me they were the only part of him that looked young. His skin was thin and wrinkled, and he looked very frail. I couldn't even guess his age. Yet he looked regal. He wore a nice suit that somehow fit well despite his inability to fill it. The shirt was pure white and his navy blue tie was tightly knotted and perfectly centered. I stared at him.

He scowled at me. "Well, don't just stand there. Let me see it." He held out his hand.

"I'm sorry. Who are you?" He obviously wasn't some soldier sent here to hold me until Cain could get his hands on the staff. On the other hand, he had the same dismissive demeanor of Cain himself.

"I'm Plan B." He laughed a scratchy high-pitched laugh.

"Plan B?" I worried that perhaps the old man was insane and had wandered into my room.

"Yes. Plan B. If Cain can't get you to follow his orders, he's going to take the staff from you and give it to me to wield." I stared at him. "For whatever good that will do him." He scratched his head. "Actually, I might be Plan C. Plan B is probably Cain trying to use the staff himself." The old man looked at me, and when I didn't respond added, "Fine. If you must know, I am also the Royal Gardener at Balmoral." His expression didn't change, but he opened and closed his hand in a reminder to hand him something. Did he mean the staff?

"Do I know you?"

"Unfortunately not." He sat up straighter but still didn't stand. "Or perhaps fortunately. Give me the staff, and I think that may clear some things up." I pulled the cane against my chest.

"I'm afraid I can't do that."

He shook his head and nodded. "Ah yes. I expected this." He waved his finger at me. "My son said the same thing after I gave it to him and asked him a few years later if I could use the staff for some particularly difficult topiary work." He shook his head. "It would have made things much easier." He sighed. "The selfishness of youth, I guess."

He gave the staff to his son? My staff? My *grandfather's* staff? Before I could ask any questions, the old man laughed. "Maybe you aren't as stupid as my son. You are starting to understand now, are you not?"

"Who are you?" I whispered the words, although I had started to put things together.

He laughed a bitter laugh. "Maybe you are as stupid as he is, after all. I'm Joseph Blacach. Declan Black, your grandfather, is my son." I felt my knees go weak, because I knew that he was telling the truth. I saw it immediately. Not just in his eyes, but the shape of his face, and even his gruff demeanor, which if I were honest, was a big part of my grandfather's personality. His smile, fleeting as it was, reminded me of my father's smile. I took a step forward.

"You're my great—"

"Grandfather. Yes. I'm also an Archmage. I've borne the staff. Blah. Blah. Blah. That's why Cain used his infernal connections to get me sent here. He thinks I'm a loyal citizen and will wield the staff for him, but the truth is—" He leaned forward and lowered his voice. "—I just came here to hold the staff one more time before I die." He held up a finger. "But I did not lie. I am the King's gardener in Balmoral." He shrugged. "As it were."

I walked over to him, and as I approached he held out his hand again. "If I'm to be totally truthful, I also wanted to see you, my great grandson. But don't tell anyone. I have a reputation for being decidedly unsentimental." He laughed.

"Plan C," I said as I held the staff up.

"As you wish, although one might think 'Great Grandfather' would be more appropriate." He looked at the staff. "Ah, still a cane. My foolish son never could figure out how to change it back I see." His eyebrows furrowed, and his jaw clenched. He looked both sad and angry. I didn't move, and he added. "The staff, boy."

I handed it to him.

I knew I shouldn't have, but I did. I cannot explain why other than to say that I knew it was the right thing to do. The staff said as much to me in its arcane and unfathomable language. He held it up and it transformed into a living branch of some flowering tree. It bloomed with white flowers, and petals fell as he pulled it close to his eyes.

Joseph—I still had trouble thinking of him as my great grandfather—smiled, and his face transformed. He breathed in deeply, his nose among the flowers. The happiness made him look years younger. He lowered the staff and it transformed into a cricket bat. He looked at me. "You are a young boy. Would you prefer this?" I didn't answer, and he quickly added, "Ah, you are American. Perhaps this is better?" The cricket bat transformed into a baseball bat. "Or this?" In short order he changed the staff into large stick, a flower, a wand, and a wooden knife.

Before he could do any more I interrupted, "I prefer the cane."

He frowned. "Making it a cane was a joke I played on my son as a reminder of his feeble ego." The staff remained a wooden knife, and Joseph tapped it on his palm. He stared at me, and again I felt uncomfortable in his gaze. His presence was at once exciting to me, but his mannerisms and attitude were disturbing. He took joy in the staff and what it could do, but he did not seem to care about me much at all.

The more I considered him, the more it bothered me that he was dismissive toward my grandfather, his own son. "I prefer the cane," I repeated, a bit more forcefully this time. "And you can give it back to me now." I held out my hand.

He didn't say anything for a while, just stared at me. When I refused to avert my gaze, he smiled my father's smile and held up the staff to me, which without my noticing had turned again into a cane. As I went to take it, he pulled it back. "Are you not curious what my mastery of the staff is?"

"I'm afraid I don't understand. What do you mean 'mastery?'"

Joseph shook his head. "How much do you know of the staff, boy?" He hadn't offered the staff back to me, although it still held its shape as a cane.

I looked at him, and all my questions, all my confusion, tumbled into my head. What *did* I know? What did Mister Ali teach me? What did my grandfather teach me from those few moments when he gave me the staff? The answer scared me. Nothing. I knew nothing of the staff. And then it hit me. *He knows*, I thought. *He is the only one who knows.*

Before I could say the words, my great grandfather pointed to the other reading chair. "Have a seat, Thomas." His voice was wistful but also kind. "I know too little of your situation to expect so much. My disappointment over Declan should not poison my view of you." He pointed at the illusion textbook lying on the floor, and it turned into rectangular piece of rich dirt. Grass grew out of it and turned it into a small piece of lawn. "Sit."

I sat down and looked at the grass. It was rich and lush—and appeared real. "Are you an illusionist?"

Joseph looked aghast. "Good Lord, no. Illusion is the creation of the unreal and thus it is weak." He sneered. "A useless magic." He turned and looked at me. "The staff in my hands manipulates the innate bits of life that are hidden in practically everything." I didn't say anything, and he sighed. "To your grandfather, the staff was wasted on me. I was little more than a gardener." He touched the table top, and twigs and branches grew up from the wooden surface.

"That's amazing!" I said. I wondered at this power of his. Could he create massive tree houses? Could he make animals grow, too? Could he touch the sea and fill a net with fish? If he could manipulate life could he also bring someone back from the dead? Could he heal injuries? There were so many things that I could imagine he could do with his power that it overwhelmed me.

"It is kind of you to say, but, unfortunately, I was ordered to give up the staff because my mastery was not quite as valuable as that of my son, who could destroy things." He ran his hand over his head, and it was the exact same movement I had seen my grandfather make over and over again as he tried to tame his wild hair.

"Is there anything you can't do with the staff?" I replied in awe.

"We don't have time for us to discuss the missed opportunities of my youth. Let me just state that the most powerful

Archmage since the staff was brought to Britain is sitting in this room." I thought of his words. They didn't sound like the boastful comments one would hear from a boor. Nor were they filled with the bravado I heard attached to those that described my grandfather. My great grandfather could manipulate life itself. Yes. I agreed with him. That was power of a frightening magnitude. I nodded. He *was* the most powerful Archmage in history.

"You nod, but I have not finished." The *second* most powerful Archmage in this room is the one that currently holds the staff." He smiled, and the cane turned into a large intricately runed staff.

It took a moment for the words to sink in. "But I can only make light."

"So I heard." He didn't add anything, and the silence became uncomfortable.

"You mentioned that the staff came to England. I thought that the staff was our family's legacy. Were we not always from England?" I was thoroughly transfixed with the opportunity to learn more about the staff and our family's history.

"The origin of the staff has nothing to do with our family." He turned the staff back into a cane and handed it to me. "Our family are thieves."

"Excuse me?" He said it so matter-of-factly that I couldn't quite believe what I heard.

"During the First Crusade, one of our illustrious forefathers traveled far to the Southeast and came back with a powerful magic item. How he got it is lost to history, but you can be sure it involved murder, torture, or probably both. Ha!"

"The staff…"

"Yes. How the fool escaped Persia with one of the few icons of power left in the world is beyond me, but he did."

"I thought the staff was one with our family and that only we can use it."

"Well, that story certainly stops people from asking embarrassing questions."

"So we aren't the only ones who can use it?"

"Of course not." As he spoke, my great-grandfather appeared nothing more than to be annoyed with the whole story. At this point, however, he looked me in the eye and held up a finger to underscore the point: "Here is your first and only lesson about the staff: Its power is its own. Not mine. Not yours. Not our family's. Different people can use it to different effect. Thankfully, very few people can get it to do anything. Hell, it sat on a mantle for decades a couple hundred years ago." He shrugged. "Perhaps the staff got bored with our family and hoped we'd pass it on to someone else." He laughed. "Of course we didn't."

"But Mister Ali's family is from Persia, and he said it was destined only be held by one of our family."

Joseph frowned. "Another reason to be rid of that staff! That we have deluded the very people we stole the staff from through lies is a stain on our family!" He waved his finger at me. "I'm too old to make a difference, but know this, Thomas. If you tell Ali or his family or anyone from Persia that the staff belongs to anyone but them, then you are party to their oppression."

The history of my family and the staff, which so thrilled and inspired me just minutes before, now made me uncomfortable. I could not believe that we stole something and then used the very thing we stole to convince those we stole it from to serve us. The idea of destroying the staff seemed to make much more sense now. "I should return it to Ali's family and tell him the truth," I said quietly.

"Good God, boy. Don't do that!"

"Why? Does it not belong to them?"

"Have you not been paying attention? The staff belongs to no one but itself. Better to destroy it and rid the world of one of the last pieces of magic that humans can control." Mister Ali had made the same argument, and while I vaguely understood Mister Ali's point about the danger of magic, I also remembered his joy of magic working with the technology of the train. Maybe my great grandfather didn't understand this exciting future.

"But magic is a force for good, too! Your own son used it to help defeat the Germans, and what about the great achievements of magic and technology working together. I rode here on a train that was as fast as the wind and flew across water!"

My great grandfather stared at me as if I were an idiot. "I would be angry, boy, but I can only pity you and your ignorance." He leaned forward, and his glare was uncomfortable. "Let me ask you this: How does that majestic train run?" He emphasized the word "majestic" and sneered when he said it.

"The engineer uses magic?" I answered weakly. I did not know but assumed it was powerful magic created by the engineer, who was some kind of transportation magician. Even as I considered the scenario in my mind, I knew it was ridiculous.

"The train is powered by a Marid, enslaved in the engine and tortured until he uses his magic to power the train and create its magic."

"Marid?" I had heard them mentioned over the past few days, but I was still unclear on what they were.

And my question was the last straw. My great grandfather's temper boiled over. "A Marid! The most powerful of the magical creatures. It was enslaved by trickery, you ignorant child! Is that the magic you are proud of? Is that the magic you want to use to gain fame and power for your family?"

"No!" I threw the cane to the ground. "I want none of that!"

Joseph held up his hand, and the cane flew into it. "It is the bargain you now live with. Here—" He handed me the cane. "Take this and do with it what you will. I'm too old. I'm not even a Plan C. I'm a curiosity. Nothing more." He stood up.

"Give it to Vingrosh. He could rid it from the world. Exchange it for my son if you want. I don't care." He turned away from me and took a few steps and then paused. "Cain wants the staff. He brought me here as insurance. To use the staff against Hitler if he could not. I came only to hold it again and to remind myself that at least one person could use the staff to create beauty and not destruction. I have done that."

I stood up as he walked to the door and ran to him. "Wait!"

"Goodbye, Thomas. I like to think that you'll make the right decision, but, alas, I don't have the energy to find out."

He was at the door when I reached him. He moved slow. He was old and frail, and I could tell that he had used more energy in the past few minutes than he had in a long time. "You said you were the second most powerful Archmage in history in the room. Did you mean that I was the most powerful?"

He looked at me, and I wanted him to smile, to say, "You are! Now use your power for good." But he did none of those things. He shook his head and opened the door. He walked out, then turned to me, and said, "How much do you know of light? Can it bend? What does its absence mean? What happens if you slow it down?" I didn't understand what he was saying, and he clearly noticed. "Perhaps it is best that you don't know." And with that, he walked toward the stairs while I stood in the doorframe. I watched him depart, wondering if I'd ever see him again.

Chapter Seventeen

VINGROSH SHOWS FEAR

I considered following him, but I knew that I had no time. Mister Ali wanted the staff to destroy it. Cain wanted the staff to use it. They were probably looking for me, and no one seemed to care about finding or rescuing my grandfather. The best thing for me to do was to look for him on my own.

Wait, not on my own. With Naomi. I quickly put my shoes on and rushed back to her room. I rapped on the door, and it opened after the first knock. "You will not believe what happened," she stated as I walked past her into the room.

I considered Cain arriving and warning her about me. Or Mister Ali chasing me down. Or someone else ruining our plans. "What?" I replied absent-mindedly, thinking of all the bad things that could happen. She walked over and fell onto the cot.

"The Head Boy stopped by. He told me that if I'd reconsider my unreasonable refusal to learn some domestic spells, he was given permission to teach me some elementary shields." She grabbed a pillow and screamed into it, shaking her head back and forth, her hair flying about her face. She stopped and tossed the pillow next to her. "I needed that." She looked at me, smiled, and then frowned again as she continued speaking. "He acted like he was going out of his way to do me some great favor, and when I asked him he couldn't even do the Blessing of Kaveh! My mother taught me that when I was ten! The entire academy is filled with incompetents!"

"You should have illustrated how to cast a detonation, using him as a target, of course."

"I was tempted."

I sat on the chair. "I had a visitor, too."

Naomi sat up. "Who? Was it Cain?"

Jake Kerr

"No. It was my great grandfather." I then described his visit, and the history of the staff. I left nothing out, because I wanted to see what Naomi would say.

She was quiet for a bit, and then replied, "A gardener and a streetlight. Doesn't sound very powerful to me." I knew she was teasing because she was smiling when she said it. "Oh well, you may as well use your instrument of oppression to free us. You can deal with your wicked family legacy later."

While I knew that Naomi was teasing, the truth was uncomfortably close to the surface for me. I decided to change the topic to more practical concerns. "So, how am I to free us?"

Naomi smiled and held up her index finger. "You blind everyone with the staff and we could just walk out while they stumble around." She held up another finger. "I could send a detonation off through a window near the main building here, as everyone runs to investigate we could sneak out." She held up a third finger. "I could just blow up everyone as we fight our way out." She dropped her hand and when I didn't reply, she added, "Actually, I rather like the third idea."

"I think there may be too many soldiers for you to blow up everyone." I shrugged.

"You're right. Looks like you get to blind everyone."

"I don't like that idea either!" I objected. "I don't want to blind anyone." I actually wouldn't have minded blinding Cain, but I didn't mention that. "I think we should just sneak out."

Naomi stood up. I could tell that I angered and disappointed her again. "Are you kidding? You expect to just walk out?" She waved her finger at me. "And you're worried about *blinding* people when Cain set you on fire and Ali set Shadows to attack you?"

She stood above me, her hands on her hips and her blonde hair a tangled mess and yet still magnificent as it framed her angry face. I wanted to do nothing more than to impress her, but the thought of hurting innocent soldiers as we escaped was repugnant to me. For the first time, I challenged her. "That's always your solution isn't it? Hurt others so things are easier for you." I stood up, and her eyes went wide. "Well, you know what? Sometimes hurting people doesn't get the job done." It as my turn to point my finger at her. "I know you're alone, and it hurts. *I'm* alone, and it hurts. But my solution isn't to just destroy things."

I turned and threw my hands up and walked away from her. "You're a powerful magician, maybe you can just cast an illusion spell!" I exclaimed, more out of frustration than as a real idea.

Naomi was quiet, so I turned to look at her. To my shock the furious clench of her jaw that somehow made her even more pretty transformed into a smile. "Yes. That's a good idea." She shook her head, slid her hair behind her ears, and then rolled up her sleeves. When I didn't say anything, she added, "I can get us out of here."

And I believed her. I had never seen her cast an illusion, and it was obvious that the various magicians all seemed to focus on one aspect of magic. The Masters were an example of that. Naomi seemed to embrace the mastery of destructive magic that Master Richard did, but I had also seen her shield spell and also the spell she did for Lord Gort. Why couldn't she be as mighty as three masters? She knew more about magic than anyone other than perhaps Cain.

"What do you have in mind?"

"It is a spell that will have us fade into the background," she stated. "I have only cast it on stationary items, and it will be very difficult to maintain while walking. I will need to keep my eyes closed while I concentrate." She turned to me. "You will need to hold my arm and guide me as we walk."

She held out her arm, and I fumbled with the cane as I moved it to my left hand. I took hold of her arm and Naomi then closed her eyes. It all seemed a bit sudden, but Naomi seemed impatient to get going.

"Let me know when you're ready," I stated, but Naomi was already making motions with her right hand and moving toward the door. I opened the door, and I guided Naomi through.

I guided us down the stairs and almost jerked us to a halt when I saw Felice pacing around the entryway, as if she were waiting for someone. I trusted Naomi, however, and continued to walk steadily toward the door. Felice didn't notice us. When her gaze wandered our way, she just continued to look around. As Naomi said, we had somehow faded into the background.

We exited the building, and I considered whether I should try to find some other way out, but the front gate was closest. Her arm constantly moved under my hand, and I did my best to guide her while not interrupting her spell.

I noticed trouble. In the distance I could see the three masters moving in a group toward the door we just exited. I did my best to increase our pace, but we were still a long way from the gate.

It was at that point that I realized the illusions surrounding the Citadel had completely confused me. I looked around. I saw the gate clearly ahead, but as I looked elsewhere it moved to my left. I had just assured myself that the gate was ahead of me, when it appeared to the left again. Surprised, I jerked Naomi's arm as I tried to change directions and get our bearings correct. She exhaled an "Oh." I steadied both of us, but it was too late. Naomi's hands started to move even faster, and as I looked at her, perspiration formed on her forehead.

We took another few steps before Naomi whispered, her voice strained, "The illusion is failing." After a few more steps she opened her eyes and looked right at me. "Run!"

We ran.

There were shouts and soldiers swarmed across the field toward us. There were a few dozen soldiers at the gate, and the nonchalance of how they stood waiting for us was more disturbing than the soldiers chasing us. It underscored the absurdity of our position: We were just running into their arms.

It was then that I saw a flash and then an explosion above the gate. Bits of stone rained down on the soldiers, and their nonchalance quickly turned to attention. Some fled through the gate while others dropped to their knees and raised rifles to their shoulders. I looked at Naomi. She was preparing another detonation.

"Hey, I didn't kill anyone!" She was breathless. I had hoped it was from effort, but a part of me knew it was from joy.

The rat-a-tat of machine gun fire sounded, and I could see the bullets hitting the dust behind us. "They have machine guns. We can't beat them with force!"

I looked at the staff in my hand, and I knew what I had to do. Cain would kill us for the staff. There was no doubt. I didn't want to think that Mister Ali would kill us to destroy the staff, but he had attacked his own family at the Persian Garden for it. Our situation was desperate. I knew I could blind everyone with the power of the staff. They would not be dead, but they would live the rest of their lives in permanent darkness. Was that something that I could accept?

We ran toward the wall as the words of my great-grandfather entered my head. I was the most powerful Archmage in history. But all I could do was create light. Wait, he said I could do more than that. Could I bend light? And what was that about absence? Then it hit me. Could I absorb light? Could I blind everyone temporarily not by burning their eyes with light but by taking the light away?

I squeezed the staff and everything went black. No, it was darker than black, a fuliginous deepness that was impossible—the total absence of light. I stumbled as Naomi said, "What happened? Have you blinded us, too?" I grabbed Naomi's arm. I shook my head in disbelief. I had blinded everyone all right, including us. "You idiot! You did it, didn't you? You have blinded us, too!" Naomi tried to pull her arm away, but I held strong.

"We are not blind. There is just no light. Keep walking. They still know where we are." I could hear shouts in the distance and the sound of boots stumbling about.

"Where does the darkness end?" Naomi asked. Her voice was hushed, and my heart leapt as I took her tone as meaning she was impressed.

"I don't know, but I wanted darkness for as far as I could see, so I believe it is to the horizon."

"Nice job, but it would be nicer if we could see." I considered the idea of just letting light enter our eyes but no one else's, but I sensed that it would be impossible. I then considered creating a cocoon of light that only surrounded us, and as soon as I thought of it I realized that the staff could make it so.

Light exploded around us, and I had to cover my eyes. It wasn't that the light was extremely bright; it was that our eyes went from no light to light in an instant. The contrast was painful, and both Naomi and I stumbled.

As my eyes got used to the light I could see that we were surrounded by a perfect sphere of light that extended about five feet around us. Beyond was perfect black. The light emanated from the tip of the staff, and as I moved the staff the sphere moved. I walked forward a step, and the light followed.

"Streetlight!" Naomi said, and while it was her insult of choice for me, I could see that she was smiling when she said it.

We made our way toward the gate, and that was when we ran into someone. As the soldier entered the sphere of light, he threw his arms over his eyes and cried out. A voice mere feet away yelled out, "What is it?" As we retreated backward from the soldier, he yelled out, "I found them!"

My wonderful magic didn't seem to be very effective, after all. We could find our way out with the light, but there were too many soldiers for us to get away without alerting them to our position or allowing them to see us.

"Make for the field. It is so large that our likelihood of running into someone is low," Naomi whispered. I led us across the lawn.

After about thirty yards, Naomi spoke up. Her eyes were darting around us. "Could you make the light smaller? That would lower the chance of others finding us." I nodded and reduced the size of the sphere to just outside our grasp. As the light settled around us, I heard a deep metallic voice.

"Hail..." The slight echo, the baritone... The last time I heard the voice was in an alley back in New York. The only difference was that the voice was now speaking in English.

"Vingrosh," I whispered.

"Archmage." The voice came from just beyond our circle of light.

I squeezed the staff in my hand, considering destroying him immediately by filling the entire countryside with a blistering magical light, but I stayed my hand. I wanted to know of my grandfather, and I had hope that Vingrosh would know his whereabouts.

"The leader of the Shadows." Naomi whispered, shrinking away from the direction of Vingrosh's voice. I nodded.

"I have been following you, Archmage, but I feared to approach." The idea that Vingrosh feared me made me smile even as it awed me. Vingrosh was afraid of me! I was not just a streetlight. Perhaps my great grandfather was correct.

"Where is my Grandfather?" I asked. My voice was not just steady but commanding. Understanding my power over the Shadows gave me confidence. I may still have been weak compared to Cain, but for creatures of darkness, I was mighty indeed.

"The *Pehlivan* is safe, but the Djinn have taken him and his shield." His shield. He meant Mister Oz. "I cannot order the Djinn to return him. They follow their own counsel." The voice had moved behind me. I swiftly turned to face it. While that would have frightened me before, now I considered it as an indication of Vingrosh's fright. "This darkness you have created…" Vingrosh paused.

"I want my grandfather back," I stated, extending the light around us slightly. There was a metallic cry, and before he could reply, I added, "and Mister Oz, too." I thought of the last time I saw them both, bruised and bloodied in the Persian fortress in Manhattan.

"I will lead you to them, but can do no more than that. It is up to the Djinn. I will speak to them on your behalf, but you must," he paused, and then repeated, an almost pleading emphasis in his voice, "you *must* build us a home of this darkness you have created." His words came in a rush. "I have followed you to discuss the staff, but this is something else entirely. This darkness. I have never experienced anything so tranquil and beautiful." There was a pause and then he repeated, "You must build us a home of this darkness."

It took me a moment to understand what he was saying. I had removed all light. I had created a shadow deeper than any possible. For a Shadow, the magical darkness I created must have been like heaven. Vingrosh wanted me to build that for him and presumably his people.

I considered the idea. I could do it. That was obvious. The staff told me so. This was the price of freedom for my grandfather and Mister Oz and perhaps others. But what of the staff? Vingrosh attacked us for the staff. Would he still try to take it?

"You will take the staff," I said flatly.

"No, Archmage. Your power is too great. No one can defeat you. We can only hope to beg your kindness." Vingrosh, his voice echoing in the hole of his existence, sounded timid and even servile. "Provide us with the dark that is darker than dark, and we will depart this world to live there."

I looked at Naomi, and she shrugged. "I will do this for you, but you must lead me to my grandfather and Mister Oz." I looked around. "And we must escape this place first."

"The Citadel's electrical light defenses were silenced by your magic." I didn't say anything, and Vingrosh added, his voice almost gleeful. "It is dark!" Seconds later I heard screams both near and far.

I didn't want him to kill everyone in the Citadel and, with horror at what I might find, I yelled out, "Vingrosh, do not kill them! We just need to escape!"

"They are not dead, Archmage." Vingrosh's voice came from in front of me, and this, more than anything calmed me. He knew I could destroy him in an instant, yet the hope I heard in his voice led him to trust me. "We hold them in our darkness. They are... elsewhere. We will return them after you depart."

While Vingrosh assured me that no one was hurt, I remembered the horror of losing all feeling in my hand as it passed into a Shadow. The thought that someone's entire body would be in that void without any feeling or sight filled me with sadness and revulsion.

Naomi interrupted my thoughts. "We need to go, Tommy. I don't know if he is telling the truth, but we need to get out of here." She grabbed my arm and tugged me toward the gate. I nodded and followed her lead.

After a few steps she punched my arm, whispering, "Not bad, streetlight! Shadows are good allies to have."

We were quiet until we passed through the gate and were a few yards down the road leading away from the Citadel.

Naomi broke the silence. "As soon as I know where we are, I'll get us to a Way Station."

"I've changed my mind. We are not taking a train." The words of my great-grandfather about the trains running on the tortured magic of Marids and the memory of the wail I heard, a wail I now knew was of horrific pain, were reasons enough for me. Using one again was something I would never do.

"Got a better idea?" Naomi looked at me, a look of annoyance on her face. The look bothered me. I wanted her to look up to me, to respect me, to want to be near me, and yet I was about to tell her that her dead mother's life was dedicated to the propagation of slavery. But I had to.

"No, but the trains—"

"You must use the rails, Archmage." The voice of Vingrosh came from nearby. "Your grandfather is at Persepolis near Shiraz in Persia. There is no better way to get there."

"I will lift the darkness, Vingrosh," I stated.

"As you wish. We are away from the lights and hold those that were chasing you."

I let light return, and saw Vingrosh, a mass of black at the edge of the road. I turned to him. "But the Marid?"

"This is about the Marid?" There was disgust in Naomi's voice. "You are concerned about *that*?"

I ignored Naomi, and waited. Vingrosh eventually replied, "You know of the slaves." There was a pause, and then he continued. "Your concern is noble, but there is no other option that won't put the staff at risk."

So that was it then. It wasn't about the slavery of the Marid for Vingrosh either. It was about the staff and, it appeared, my ability to create a perfectly dark and safe home for his people. Was I the only one who cared? I shook my head. "We don't appear to have a choice if I'm to save my grandfather, but I will talk to the Marid before we go."

"The Marid will not listen, Archmage," Vingrosh stated. "Your words enslave them."

"Talking to the engine? This I have to see." The sarcasm in Naomi's voice was clear, and I found her callousness painful. Did she not see magical creatures as people? We were having a conversation with one. She had called the Shadows great allies. How could she not see that enslaving them was evil?

Knowing this wasn't a conversation we needed to have at that moment, I changed the subject. "We still have to find a

Way Station first." I looked down the road. "Maybe we can find a street sign or something." In response, Naomi strode ahead and didn't seem inclined to have me catch up.

After a few minutes, I spoke up. "Why are there so few magicians?" It was a question that had bothered me since I discovered that beyond Cain there were only three masters in England, and two of them were Persian.

Naomi slowed down and answered, although she still didn't turn to look at me. She was still angry, and she spoke to me as if lecturing a child. "Perhaps it is because it is almost incomprehensibly difficult." She kicked at the dirt. "And why bother training five years to learn a single detonation spell when they are no more powerful than a rifle, which any idiot can use?" The bitterness in Naomi's voice was thick.

I didn't reply and gave Naomi her space. Her answer reminded me of my experience with my Grandfather at Coney Island. He had told the illusionist to use magic on the water that couldn't be replicated by science, and the magician couldn't do it. Was that the secret to the disappearance of magic? That it was archaic and ineffective compared to technology, like a horse-drawn carriage or gas streetlamp? The thought that it was all just a waste of time made me realize how hard it must be for Naomi. She spent her life studying something that was completely useless.

I felt bad for her, even as I still found her attitude toward the plight of the Marids troubling. Maybe it was all of a piece. She was desperately clinging to magic, no matter what the source. I found it all too complex and difficult to understand. Luckily I saw a road sign in the distance, which was not only an opportunity to get our bearings but was also a way to get our minds off our troubled thoughts.

"There's a a road ahead," I said as I jogged up next to Naomi. She didn't say anything but didn't increase her pace to get away from me either. It was something.

There was a sign at the intersection. "London Road," I added, reading it as we approached.

"That's not very helpful," Naomi noted. "It's probably miles long and extends all over the city."

"Yes, but *that* is." I pointed up London Road. There was a sign that said *Wentworth Club*. "Is there a station in Wentworth?" I asked, turning to Naomi.

"No, but there's one in Sunningdale!" She pointed to a smaller sign that had an arrow pointing down London Road in the other direction. It said *Sunningdale Golf Club*. We turned up London Road and marched along the side. A few automobiles and horses passed us, but for the most part we continued on in silence, the sniping of our previous conversation not being something that I, at least, wanted to repeat. We reached the station, and I knew what I had to do, whether it permanently alienated Naomi from me or not.

Chapter Eighteen

BEAUTY AND PAIN

After King's Cross and the Citadel, Sunningdale station was a rather drab affair. Naomi and I entered through the white painted double doors and found a mostly vacant room with a ticket booth to the right. Without waiting for me to say anything, Naomi went up to the woman at the ticket counter and asked, "We need to see the Way Master."

The woman looked confused. "I'm sorry. I don't know what you mean by Way Master, but the Station Master is busy. He's overseeing a rail line inspection."

Naomi smiled. "Thank you." She then turned and said to me, "Follow me."

I shrugged and followed her. She was, after all, much more familiar with Way Stations than I was. As we exited through the large doors that led to the tracks, the ticket woman yelled out, "Excuse me! You aren't allowed out there." Naomi didn't bother to respond and just continued on.

I followed. She stopped at the edge of the tracks and looked left and right. There was a train at the station, but it appeared to be ready to depart any second. Naomi shook her head. "No time to talk to the Way Master." She turned to me. "Be intimidating." She then looked at me and shook her head, smiling slightly. "Okay, *try* to be intimidating." She continued to the engine car.

As I rushed to follow her I tried to understand her smile. It was maddening. Did she find me amusing in a dismissive way or did she like me? And why did I care? She discounted the slavery of the Marid. That was hard to forgive. The thought of the Marid reminded me of what I needed to do.

Naomi climbed up and pounded on the window of the engine and then hauled the metal door open. I heard a "Hey!" but she just pulled herself in.

I paused but she poked her head out. "You need to talk to the engineer."

I scrambled up and entered to find Naomi making a fist and looking up at a tall man. "This is an emergency. The Archmage is here and needs immediate transportation to Shiraz."

The man looked like a giant made of all muscle. He had thick black hair, and while his coveralls hid his build, it was clear that he was a physical force, and the look on his face made it clear he was someone not used to being confronted. "Look, young lady. I haven't heard the Shiraz stop and the *Pehlivan* mentioned in the same sentence in nearly thirty years. I don't know what kind of game you are playing, but—"

"I am the Archmage." I tapped the cane to the ground and lit a light from it's top. The light was intense and filled the whole small compartment. The man towered over me, but he clearly recognized the staff. His jaw dropped open as I lifted it up toward his face. "And this is an emergency. We need to travel to Shiraz, and if you don't take us there immediately, I will—" I tapped his chest with the lit edge of the cane, which made him flinch. "—*melt* you."

I immediately felt foolish saying the words. They sounded so silly to my ear. Melt him? But as I was beating myself up over my inability to intimidate him, he replied, "Of course, Archmage. But we have passengers. I'll need to disconnect them from the engine." I didn't say anything, and he added. "We can't take them to Persia!"

"Oh. Of course. Of course." I moved to the back of the room. "Naomi," I yelled out. "Please keep an eye on the engineer as he disconnects the train. When he's done escort him back here. I'm afraid I don't trust him."

Naomi smiled like I had just given her a birthday present. "Sure thing, Archmage." As the engineer made his way out, it hit me that this was the first time that Naomi had called me anything other than "streetlight" or "Tommy." I felt a rush of confidence.

I opened the door to the next room, looking for the mighty imprisoned Marid. I walked through and closed it behind me, not allowing Naomi the opportunity to follow if she returned quickly. Thankfully, the living area was empty. This train was apparently only operated with a staff of one.

The door at the back was thick, and it took some effort to haul it open. I immediately saw why—it was solid iron, with only the side facing the living area lined in wood paneling. The room was filled with gauges and tubes. It was also very hot. I dared not touch the tubes, as I knew they would leave me with blisters. The tubes appeared to come from the room behind the one I was in. It was all new to me, but one thing was clear: Whatever was in the next room powered the entire train.

The door to the Marid was iron, and the handle to open it was a spiral of coils, such like you sometimes find on fireplace pokers. The door slid open to the right, so I grabbed the handle and pulled with all my strength. Thankfully, despite its thickness it wasn't hard to open. Once it was open, however, the hot air slammed into me with tangible force. It was almost impossible to breath, and my instinct was to back out and shut the door.

I walked through.

The entire room shook with a low rumble. Across from me was a massive furnace with a small opening glowing yellow orange. The air was so hot that everything looked insubstantial. Solid surfaces wavered in front of me. I closed my eyes as sweat started to drip down my face. I closed the door, both out of a desire for privacy as well as concern over the heat damaging something in the other room.

"Marid, you may not understand my language, but it is important for me to tell you this, whether you can understand or not." I squeezed the cane in my right hand. I hoped that my sincerity would be understood even if my words were not. "I have taken charge of this engine because I have no choice. I don't want to use your power without your permission. I think to do so is—" I paused, choosing the word carefully. "—evil. So I ask you, please carry us to Persia. My grandfather is a captive there, and I wish to bring him home." As soon I spoke of his temporary captivity to the Marid I felt embarrassed. How could I express concerns over Grandfather's captivity to a slave? I made a decision, one I knew was right. "My needs are unimportant compared to your own, however. So I make this promise to you: If you do not wish to make the journey, do not move the train. Leave it here. I release you from your bondage. You are free." I opened my eyes, the sweat and heat filling them with tears. "But if you do take us on our journey to Persia, you are still free. Either way I release you. I will not force you to make this trip."

I turned to leave, the furnace burning but silent. The heat had become overwhelming, so I pulled the door open quickly. I exited, but before I closed the door, I leaned in and whispered one word, in a voice barely loud enough for my own ears to hear: "Please."

Naomi and the engineer were waiting for me in the first room. I didn't enter as it was a tight fit. I leaned against the door jamb. Naomi had her hands outstretched toward the engineer, who was holding his hand against his left shoulder. "Problem?" I asked.

"He attempted to yell for help," Naomi replied. "I stopped him."

"You cannot use this station without approval from Cain," the engineer stated, his voice unsteady.

"Do you think he was trying to get warning to Cain?" I asked Naomi.

"I hadn't thought of that, but it is possible. We are very close to the Citadel. It would make sense that Cain controls this station."

I turned to the engineer. "We leave now or I'll let Naomi practice her detonations on you." I glanced at her, hoping that she would go along with my plan. Without looking at me she started making the familiar hand movements of creating a detonation.

The engineer was clearly familiar with the process, as he screamed out, "Okay, okay. I'm firing the engine now."

Firing the engine. The words disgusted me. That's what he called whatever process they used to get the Marid to move the locomotive. The engineer pulled a lever, and the train shuddered but didn't move.

Naomi squinted at the engineer. "What are you up to? We need to move now."

"I don't know! The engine is not responding!"

My heart fell. I knew what had happened. The Marid understood me and was preparing to free himself. He had no intention of taking us to Persia. We would need to find a new way to get to my grandfather. The engineer pulled the lever again, and the engine shuddered but again didn't move. Before he could yank on the lever again, I spoke up. "Stop. Let me check something. Naomi, please keep an eye on our friend. If he moves feel free to blow up the offending body part." She smiled.

I assumed the Marid had decided he wanted to be free. Perhaps he was still enslaved in the furnace. Knowing my opportunity for escape was now gone, I could at least help free him. However, before I had taken one step, an ear-splitting wail filled the air, similar to the one I heard on my previous rail trip, but this was different. Where before I was hearing rage and pain, this time I heard something different—passion? Joy? Effort? Whatever it was, the sound was still fearsome.

The train shot forward, nearly knocking everyone off their feet. The engineer turned to me, his eyes wild. "What did you do? I haven't even engaged the engine, and we are moving at extraordinary speed!" I looked through the window at the track ahead of us. It was true, the scenery was flying by.

"I used a different method to *engage* the engine." I stared at the engineer, whose eyes went wide. I was enjoying being the intimidating Archmage. I could only imagine what was going through the engineer's head as he pictured what kind of magical torture I used on the Marid to have him move the train faster than it had ever moved before.

"Naomi, we need to talk," I stated.

She looked at me. "What about him?" She nodded toward the engineer.

I looked at the engineer who looked nervous but not scared. I needed to change that. "Engineer. You saw how fast we exited the station. Imagine the torture spell I placed on the Marid to make that happen." The engineer nodded slightly. "Now imagine that spell applied to you. If we aren't heading to Shiraz, that is *exactly* what will happen." The engineer glanced toward the rear of the train, then at the gauges, and then at me. He nodded again, and I believed him.

I left and went back to the living area, Naomi following but quiet. I sat down in one of the ubiquitous reading chairs. All magical living areas seemed to have them, along with a small table containing a book on some arcane topic. The one next to me, however, was empty. I ran my hand through my hair and rubbed my eyes. I wanted to make Naomi understand about the wrongness of imprisoning the Marid, but I worried that she wouldn't understand.

"You look pretty dark for a streetlight." I looked up. Naomi was standing directly in front of me, magical energy crackling in her palm.

"Is that a detonation?" My question seemed to surprise her, and she glanced down at her hand.

"Oh, yeah. Sorry. I wasn't going to use it on you if that's what you were worried about." She sounded amused but I didn't see a smile. She sat in the other reading chair. "It probably sounds odd, but I find them calming. Although, to be honest, it's more calming when I actually get to cast them and blow stuff up." I looked at her, and she forced a smile.

"I find it calming to watch you blow stuff up, too." I looked at the cane. "I can't believe Mister Ali betrayed us," I blurted out. Not me. Us.

"He is a deluded foolish old man."

"Was he right, though?" My voice came out scratchy and soft. I was confused and didn't know what to think. Magic enslaved the Marid and who knew how many other magical creatures. All they wanted was to be left alone, and we were dragging them into our world by using their power.

Naomi squeezed her hand into a fist, and the crackling energy disappeared. "Of course not! How is ridding the world of the staff going to solve anything? Will that save the Shadows from the floodlights of German armies? Why is magic the villain here?" She looked me right in the eyes. "I've spent my whole life working with magic. It's all I've done. I do it because I know that magic is more than power. It's an art. It is my *life*, Tommy. All you see me do is detonations and shields, but there is so much more to it. There is so much more *beauty* to it." She paused, and then repeated, "It's my life." She made some hand movements, and the concentration it took really did calm her.

I thought of my great grandfather, who used magic to create and shape beautiful living things. Naomi's words about using magic for beauty echoed his, but he was disgusted at the cost. Naomi didn't see that. Or refused to see it.

Regardless, I was still confused. Were we destroying the good out of fear for the bad? As I considered the importance of the question, Naomi stopped working with the magic in her palm and put her hand on my knee. "There are so few that can even do magic. How do you think that makes me feel? Do you think I'm blind? I'm as good as the masters, and yet there are, what, only three of them in all of England? How many magicians are left in the world? Ten? Twenty? Do we really want to see magic die? How is it even a threat?" She went back to practicing with her hands. "I feel like I am the last practitioner of a dying art."

I considered her words. At a basic level they were true, and her heartfelt passion and the pain behind them made me want to agree with her, but the history made me uneasy. How could I ignore that? Magic was stolen from the Persians. Were we preserving the art or were we just using that as justification to steal another's power? I didn't have an answer, and the quiet was making things awkward. I changed the subject to a more immediate question.

"What of the staff? It has real power and could do damage. What should we do with it?" I expected a vociferous response about the artistry of magic and the stupidity of giving up on it, even through the vehicle of the staff. She obviously believed these things. So her restraint surprised me.

"You know, streetlight, I'm not naïve." Her head was lowered as she spoke the previous words, but she then raised her head and looked at me again. The intensity of her eyes and attention was intimidating, and I turned away. "Magic is dying, but the staff won't make any difference at all. It can do harm, and it can do good. It just is."

"That's refreshingly cynical of you." I smiled as I replied, hoping to lighten the moment.

"Tommy," she said. I turned, and she again looked sad. "I'm a realist. The kind of magic that I can do—the kind the masters can do—has no practical use. Rifles are as powerful as detonations. Hollywood can create illusions that fool people as well as magic." I thought of Cain and was going to disagree, but didn't want to interrupt her. She had never been this open with me.

"Thanks to technology, magic no longer has power. It is an art. The only real powerful magic is done by magical creatures and artifacts like the staff. I know this. Do you understand?" I didn't, and shook my head. "People want magic for power, but magicians have no real power, so we use artifacts and magic creatures. The only way to change this is for magic to fade away and be forgotten because then we won't be tempted by the power of the magical creatures."

I was excited that she was seeing the heart of my conflict. I loved magic, but I didn't love the impact it had on the mostly unseen magical world. I was about to comment to that effect, but Naomi continued, "But those are two different things, and

I don't agree with the idea that we should sacrifice one for the other. That's like saying we should stop using horses because they don't want to carry riders."

My heart fell. She didn't get it. "But, magical creatures can think. You've heard me talk with Vingrosh."

"*Shadows* can think." Her tone was of a teacher. "I'm not talking about Shadows."

"I set the Marid running the locomotive free," I blurted out. I don't know why. Perhaps I wanted to shock her. Perhaps I wanted to let her know that I didn't agree with her.

She tilted her head as she looked at me. "When?"

"In Sunningdale." I said the word as a challenge, but her response deflated me.

"And yet the train is rushing toward Persia." She stood up. "If the Marid could understand anything more than binding words we wouldn't be moving. He would have freed himself." I didn't reply as she moved toward the engineer's cabin up front. At the door she stopped and turned back to me. "He didn't understand, Tommy. He *couldn't* understand. He's an elemental. If he did, he'd be free, and we'd be dead."

She walked through the door and closed it behind her.

Chapter Nineteen

NAOMI WEARS SPECTACLES

I tried to picture how our arrival would go in Shiraz. Vingrosh had said that the Djinn were holding my grandfather and that it was up to me to secure his freedom. But I had no idea where Vingrosh was or how to do that. Would Vingrosh meet us or was he too far away? For that matter I didn't know how Shadows traveled.

I figured we would find out when we arrived. The fact that we didn't really have a well-thought out plan didn't much bother me. The last organized plan I could remember was the one my grandfather and I had to watch Errol

Flynn and then have lunch at the Persian Garden. That one didn't turn out too well.

A few hours later the door opened and Naomi came back. She was frowning. "It appears our engineer decided to take a detour, which has cost us about ninety minutes of travel time. The idiot tried to lie to me." She shook her head. "I know the routes better than he does."

"That's not too bad," I replied. A delay seemed like a minor annoyance. We had at least escaped Cain and the Masters.

"But *why* would he try to delay our arrival? He knew that he couldn't stop anywhere else or you'd do some fearsome Archmage magic to him."

"I don't know," I replied.

She sat down on a chair and leaned her head back. It looked like she was staring at the ceiling, but her eyes were closed. She tapped her foot, and her blonde hair swayed beneath her head. "Ah!" She stated, opening her eyes and lowering her head in a rush, her hair flowing across her face. "He's giving Cain and the Masters time to beat us there!" she said, as she pushed her hair back from her face.

"Oh." I felt stupid for not thinking that Cain would try to chase us. I had trusted so much in our magical rail transport that I didn't even consider that they would have similar or faster travel. One thing bothered me, though. "How do they know where we are going?"

Nodding to the front of the train, Naomi replied, "I'm guessing the engineer let them know somehow."

"We should keep an eye on him." I stood up.

"Well, I scared him a bit when I found out we weren't heading directly to Shiraz." She smiled wickedly. "But you're right, we should probably stay up front." I nodded and walked past Naomi when she grabbed my arm. "This might get messy. They know your darkness trick, and they know you have the Shadows on your side. I'm not sure if they can actually do anything to stop them or you, but they'll try, so we need to be prepared."

"Of course," I replied, trying to sound confident. Naomi stared at me, as if sizing me up. It was difficult not to look away. While she was probably thinking about how well I would do when faced with hordes of Djinn, I was thinking how I didn't want her to let go, that I could feel her fingers squeezing my arm, as if I were escorting her to the prom.

She let go and walked toward the engineer's cabin. I couldn't tell what she was thinking. It was maddening. Did she have confidence in me? Was she as thrilled to hold my arm as I was to have it held? Could she picture me with her at the prom? All these thoughts and more filled my head as I followed her into the cabin. I pressed against the far left wall due to the small space. Naomi stood near the engineer, rhythmically moving her hands, the energy occasionally crackling loud enough to be heard over the wheels of the train. The engineer kept glancing down at her hands.

"You can lower your hands now, miss." There was fear in the engineer's voice.

"I don't think so. I find it calming."

"Is that the station?" I pointed ahead. We were rushing across desert, and in the distance was what looked like a station the size of Sunningdale, at the edge of a large city. The heat coming off the rails was so great that the station flickered on the horizon.

"Yes," Naomi replied. "This is a famous station. It has served Persepolis for many years."

"Nice job, engineer," I stated, slapping him on the back.

He turned to me, a smile on his face. "I know."

He pulled a lever, and the train started to slow.

The train stopped, and Naomi jumped down, her hands at the ready. Her eyes darted all around, including the sky. "The station is mostly empty. Looks like we beat them, so we should move."

I stayed behind. I looked at the engineer, who was grinning. I couldn't stand his arrogance, so I said, "Enjoy our departure, but you won't be heading home. I freed the Marid."

His grin grew even wider, if that was possible. "The elemental is bound by a word of power, and only the engineer can free him." He leaned down, his grin turning to clenched teeth. "And I won't free him no matter what you threaten me with. I am not suicidal."

"Tommy, we gotta go!" Naomi yelled from the landing.

It was at that point that a massive banging and squeal of iron and steel came from the back of the engine. I tapped the engineer on this chest with the cane. "I guess on this trip I was the engineer." I almost fell as a tremendous blow shook the whole cabin. I rushed off the train, the engineer close behind. Naomi stared at the back of the engine as a flash of light and a wave of heat hit us. The Marid shredded the metal, melting the iron as it broke free.

It was magnificent, at least three times the size of a Djinn, its body shrouded by a mantle of flames. It leapt down to the ground, and with two massive blows knocked the train onto its side, metal screeching under the strain. Its power was astonishing. I now understood why everyone was frightened at the Persian Garden when we were told a Marid approached.

With a howl that sounded part train whistle and part triumph, the Marid spread its wings and lifted itself into the air. It swooped toward us, and we all threw ourselves to the ground, the engineer crying out. I could feel the heat as it passed over me, but it didn't land or shoot fire at us. More than anything I felt like it wanted to remind us of its power before it left for its life of freedom. I glanced up, and the flaming wings beat on toward the horizon away from the city.

I felt a hand on my arm, and Naomi looked at me. She looked like she was in shock. "You freed it, and it didn't kill us."

"More than that," I replied, smiling. "It did me a favor in bringing us here." She didn't reply, but I could tell that she was doing her best to fit the intelligence—and more importantly, the generosity—of a recently freed slave Marid into her view of the world.

I stood up, brushed the dust off my pants, and held out my hand. Naomi took it, and I helped her up. She was surprisingly light. I guess I saw her as larger than life, mighty and powerful.

She looked around. "I don't see any Shadow greeting committee, so we should probably head for Persepolis as quickly as we can." I nodded as Naomi started toward the double doors into the station.

We entered, and Naomi said, "Something feels wrong," just as a Shadow flowed over to us from a corner. We waited as it raised itself into the semblance of a human.

"Archmage," the Shadow said. It didn't sound like Vingrosh, but it had the same metallic voice, so I assumed he had sent a message ahead.

"Have we met?" I asked.

"No, Archmage. I am here to escort you to Persepolis. Your grandfather is held there."

I nodded. "Do we have transportation? I am afraid we are pursued." I looked toward the track. The engine we arrived in was a twisted wreck. I hoped that it would slow Cain and any-one else down at least a little bit.

Before the Shadow could reply, Naomi stopped, turned, and pointed to the ceiling. Alarm filled her face. "Tommy, these are electrical lights!"

I looked around, and she was right. The entire room was lit with electrical lights. I looked at the Shadow, and it wavered a bit. Then a patch of black shot out and knocked the cane from my hand. It skittered across the floor. I turned to run for it when a fist glanced off my head. I sprawled to the floor. I heard the explosion of a detonation as I scrambled toward the cane.

"Tommy, this whole station is an illusion! Cain is here!" Naomi was glancing around, launching detonations at any-thing that moved.

I looked toward what I thought was a Shadow just as a det-onation exploded into its chest. It flew backward, turning into one of the Masters as it slid along the floor from the force of Naomi's magic. It was the Master of illusion. He lay unmoving on the floor. I turned back to the staff. I had to get to it.

Cain stood holding it.

"Enough!" he shouted. Naomi lifted her hands to fire a detonation only to have her arms bend downward as if made of rubber.

"Quite difficult to do things when your arms don't cooperate isn't it?" Cain laughed and tapped the cane on the floor. I stood up and looked at him. He looked like he did back in London, his eyes had the same tic, and his body jerked and spasmed every so often.

He walked over to me. "Let this be a lesson to you, boy. *Real* magic is power. Detonations? Please. And this?" He waved the staff in front of me. "Light? Seriously? Did you think tricking me with light and darkness could stop me? Even if you wanted to join me you would be useless." The disgust in his voice was clear.

I gauged whether I could grab the staff from his hand without him hitting me with some painful illusion, but he stayed far enough away that even the attempt would have been foolish. Cain waved his hand, and the entire building disappeared around us. It didn't even exist. What we thought was a station was a just bare land in the desert. We could have been miles from Shiraz. We just thought we had arrived there.

As the station disappeared, I could see an army truck in the distance. A plume of smoke came out from behind as it moved toward us. Cain turned to Naomi. "You, foolish girl." He pointed at her. "Over here next to our esteemed Archmage. And if you don't move quickly, I will illustrate what happens when you face an illusion of being burned alive." She walked over to me, pure hatred in her eyes.

Cain looked at her. "You have talent. Simin had a fairly strong shield on, and your detonation ripped right through it. Impressive." The truck pulled up.

"Jonah!" Cain yelled out, and the engineer emerged from behind the wreckage of the train. "You did well. I'll make sure you are promoted to a major London station for this." The engineer named Jonah walked over, his face red. He wore glasses that I had not seen during the entire trip.

Cain marched over to him. "Where did you get those?"

Jonah put a hand up and touched the wire frame of the lenses. "They are a family heirloom."

"They are a weapon against magic," Cain replied as he grabbed them. The engineer cried out as Cain tossed them to the ground. "You have no need of these. I released the illusion.

You won't trip over some nonexistent step." Cain slammed his boot onto the glasses, crushing them into the dirt.

I recognized the spectacles. They were identical to the glasses that the quartermaster had given me at the Citadel. He had told me to wear them for my meeting with Cain, but I had forgotten. Now I knew why he had said that. *They allow you to see through illusions.* I patted my pocket; the glasses were still there.

"Those are priceless!" Jonah exclaimed.

"They should be more than priceless. They shouldn't exist." Cain turned and made his way back to us.

Jonah yelled out, his voice strained. "He released a Marid, Cain."

"Richard has handled Ifrit easily. I'm sure a Marid would be no more difficult. Let it attack."

Jonah looked alarmed. "This is a Marid, Cain." To reiterate his point he repeated, "A *Marid.*" Cain waved his arm at him in response. Cain's response shocked me. *Had he never seen a Marid?* If he had he certainly wouldn't have been so nonchalant about it. I noted to myself that if Cain lacked knowledge of magical creatures, perhaps he had other blind spots, as well.

"It worries me not, but you are right that we should leave. It is safer for us in London. Once we reach the station, you can make arrangements with the Way Master there." He turned to me. "We are leaving for Shiraz Station. I hope you enjoy the irony of that, young man." He turned to the truck; the other two Masters were standing next to it. "Place these two in the back. We can leave them with the Persians to deal with." Cain turned to me, and bowed slightly. "You see, Tommy. I'm not a monster. I'm not going to kill you, just leave you with the natives." He turned to the Masters. "Don't worry about the Archmage. Without this—" He held up the staff. "He is just a boy."

The Master named Richard came over and motioned for us to move to the truck. As we were led away, I could hear Cain behind me. "Poor Simin, defeated by a girl." And then: "Leave his body here. We don't have the time or resources to bring it back."

The truck was the kind designed for transporting supplies or troops. It had a small cabin in the front and a flat bed in the back with bleacher type seats down both sides. Above the cabin were large electrical lights that looked dim in the sunlight, but I was sure were bright—bright enough to keep away

Shadows. "Climb on and move to the front," Richard said, his hands crackling with the energy of an unreleased detonation.

There was a small step, and I climbed on without much trouble. Naomi had difficulty due to her arms and hands wobbling around like rubber. I assisted as well as I could and we eventually settled near the front. Richard sat toward the back, his eyes on us the whole time. I sat to Naomi's left, between her and the Master.

The truck turned hard and moved along what appeared to be not so much a road as a narrow path that had fewer rocks and brush than elsewhere. The jostling was heavy and constant. Every so often I would glance at the Master, but no matter how much the truck bucked, he kept his hands steady and in front of him.

I leaned over and whispered to Naomi. "I have spectacles in my pocket that will break your illusion. Pretend to fall into my lap, and I'll put them on you." I turned slightly so that the Master couldn't see and slid the glasses into my hand, providing Naomi a glimpse.

I leaned back and looked to make sure she understood. For a moment she looked uncertain, but then I noticed a small smile form on her mouth. I waited and not long later the truck hit another rock and bounced. Naomi cried out and fell forward into my lap. I slid the spectacles on her nose and over her ears. She yelled out, "Don't be so clumsy, you oaf!" as she slid off my lap and down onto the floor of the truck.

Her back was to Richard, and I could see that she was preparing a spell. It looked like a detonation, only different. "Don't just sit there, help me up!" Her voice sounded forced. I leaned over and grabbed her waist. I could tell she was tensing her legs as I helped her up. She turned in a crouch and unleashed her spell at the Master. He didn't have a chance. The last thing I saw was his eyes go wide and then an orange ball of fire hit him in the head. The spell threw him back with enough force that as his legs hit the edge of the truck he flipped into the air and landed in the dirt behind us.

I looked at Naomi, but she had already turned to the front of the truck. Before I could stop her she launched another fire type spell at Cain and the final Master. The ball of flame hit the back of the cabin and tore a huge hole into it as it continued through and into the engine. The force drove the front of the truck into the ground, stopping us from moving forward.

The momentum lifted the back of the truck into the air with a screech of metal. Naomi and I went flying into the air.

I landed in the dirt and rolled to a stop. I was dazed and bruised but not seriously injured. I stood up and looked around. The truck looked like it had been hit by an artillery shell. It was on its wheels, but the front was twisted and melted. The wheels were flat and bent to the side.

"I broke your glasses." It was Naomi. She was walking toward me, holding out the spectacles. The metal frame was bent, and the lenses were spiderwebbed with cracks. I slipped them into my shirt pocket and then ran over to the truck. I had to get the staff.

Cain was in the passenger side of the truck, unconscious and bleeding from his head. The master was on the ground, also unconscious. I pulled Cain from the seat and dropped him on the ground. Naomi walked up. "There's your staff." She pointed to the ground near the front of the truck.

I rushed over and picked it up. I didn't realize how empty I felt without it. As my fingers squeezed the wood, I could tell that it was unharmed and, more importantly, that one of my senses had returned, as if a blindfold were removed from my face.

"Are they okay?" I walked over to Naomi who was bent over Cain and Master Behnam.

"I don't know." She reached down and put her fingertips against Cain's neck. "They're alive at least."

I looked around again, this time taking in our surroundings. We were in the middle of a flat plain, and I had no idea how far we were from Shiraz. "So streetlight, do you have a plan?" Naomi brushed some dust off her clothes as she spoke. "Looks like we're surrounded by a whole lot of dirt."

I was about to just say we had no choice but to follow the train tracks to Shiraz when a black shape flowed toward us from a small tree.

"Archmage," the deep metallic baritone voice from the Shadow said. "I have unfortunate news."

Chapter Twenty

AN OLD MAN GIVES US A RIDE

"Vingrosh," I replied. "Where have you been?" I walked toward him, but Naomi held back, staring at the pool of black in the dirt.

"The magicians held me at bay with their lamps." I glanced at the now shattered lights on top of the truck.

"What is the unfortunate news you mentioned?" I wanted to ask him about nearby settlements or if there was someone we could seek out to help Cain and Behnam, but I was most worried about whatever news he had. I filled myself with hope after Vingrosh mentioned that the Djinn were holding my grandfather and that he was alive, but now I felt an emptiness as I waited for his words. I knew he would say that Grandfather was dead.

"I attempted to intervene on your behalf, but the Djinn will not listen to reason. They will not return your grandfather unless the staff is destroyed. It has killed too many of them, they say. It is an instrument of destruction, and you are not to be trusted."

Naomi spoke up. "Can we just attack them?" She started practicing her magic by twisting and turning her fingers.

"That is unwise," Vingrosh replied. "They hold the *Pehlivan* at Persepolis." He didn't add anything, as if the meaning was self-evident.

"Is that bad?" I felt foolish asking, but I had no choice.

"That's their ancestral home," Naomi added, sounding once again like I was an idiot. "Most magic traces its roots back to there. We'd have to defeat an army of them."

I remembered Mister Ali mentioning Persepolis and others taking notice, and I also remembered my great grandfather talking about how the staff was stolen during the crusades. Could it have come from Persepolis? I had never connected magic so directly to Persia, but now it all started to make sense. Two of the masters were Persian, the respect that my grandfather had for Mister Ali and his family was evident, and even when Mister Ali was dismissed by people, his mention of Persepolis made them pause.

"Perhaps I should give them the staff."

"No!" Naomi exclaimed. I looked at her, and she lowered her head. "I was wrong. The staff can make a difference." She looked back up at me. "You can't let magic die, Tommy," she added in a whisper.

I looked at Vingrosh. "You have promised to create us a home," he said, although it was difficult to assess the tone of his voice. He added, "The Djinn will speak with you. Perhaps you can convince them."

Naomi took a step forward. "*Speak* with them? So we are to go to this Persepolis, meet with an army of magical creatures with massive jaws and claws, tell them we're sorry we killed a bunch of them but let's let bygones be bygones, and then ask them to give up the very same person who was the one who killed so many of them? Is that your recommendation?"

"You are mistaken," Vingrosh replied. He slid closer to Naomi, who took a step back in response. "The *Pehlivan* never attacked the Djinn. He defended himself, and that is all. They understand this. Their concern is with the power of the new Archmage and the staff itself."

"That settles it then," I replied. "I will talk with them and convince them that I am a friend. They will let Grandfather go and trust me with the staff."

I tried to sound confident, but I was unsure I succeeded, as Naomi replied, "And when that doesn't work, I'll blast our way out."

I looked toward the empty horizon. "But how do we get there?"

"I could alert the Lords of Persepolis," Vingrosh stated. "They are friends of the Archmage and would send help. Others would help, as well. The staff and Archmage are famous in Persia."

"No!" I replied. "That is Mister Ali's family. He wishes to destroy the staff, not help us." I frowned. "You know this, Vingrosh. He plotted with you to do it!"

"The situation has changed."

"For you, perhaps, but not for him." Mister Ali's words in Lord Gort's office still stung. He didn't care about my grandfather, and he didn't care about me. All he cared about was ridding the world of the staff and magic. "But you can tell them about Cain and Behnam. While they are saving them, we can meet with the Djinn."

"It shall be done," Vingrosh replied, and he slid across the dirt, merging with the shadow he came from. I assumed he had left.

Naomi shrugged. "Time for a walk."

We settled into a brisk pace, but the sunlight was overpowering and before long I was soaked in sweat. Naomi was, as well. After about an hour we came to a real road. It was still dirt, but it was clearly used by vehicles.

Naomi pointed to our left. "That way follows the tracks." I was too hot to do anything more than nod.

Twenty minutes later we came to a few wooden houses. I went up and knocked on a door. An old woman answered. I started to say hello in Farsi when her eyes went wide as she glanced at the cane, which I had taken to leaning on ever since I hurt my leg.

"*Pehlivan!*" she cried out. She opened the door wide and yelled out a few words in Persian. An old man, more thin and frail like my great grandfather than vibrant like Mister Ali, limped forward.

He looked at the cane and then at me. "Where is the *Pehlivan?*"

I shook my head. "I am his grandson. I need to get to Persepolis to save him."

He turned to the woman, who I assumed was his wife, and said a few words, the only one I understood was "archmage," which he said before glancing at me. She nodded when he finished.

"Amir," the man said touching his chest. "Afra," he added, pointing to the woman.

"Tommy," I replied, holding my palm against my chest. I then introduced Naomi.

"Wagon," he said, turning to me, and then pointed off in the direction we were heading. "Persepolis."

I grinned. "That would be great!" I added, "Kheili mamnun," which was Farsi for thank you.

"*Pehlivan,*" the old man muttered, as if that explained everything. He pointed to the road and held up his palm.

"He wants us to wait by the road," I said, turning to Naomi. She rolled her eyes. "I guess that was pretty obvious."

She smiled, replied, "Streetlight," shook her head, and started toward the road.

About twenty minutes later a single brown horse came around from behind the house pulling a flatbed wagon. The old man sat in the front with the reins in his hand. He stopped near us and pointed in the back. We climbed up and settled in. Naomi sat across from me. The heat was so stifling that she didn't even bother practicing her spells.

"Long trip," the old man said, and then he snapped the reins and we were off.

We crossed the rail tracks at one point. Later, as I glanced up, I noticed a city far off in the distance. "Look," I said, pointing. "That must be Shiraz."

Naomi looked up. "Yes. I guess the old man is taking us around the city. Probably smart." It wasn't until later that I learned the extent of my grandfather's fame in Persia. He was the *Pehlivan*—the hero—to practically everyone. Many felt that he was the one who freed them from occupation after the Great War.

At one point Naomi leaned over and whispered, "You know we have to destroy all the Djinn."

"No, I do not know that," I replied.

"Don't be naïve. They aren't going to understand anything but saving themselves. You've seen them up close. Sure, Vingrosh may have been able to bargain with them, but they will only want one thing from us—to destroy us and the staff."

"I don't know if that's true."

"It *is* true. Look, I have a plan. We get close enough that you can toss the staff to your grandfather, and he can destroy all the Djinn."

Naomi's implication that my grandfather could save us with the staff but I couldn't didn't bother me as much as her prejudice against magical creatures. It reminded me of my great grandfather talking about the fear of the Shadows. It was based on nothing but stories and myths. I replied, "They may not even let me that close, and, besides, what if he is hurt? And what if the Djinn actually are willing to talk?"

Naomi shook her head. "You're an idiot." We didn't say anything to each other for the rest of the trip.

It was early evening and several hours later when the old man reined in his horse. He pointed to stone ruins in the distance. "Persepolis." He then pointed to the road. "Out." I smiled. His limited English made him sound like a stern father kicking out a misbehaving child, yet the reality was that he had helped us more than he probably imagined.

We climbed out and I told him thank you. He bowed his head and said, "*Pehlivan.*" I couldn't tell if he was referring to saving my grandfather or he was calling me that term. Either way, I was immensely thankful for his kindness.

I turned to Naomi. Her hair was pulled back behind her ears, her sleeves were rolled up, and she was staring off at the ruins. "Ready?"

Naomi's hands crackled as she prepared her magic. "I have everything I need," she replied.

"Should we wait for Vingrosh or walk toward the ruins?" I asked.

"Walk," Naomi said. I was worried, because it was clear she was itching for a fight. I was angry at her lack of self-control when it hit me—Djinn had killed her mother. How could I have forgotten that important point? Was it even safe taking her with me when she could lose control in a vengeful rampage? I wanted to think she wouldn't do such a thing, but the truth was that I didn't trust her. She was too passionate, too emotional.

"Maybe you should stay behind." I tried so hard to make my words sound reasonable and calm, but it was clear I failed miserably. Naomi turned to me, looking like I had slapped her.

"You don't think I can handle myself?"

"No! That's not it!" She advanced on me, and I backed up a step. I didn't want to tell her that her behavior was proving my point as that would have just made it worse. "It's just with your mother—"

"My *mother*? You think I'll just attack them out of anger?" I paused, and she used that as evidence of agreement. "Listen, streetlight. Djinn killed my mother, and yes, I would very much like to see a large number of them die for that. Maybe it won't make me feel better, but maybe it will. However—" She turned her head away. "I am here for you and your grandfather. I don't want you to lose *him*."

She turned back, and I saw disappointment in her face. She wiped at her eyes and turned away. "Forget it. Just go yourself."

She started walking in the direction of the retreating horse and wagon.

"Wait!" She didn't wait. I ran up to her. "Hold on!" She kept moving. "Naomi, please!" I grabbed her arm, and she whirled around. Her face set in the intense look that was both intimidating and beautiful. There were tears on her cheeks. She didn't even bother to hide them, and that made me think that something had changed between us. I desperately wanted that change to be a good one. "I need you." I said, quietly. She stared at me. I held up the staff. "I'm just a streetlight."

A small smile formed at the edge of her mouth. "Of course you need me." She walked past me toward ruins. I rushed up to her, but didn't say anything. After a few paces, she added in a whisper. "And you're more than a streetlight." I turned to look at her, but she jogged ahead, adding, "Just try to keep up and stay out of the way."

Chapter Twenty-One

THE MOST POWERFUL ARCHMAGE

———————————————•

There was a small copse of trees between us and the ruins that seemed out-of-place. I considered that they may have been illusions and pulled the spectacles out of my pocket. However, they looked the same with them on, but whether that was due to the glasses being broken or the trees being real I had no idea. I expected Vingrosh to emerge from the shade of the trees, but he never appeared.

We exited the trees and approached Persepolis, passing sand colored pillars and walls in advanced states of ruin. With every step I noticed the staff getting warmer. I also felt strangely calm, as if I was returning home after a long trip away. Nothing looked familiar, or even livable, yet it all seemed comfortable.

As we passed the remains of an entryway flanked by what appeared to be horses or bulls with human heads, a large Djinn emerged from between them. Naomi crouched and prepared a detonation. I touched her arm. She shook me off, saying, "I'm just being careful." I took a deep breath, thankful for her presence—the Djinn was massive, all claws and muscle. It's mouth was pulled back, exposing its teeth in a deadly smile.

"You do know how stupid this is," Naomi muttered from my right. I didn't look at her, but I could picture her rolling her eyes once again at my foolishness. The thought actually calmed me.

Before I could reply, the Djinn held up its arm and beckoned us forward with a single dagger-like talon. After it turned and took a few steps, I yelled out, "We are waiting for Vingrosh." The Djinn stopped, turned, and shook its head. It completely ignored any further response, turned, and continued walking in its predator-like crouch.

"It isn't a creature you can reason with, Tommy," Naomi said.

"What should we do?" The Djinn continued to walk further into the ruin.

"I don't like this at all, but at this point I don't think we have much of a choice." Naomi looked around.

"Well, if it turns out badly, I could blind them." I held up the staff, not entirely confident it could save us from a mass of Djinn in an open space.

"He's getting away from us," Naomi replied, her voice calm.

"Let's go," I said, more out of a desire to do something rather than reasoned planning.

We jogged to catch up to the Djinn. I couldn't imagine where he was taking us; the whole area was nothing but a multitude of sand-colored columns and collapsed walls. The roof had caved in ages before, and the sun beat down on us. In the middle of what at one time must have been a large building filled with columns, the Djinn stopped.

I looked around, but there was nothing to see. Naomi muttered, "not good." I figured that there may be an illusion in place, so I grabbed the spectacles again. I put them on, and everything seemed the same except for one corner section of glass in the left lens. There was a flash of movement in it.

I pulled off the glasses and held that small section of the shattered lens in front of my right eye. I closed my left eye and looked around.

We were surrounded by Djinn. Hundreds of them. Large, small, grey, red. They were all crouching on and around the bases of the collapsed columns. "Naomi," I whispered. She looked at me. "Look through the lower left corner of the left lens." I handed the spectacles to Naomi.

As she put them up to her face, her jaw dropped and her eyes went wide. She handed the glasses back to me and said, "I think a shield is a good idea right now." She knelt down and spread her arms, starting her spell.

I raised the staff. I hoped it still elicited fear. As if in response, a creature flew in low from the forested section of the ruins and landed near the entryway. It was enormous, almost twice the size of the Djinn, and while it didn't seem to have the claws and teeth of the Djinn, fire flickered over its entire body, with flames gathered at each extremity. The glow of the flames gave it a red tinge. Unlike the Djinn, its face appeared

0.25

more human-like, although that was mostly due to the lack of gaping jaws. It still looked frightening. I had seen this type of creature once before—the magical creature that shot fire at me at the Persian Garden.

It folded its wings tight against its back and walked toward us. Naomi was still facing the Djinn as she concentrated on finishing her shield spell, while I simply stared. The giant Djinn stopped about twenty feet away. I could feel the heat from its flames.

"You may as well stop your shield spell, magician." The monster spoke in perfect English. In fact, it had an academic East coast American accent. It sounded like one of the instructors from my high school. Naomi ignored it. "The Mantle of Anaitis cannot stop an Ifrit." It sounded amused. "You should know this." Naomi dropped her hands, stood up, and turned. She looked drained.

"You are an illusion. Djinn and Ifrit do not speak. They are bound by our words."

That made sense to me. I was raising the broken glasses to my eye when the Ifrit laughed. "Just because we do not speak does not mean we cannot." The Ifrit spoke while using it hands, and that, combined with its voice, made it appear even more human. A glimpse through the lens confirmed it was what it appeared to be. "We have been enslaved and forced to grant wishes for millennia before we realized that our voices were the things that betrayed us and bound us to your commands. That I am speaking to you now should illustrate the gravity of our situation. You—" The Ifrit pointed at me. "Archmage. You are here for the *Pehlivan.*"

"I am," I replied. The fact that the Ifrit spoke in a reasonable manner didn't distract me from the fact that we were surrounded by teeth and claws, which I glimpsed once again in the spectacles.

"We will free him if you give me the staff." It held out its arm and opened its hand. Flames rose from its fingertips. "We cannot destroy it or return it to its home, but we can keep it away from humans."

I shook my head. "I have promised the Shadows I would use the staff for their benefit. Perhaps after I do that, we can discuss what to do with it." I looked around, hoping my words would inspire Vingrosh to show himself. I glanced back at the

Ifrit. Perhaps his flames emanated magical light? Whatever the reason, Vingrosh remained absent.

"Vingrosh has agreed with us that the staff should be removed from human hands."

"He has changed his mind, and you know this. Why do you lie?" I replied. I heard a crackle and glanced to my right. Naomi was preparing a detonation. The Ifrit seemed unconcerned.

"It matters not." The flames from the Ifrit grew brighter, and its skin reddened. The heat was powerful enough to be uncomfortable. "You will now drop the staff, Archmage."

"Now would be a good time for darkness, Tommy," Naomi whispered.

I held up the staff and brought the utter blackness of no light to the entire area outside of the two of us. There was the sound of scrabbling claws, a few howls, but what frightened me the most was the flaming image of the Ifrit approaching. The staff did not remove the magical fire of the Ifrit or the light that emanated from it. And I knew why because the staff told me as I held it.

The flames are its life force. That isn't actually light! I found the concept interesting—a fire elemental where its flame and light were part of its being, not based on the science of light. As I was being distracted by the staff and my own mind, Naomi unleashed her detonation. It was larger than I had expected, and it hit the Ifrit directly in the chest.

The blow from the spell staggered the Ifrit, and it fell backward. There was another howl, and the Ifrit yelled out as it stood up. "No! I can handle the humans." It stood up, and before Naomi could launch another detonation it shot a ball of flame toward her. The ball hit her in the chest before she could react, and she flew back far enough that she entered the darkness that I had created.

"No!" I cried out. I removed the darkness and looked toward her. She was lying on the ground, her body in a heap. I turned to the Ifrit, which approached. I held up the staff and was about to bring forth the pure intense light that blinded the Djinn when I felt something hit me so hard in the chest that I knew I was about to die. The staff became intensely hot and vibrated violently in my hand. I landed on the ground, and while I felt horrible pain only one thing filled my mind: The sound of the staff clattering as it bounced away from me on the ground.

I forced myself up, only to see the Ifrit approach, its flames even brighter. It paused, even though it was already close enough that I felt my skin redden in a burn. "The staff has saved you." I felt my chest, expecting a hole or, at best, a deep burn. But I was unharmed. "It will not save you again."

I rolled toward the staff and grabbed it as a ball of flame hit the floor where I had just been. I held it in my hands and scrambled to my knees. The Ifrit laughed, but before he could say anything, I yelled out, "Before you kill me, let me see my Grandfather! It is my last wish." I was stalling for time, desperately hoping the staff would provide me with some guidance.

My words seemed to hit it as hard as Naomi's detonation. It paused, and then retreated a step. "I will do this, but only out of respect to the *Pehlivan*. You have earned no such request." The Ifrit waved a hand and said something in a language that seemed based on growls. I looked at Naomi. A wisp of smoke floated out of her slightly open mouth.

I forgot about escaping. I forgot about destroying the Djinn and the Ifrit. I looked back again. *No!* Naomi couldn't be dead. She was the true hope for magic in the world. She was already one of the best magicians alive, and she was only my age. She had achieved more than me. Worked harder than me. Earned honor and accolades more than me. My eyes burned, and I wiped them with the back of my hands. *No! No! No!* I stood up, my knuckles white as I clenched the staff.

"My little Archmage!" I turned to see my grandfather approaching. He looked the same as when I had last seen him, his hair just as wild, his suit torn, his eyes fierce. He wore a huge smile. Mister Oz was with him, a step behind. He looked weary, but was also smiling.

"Grandfather! Mister Oz!"

I took a step toward him but the Ifrit spoke in a booming voice, "Do not approach the *Pehlivan*."

"It's okay, Tommy. They fear you'll give me the staff." I nodded. "I knew you would get away and save me." He smiled and ran his hand through his hair, and I couldn't help it. I cried. I had seen him make that same movement hundreds of times in my life, his poor attempt to tame his hair. But seeing that simple motion after assuming I would never see it again was almost too much. And with Naomi gone, I had lost one friend even as I had regained another.

Mister Oz walked to me, and the Ifrit let him pass. He gave me a big hug. "Tommy, why in that uniform you look like a young man now!" He smiled his smile and then looked around. "But where is my father?"

All the energy left me as I faced that question. I stammered out a "He is still in London," which elicited a hesitant nod in return.

A booming voice interrupted any further questions. "I have done my kindness. Now throw the staff over there. He pointed to my right, a direction well away from my grandfather. Mister Oz whispered, "Don't give up the staff, Tommy." I nodded.

"What will you do with us?" I asked.

The Ifrit laughed. "Why I will kill you. You didn't expect me to let the *Pehlivan* and his heir leave when the Shadows refuse to rid the world of the staff?"

I put every ounce of being into begging the staff to give me guidance. Anything. An escape. An attack. A shield. I held it up, hoping to buy more time through intimidation. "Then I fear you are going to have to take it from my hands yourself, Ifrit."

"As you wish." I saw a glow and then the staff once again bore the brunt of the Ifrit's attack. It burned hot in my hand, but unlike last time, I did not let go. The force still knocked me to the ground. I looked up to see the Ifrit approaching. While I knew it could not hurt the staff, it was only a matter of time before the pounding knocked it from my hands.

I looked up, and my grandfather was running toward me, his hand outstretched. I knew what he was doing. He wanted me to give him the staff. *Stop*, I thought. *You are too far.* The Ifrit turned to my grandfather and raised its arm. *Stop*! I thought of my grandfather. I thought of Naomi lifeless behind me. I didn't want to lose him. I was alone. I didn't want to die alone.

I closed my eyes, not wanting to see Grandfather die. I reached out with my hands, the staff cold in my hands. "Stop," I whispered at the Ifrit. And then, to no one in particular, "Please make it all stop."

A feeling like a minor shock went through my hands. It tickled more than anything. The sounds surrounding me slowly muted, as if a song on a record player was fading out. I opened my eyes, and the entire world was frozen. My grandfather was mid-step heading toward the Ifrit. The Ifrit had a ball of fire inches from his hand and aimed at my Grandfather. I looked around. Nothing moved.

I tapped the cane on the ground, and it let out a sharp crack, but that was the extent of movement in the world. I looked at the staff and tried to work out what had happened. My last thought was wanting everything to stop. And that's when it hit me. *I had stopped time.*

How could I stop time? Was light related to time somehow? Did I stop light and did that stop time? I didn't know what I did, but the more I thought about it, the more I realized that it was true. The staff's connection to me made it clear.

I walked over to my grandfather, and as I approached I freed him from time. Again, I don't know how I did it. Heck, I didn't do it. As my great grandfather had said—the staff belongs to no one. I had wanted my grandfather free, and the staff made it so.

He stumbled forward and then stopped. He looked around, his eyes wide in shock. "Tommy, what has happened?"

"I stopped time." My grandfather's shock turned to awe. I had impressed him, and that meant more to me than anything. And that thought made me miss him all the more. I ran up and gave him a hug.

"What should we do Grandfather? Should I give you the staff so you can destroy all these Djinn and Ifrit?" I held out the cane.

"No, Tommy." He tussled my hair with his hand. "Can you free Baraz? Then we could just walk away."

I was shocked that he didn't want to destroy them all. I remembered the painting in the Citadel, his face joyous in destruction. It was the same face I saw during the attack on the Persian Garden. "Wouldn't it be safer to destroy them?"

Grandfather shook his head. He looked sad. "No, Tommy. They just want to feel safe. We don't kill people just because they want to be free of fear or domination."

I nodded. "Let me free Mister Oz!" I turned to assist Mister Oz and saw the body of Naomi in the distance. I ran to her and put my hand over her mouth. She wasn't breathing, but I couldn't tell if that was because she was beyond the reach of time or if she was dead.

"A friend?" my grandfather spoke from directly behind me. I nodded without saying anything. He knelt next to me and looked at her. "She took a full Ifrit detonation. She must have been shielded or she'd be in much worse shape." I looked at her scorched shirt and reddened face and burnt hair and wondered what could be worse.

"She's dead." I said, flatly.

"We should ask Baraz. He has talent as a healer."

Without even turning I freed Mister Oz. I heard him groan, shout out Grandfather's name, and then limp over to us. Before he could say anything else, I asked, "Is she dead?"

"My dear Tommy. What is happening? How can I tell if someone is dead, when I'm not even sure if I'm alive." I explained that I had stopped time, and Mister Oz just stared at me. "You stopped time?" I nodded. "Archmage," was his response. He then knelt down and looked at Naomi.

After feeling her neck and looking in her eyes, he held his hand about six inches above her chest and made some motions. When he finished, he looked up at me. "She is gravely injured. Her shield did not protect her enough to stop the damage inside her."

"Gravely injured?"

"She will die, Tommy. I am sorry." He lowered his head.

"Isn't there someone who can save her? A healer? Wherever they are, we can go there!" I looked at Mister Oz and then my grandfather and then back again. Neither of them moved. "Isn't there anyone?"

Finally, Mister Oz spoke up. "I'm afraid there is no one with the power of life forces in the world today to heal this much damage, Tommy." He put his hand on my shoulder. "I'm sorry."

As he stood up, his words echoed in my head. Power. Life forces. Heal. I smiled and stood up. "The second most powerful Archmage," I whispered to myself. Grandfather looked at Mister Oz.

"Tommy, what are your talking about?" My grandfather ran his hand through his hair as he peered at me.

"I will tell you on the trip back. It's a long story. For now I will keep Naomi outside of time as we transport her to England. That way she won't get any worse. There is someone in England who can heal her."

"Tommy, Cain is powerful, but he is an illusionist."

"I am not talking about Cain." I turned to the two of them and added. "Can you help me carry Naomi out, please?"

I reached down and took Naomi in my arms for the first time. It was not at all like it was in my dreams.

Chapter Twenty-Two

THE SECOND MOST POWERFUL ARCHMAGE

There was a small village near Persepolis, and Grandfather was, as expected, received as the hero he was. We were offered a cart ride to the train station, which we gladly accepted. Mister Oz and a young man from the village laid Naomi gently on a few thick blankets, her head resting on a colorful pillow.

"So tell me about your girlfriend," Grandfather asked.

I sputtered a denial but decided that it would be useless to object. Grandfather always did what Grandfather wanted to do, and if he wanted to believe Naomi was my girlfriend I couldn't stop him. Besides, I liked the thought, although I never would have told him that.

"She is a magician of Master-level strength!" I enthused.

"Master level? I find that hard to believe in anyone that age," my grandfather replied. Mister Oz nodded.

"She did a concealment illusion as we escaped, which I'll tell you about later. She is extraordinary with detonations! I've seen her create a mantle shield that she maintained for thirty minutes!"

"The Mantle of Anaitis?" Mister Oz asked.

"Yes. That's the one."

Grandfather laughed. "That's longer than you can hold that spell, Baraz!"

I nodded. "She is powerful."

"Indeed." Grandfather slapped my knee. "Putting magic in the hands of a girl, though? That reminds me of when my father gave me the staff when I was about your age. Many people thought it was foolish to put magic in the hands of someone so young." He winked at me. "But we both know that's not true, do we not?"

I couldn't have smiled any wider. I knew my Grandfather would understand, even after all the others saw her as little more than a domestic magician. With my grandfather's questions about Naomi answered, I told my entire story to Grandfather and Mister Oz as we made our way to Shiraz.

I had just finished describing Mister Ali's and my meeting with Cain, and the two of them bristled. Grandfather punched his fist into his palm. "When I am done with Cain he will wish that the bullet in that gun you fired was real!"

Next came the part of the story I least wanted to tell—Mister Ali's betrayal. I watched Mister Oz's face as I outlined that Lord Gort and Mister Ali had planned on destroying the staff. My voice trailed off after I said that I ran from the office.

"It does not surprise me," Mister Oz finally said, sadness in his voice. "He experienced so much pain and violence during the Great War. Taking away one more instrument of violence would seem perfectly reasonable to him." He turned to my Grandfather. "Indeed, we knew this of him for quite some time."

Grandfather nodded. "His goal is unsurprising, but his methods are. I can only imagine he let things get out of control. I doubt he intended for his own son and best friend to be injured in his quest to destroy the staff."

I wasn't so sure, but I didn't challenge my grandfather's position. Mister Ali was still a father and friend. I then turned to my grandfather and said, "Next I met your father." I couldn't help but grin as he almost fell off his seat in surprise.

"What? Why?" I outlined Cain's Plan B and the conversation with Joseph. I ended by saying, "I hesitate to ask you this, Grandfather, but you understand his power, don't you?"

He still seemed to be in shock, but he looked at me, a frown on his face. "Don't be disrespectful Tommy. Of course I know his power. He makes things grow. That's why he is a Royal Gardener and not bearing the staff."

I didn't answer but instead continued with my tale. He'd understand in London.

We were at the station when I finished my story and answering the many questions that Mister Oz and Grandfather threw at me. Without waiting for either of them, I marched into the station, copying what Naomi did in the previous Way Station.

The engineer hesitated until he saw my Grandfather. He was Persian and immediately recognized him. He apologized profusely and served us fresh water and fruit, after which he went down to unhook the engine from the rest of the train.

"Excuse me, Grandfather, I have to do something," I said as I stood up. He nodded but didn't say anything as I made my way to the rear of the engine.

I spent more time with the Marid this time. I told him of his mighty brother, destroying the train as he tore through to his freedom. I discussed being alone. I talked of my friend, near death in the room up front. I apologized for his imprisonment. I asked of him a favor.

And, of course, I set him free.

We arrived in Scotland in what the engineer claimed was record time. He could not understand how the train had traveled at such great speed for such a long distance. "Must be the honor of having two Archmages on board!" he noted as we departed. I knew it was the honor of being free that sped us along.

I had argued with my Grandfather on and off the whole trip on the train. He felt it was foolish to think his father the gardener would be able to heal Naomi. I did my best to respectfully disagree, but the forcefulness of his reply and his inability to understand reason led me to just nod and stay quiet. Clearly their relationship was strained, and it made me sad.

We hired a carriage at the station, and as we pulled away, there was the sound of a mighty crash and then a harrowing scream that was part train whistle part howl. Both Mister Oz and Grandfather looked back toward the station, but I just said, "Let others deal with that. Naomi needs help." My voice was desperate, and the two of them turned away.

The castle was under heavy guard, and the guards would not let us past nor would they send a message to the Royal Gardener. It didn't help that my grandfather refused to leave the carriage. I was certain that they would have recognized him, but for some reason he wanted very little to do with this trip. At one point I thought we were going to have to fight our way to my great grandfather, but just when things were at their bleakest my Grandfather stormed over and said loudly, "I am the Archmage. I received the staff from my father, the Archmage whose magic and talent built your magnificent gardens. He is old. I am old. Can you please tell him that his son has traveled from America and would like to see him." The guard peered at Grandfather and then his jaw dropped.

Ten minutes later we were at the door of a small cottage. Mister Oz carried Naomi, who seemed so frail and tiny in his arms. I continued to halt time from touching her, hoping that I was keeping death at bay, as well.

Grandfather knocked hard on the door. It opened slowly, and I couldn't believe it was the same man who I saw in my room in the Citadel. Joseph was even more frail, stopped and thin and weak. His eyes went wide when he saw Grandfather.

"Declan!"

"Hello, Father."

"What are you doing here?"

"Nice to see you, too, Father."

Their banter was going downhill, so I stepped in. "Archmage Joseph, I am in dire need of your mastery of the staff." Both my grandfather and great grandfather turned and stared at me.

"What are you talking about? I have no time or power to go off fighting on the continent."

"Please." I stepped aside so he could see Naomi. "My friend is near death and needs you." I held out the staff to him. He stepped forward and looked at Naomi.

"She looks dead. Why are you wasting my time? I cannot raise the dead."

I motioned to Mister Oz, and he stepped forward. "She is alive, but I stopped time from touching her so we could make the trip to see you. Please, Great Grandfather. I know your power with the staff, even if others don't."

My great grandfather smiled and looked at Grandfather. "Thank goodness he didn't inherit your brains." He stepped back and waved us in. "Come in. Place her on the sofa in the living room."

We walked in, and as I passed Joseph, I tried to hand him the staff, but he waved me off. "Keep her safe a bit longer." I nodded and stood next to the sofa as Mister Oz lay her on her back. Joseph leaned in and looked me in the eyes. "So you figured it out, did you?" I nodded, and he smiled. "I knew you would."

Grandfather plopped into a chair and said nothing, watching with what appeared to be a healthy amount of doubt. While Joseph made his way in, I brushed Naomi's hair behind her ears. I wanted to kiss her forehead but was too self-conscious to do so.

Joseph sat on the couch next to Naomi and closed his eyes. Without opening them, he said, "Hand me the staff, Tommy.

It will release her, and I will begin." The moment the staff left my hand Naomi let out a small whimper.

I looked at Great Grandfather and noticed his knuckles were white around the staff. I couldn't tell if anything was happening, but I knew from my own experience that this meant nothing. The staff acted in its own way. Naomi coughed and then started to breathe deeply.

"She is healed, Archmage Thomas." Great Grandfather's eyes were open, and he was smiling. He held out the staff, and I took it in my hand. I knelt down and leaned on the staff. A small bright beacon of light shone from its end as I looked on Naomi breathing gently.

She opened her eyes and smiled at me.

"Streetlight," she whispered.

The End

— 375 —

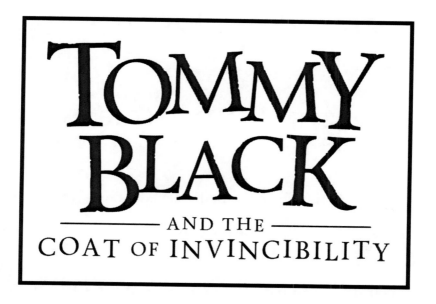

Turn the page for the first chapter from book two of the Tommy Black series, *Tommy Black and the Coat of Invincibility*.

Available Now

www.tommyblackseries.com

Chapter One

VISITING AN OLD FRIEND

As the watery mud seeped into my shoes I couldn't help but laugh. I had expected an unpleasant visit. I just didn't expect it to start the moment I stepped out of the taxi. The driver stayed in the warm, dry car, holding his hand out the window, his palm collecting rain drops. "Are you certain you don't want me to drive you closer?" he asked. "A storm is brewing."

I motioned over my shoulder as I paid him. "It's a surprise visit." He nodded but then stopped as he caught sight of my cane. He continued to stare as I started up the road, but I couldn't tell if it was because he recognized me as the Archmage or whether he just thought it was strange for a sixteen year old to be using a cane.

Setting a brisk pace, I approached my destination, the mighty Citadel of London. With each step the tapping of my cane on the cobblestones made small splashes. My hope was to get the whole unpleasantness over with as quickly as possible.

It had been two years since I had walked through the gates of the Citadel. The previous time I had the help of friends. This time I would be on my own. I didn't want to be alone. My friend Naomi had helped me escape before, and I wished she were with me now, but I hadn't seen her in a long time.

I knew that she was studying magic in England, but I didn't know where, and she didn't seem interested in letting me know. I was in England, too, and Naomi knew that she could reach me through my great grandfather at Balmoral. Every visit to my great grandfather I would inquire about a letter or telegram from her, but he would shake his head, shrug, and change the subject. I eventually stopped asking if Naomi had contacted him, and the fact that she didn't made the distance seem an unbridgeable chasm between us.

She was an extraordinary magician, and I missed how she would casually prep dangerous spells to relax herself. I missed her wit and sarcasm. I missed her strength and spirit. I missed how beautiful she was, and I missed how she drove me crazy.

Naomi never said so, but I believe she left because I had saved her life. While she was thankful, it seemed like she saw it as a challenge or even an affront. When she went off by herself to study it was my belief that her goal was to never have to be saved by someone ever again. I admired that, but I still missed her.

The modest entrance to Fort Belvedere—the Citadel—soon revealed itself. It was an illusion, of course, hiding a mighty fortress behind the facade of a country estate, an illusion created at the hands of the man I was going to meet: Cain.

I still didn't know Cain's role in the English government. I assumed he was some nebulous member of the Army Council, in charge of magic. With magic all but gone from the world I figured everyone just left Cain alone.

And Cain left alone was dangerous, as I had experienced first hand.

During my previous visit, Cain had done his best to intimidate me into giving him the artifact I now carried. Rather than work with him I had spent the past two years freeing the enslaved Marids—magical creatures that powered the trains in England and the United States.

He had sent master level magicians to stop me, but I had learned much and escaped them easily. My power with the staff, which I initially considered to be the useless ability to create light like a mere lamp turned out to be much much more—by manipulating light I could defeat practically any creature, magical or otherwise. Each day brought me more confidence.

Having freed the Marids, I intended to move on to the next victims of magical oppression, whoever they were. Were the mighty furnaces in Forest of Dean powered by Ifrit? I didn't know, but I had an idea that Cain would. Hence my visit.

I decided it was safest if I stopped time from flowing around me. It was an extraordinary power I discovered by accident and was one of many things that turned the seemingly useless trick of manipulating light into something much more powerful. Inspired by the words of my great grandfather, who nonchalantly asked me if light could bend, I studied Einstein, whose theories of space and time were based on the constant of the speed of light. Einstein taught that my power with the staff was truly awe-inspiring.

As powerful as it was, I hesitated to use the Staff. My great grandfather had also told me that the staff was ultimately in control of its own magic, and as I used it over the previous two years I could sense it more and more—the staff was affecting me. How, I didn't know, but it was there. But there were times when I had no choice. Facing Cain was one of them.

I closed my eyes and stopped time, the motion of light held still by the power of the staff. I opened my eyes to a frozen tableau. It was always uncomfortable living in a world of stopped time. The sense that it was wrong seemed to permeate everything. Still, I never failed to marvel at the stillness of the world around me.

Splashing mud from marching boots looked like chocolate milk. Rain was suspended in the air like glass beads. Even the dark clouds above me appeared to be blobs of paint smeared across a drab canvas. The activity around the Citadel appeared frantic even as it was frozen in time around me. We were at war with Germany, and troops were everywhere. The expansive lawns of the estate, which had been mostly empty during my previous visit, were full of columns of soldiers. Everything smelled of gunpowder, and the grass lawns were ground into dirt under the constant pounding of boots.

There were no magicians in view, just soldiers and guns and cannons. Technology had eliminated the need for difficult-to-learn magic, and magicians were for the most part nothing more than street performers—certainly not powerful soldiers.

I approached the door that led to Cain's office and paused, holding the cane tight. Despite my developing power, he was still frightening. He truly was an awesome illusionist, as great as any among the ages.

The last time I had visited him he had set me on fire with nothing more than his mind. I was sure that he was still outraged that I had freed the Marids, and with his power I needed to keep him off balance. I didn't want to find myself on fire again.

I passed through the doorway and into Cain's section of the building. There were no magicians on duty, which surprised me. The entry was guarded by a bored looking soldier, his hand caught in the act of scratching his bushy mustache. I wondered if there were any powerful magicians remaining in England.

There was one other change I noticed: The electrical lights that were previously attached to the pillars of the long hall that led to Cain's office were gone. They were no longer necessary, as I had created a home for the ominous Shadow creatures, creatures that could absorb anything and move it to a place without any feeling at all. Their leader, Vingrosh, had requested a home without light, and I had given them one. The Shadows had not been seen since.

Opening the door to Cain's office, I walked over, and sat in the chair facing his desk. I leaned forward and looked at him. Even with Cain frozen in time, my hands clenched the staff. He looked older—more drawn and with thinning hair—but he still oozed power. He was writing a note, the pen stopped mid-stroke. The office itself was little changed. As I looked around, I tried to assess what Cain's role was with the English government, but it was impossible to tell.

I took a deep breath and let light flow again.

"Hello, Cain." His head jerked up, but only for the slightest of moments. As a magician, his self-control was extraordinary. He looked me over, smiled, and leaned back in his chair.

"Tommy Black. What a pleasant surprise." He put his pen down and folded his arms across his chest. His shoulder twitched in one of the tics that I was told were a sign of his years of doing illusions. "Why look how you've grown. How old are you now?"

"Sixteen."

"Sixteen years old, imagine that. Did you know that when I was your age I was helping our war effort in France by creating illusions to fool the German scouts?"

I shook my head and remained alert. Cain's power was not to be underestimated.

He frowned. "Contrast that with you, a traitor and coward by any definition. You've destroyed our rail infrastructure while we're in the midst of a war." Cain stared at me, his eyes narrowed in a challenge.

My confidence withered under his gaze, but in the end I knew that what I had done was right. "I freed slaves, Cain. That is all. There are other ways to power locomotives."

Cain leaned forward and slapped his palm on his desk. I flinched at the sound. "There is blood on your hands, Black. Mark my words."

I shrugged, doing my best to present nonchalance, although the idea of having caused deaths troubled me. There was a war, after all. Still, I held my ground. "I was helping others."

Shaking his head, Cain replied, "You foolish boy. Do you know how long it has taken to refit our trains? While we were rebuilding our supply lines, Germany took over half of Eastern Europe. If you had any honor at all you would use your powers to assist us." Cain picked up the pen and started writing again. "I don't have time to deal with children."

"I am not a child. I am the Archmage." Even as I said it, I felt rather embarrassed. I was relying on my title and not my actions or the moral power I felt lived behind them.

Cain calmly placed his pen down, and looked at me again, his intimidating stare only interrupted by a twitch of his eyebrow. "You are nothing but a coward."

I tapped the end of the cane on Cain's desk and he glanced down at it, startled for the barest of moments. His fear, fleeting as it was, helped restore my confidence. "I am not a coward, as you well know. I simply disagree with your methods." Cain said nothing, and I continued. "I would like to help, Cain, but there are other battles. My legacy demands that I free the enslaved magical creatures."

I had returned the conversation to the reason for my visit. I didn't expect Cain to understand, and if I were honest I didn't expect him to help. But I had hoped he would respect my mission.

Cain lowered his head and squeezed the bridge of his nose between his thumb and forefinger. "I'm tired, Black. I have a war to fight and don't have time to pander to some pointless crusade to restore your family's honor." He looked up, appearing more disappointed than angry. "The legacy of the Archmage demands no such thing of you."

I had expected this reply. Cain's comment was true at its heart. My family had wielded the cane for centuries, and our only true legacy was to use its power. But it was my great grandfather who told me the truth about our history, of a magical artifact—the staff in the form of a cane—that had been stolen from Persia. When I realized that the most powerful magic in the world originated not from magicians but from powerful magical creatures that had been enslaved to do the bidding of man, I realized that the stain of my family legacy could be only be erased by doing good and freeing them.

I was about to explain this when Cain held up a finger. "However, perhaps our goals are not in conflict."

"What do you mean?" I had expected further argument. I was hard-pressed to consider any common goal with someone like Cain.

"You do realize there are trains in Germany?" Of course. I had focused on my own home of America and ancestral home of England, but there were enslaved magical creatures across the globe. I was guilty of the blinders of nationalism that I was trying to remove from others.

I nodded. "And they are powered by Marids?"

"Marids, smaller ones by Ifrit. You don't think the vaunted German productivity is simply due to calloused hands? Their abuse of magical creatures is well-known." I expected that Cain would exaggerate to get me to be in line with his goals, but the concept that there were enslaved magical creatures in Europe made sense. My former teacher, Mister Ali, had told me the story of how the Shadows were hunted down by the Germans over the previous centuries.

"I will travel to Europe, but I don't trust you, Cain. I will do nothing without my own confirmation." Cain once again leaned back, smiling.

"That's the least of my concerns." He laughed. "My goodness, I'll even arrange transportation. I had hoped on using you to support our offensive, but this may be even better." He stared at me again, only this time the intensity was of excitement, not intimidation. "What if I told you that the ironworks in Volklingen uses scores of enslaved Ifrit to power their furnaces?"

"I would say that I would free them." If possible, Cain's smile spread wider.

"I can have you escorted to Reims. From there you can find your way to Volklingen. Free those Ifrit, and you will have England's undying gratitude. After that you can do whatever you like."

"Cain, I will do whatever I like regardless."

He shook his head. "The arrogance of the Archmage and the impetuosity of youth. But it matters not—of course! Do whatever you like! There are enough magical creatures there that will need your help to keep you busy for years. Frankly—

and I'm sure you share the sentiment—I'll be glad to have you far away from me."

I couldn't help but smile. "I think we have an understanding." I stretched my legs. I hadn't realized just how tense I was. "When can I depart?"

"Give me a few days to make the arrangements. In the mean time I'll have Lord Ainsley find you lodgings." Lord Ainsley! I fondly remembered his kindness toward my grandfather and me. I looked forward to seeing him again.

"That works." I stood up, while Cain remained seated. I didn't expect him to see me out.

Before I turned to the door he spoke up. "Black, did you know that I talked with your great grandfather after you escaped the Citadel?" I turned and looked at him. He looked bemused as I shook my head. "He didn't say much, but he did say one thing that I considered interesting."

He paused again, so I played along. "And that was?"

"He said I should fear you." Cain scratched his chin. "Do you think I fear you?"

The idea that someone as powerful and arrogant as Cain would fear anyone was laughable. I shook my head. "I don't think you fear anything."

"Ah, Black. Such an attitude is foolish and a recipe for dying young. You would do well to remember that on the continent. Be that as it may, I do not fear you. Do you know why?"

I shook my head, not even bothering to answer. I had no desire to take part in any verbal games. "I don't fear you because you have a good heart, Black. You are predictable that way." He waved his hand as if dismissing me. "But I know more about magic than anyone else on the planet, and I assure you that while I don't fear you, I do respect your power." He nodded. "So I have confidence that you'll be able to handle what you are about to face, even if you cannot fathom just how dangerous it is."

I left and walked down the path to the wing with Lord Ainsley's office. I didn't spend much time thinking about Cain's warning. I had faced master magicians, Shadows, Djinn, Ifrit, and even mighty Marids. I couldn't wait to get going.

www.tommyblackseries.com

About The Author

After fifteen years as a music industry journalist Jake Kerr's first published story, "The Old Equations," was nominated for the Nebula Award from the Science Fiction Writers of America and was shortlisted for the Theodore Sturgeon and StorySouth Million Writers awards. His stories have subsequently been published in magazines across the world, broadcast in multiple podcasts, and been published in multiple anthologies and year's best collections. In 2014 he released his first novel, *Tommy Black and the Staff of Light*. His fantasy series, *The Guildmaster Thief*, was launched in 2015.

A graduate of Kenyon College, Kerr studied writing under Ursula K. Le Guin and Peruvian playwright Alonso Alegria. He lives in Dallas, Texas, with his wife and three daughters.

www.jakekerr.com

@jakedfw

This text of this book was set using 12.5-point Haarlemmer, a rarely used metal typeface designed by Jan van Krimpen in 1938, the year in which *Tommy Black and the Staff of Light* is set. The typeface was digitally recreated by Frank Blokland for the Dutch Type Library.

CPSIA information can be obtained
at www.ICGtesting.com
Printed in the USA
LVOW10s1802210317
527965LV00008B/1519/P

9 780692 316665